MW01226272

An Emergence of Daisies ©

Copyright © 2022 Sydney Ducharme

978-1-7780827-2-6

978-1-7780827-1-9

978-1-7780827-0-2

Place of Publication: Lacombe, Alberta, Canada

Table of Contents

To my Book Club,

Who made my dream a reality.

Chapter 1 - High Expectations

The house on the hill at Stratford and Glenn was never a happy home. However, today was a particularly dreadful day for one of the residents.

Daisy had always enjoyed spending time outside; though, it was highly frowned upon by most for a lady of her status. She had been in the garden with Susan, her lady's maid, picking flowers when another servant informed Daisy that her mother required her immediate presence in the parlour. Daisy took a deep breath to calm her nerves and made her way inside.

Daisy quietly entered the parlour, hoping not to catch the immediate attention of her mother, Duchess Margaret Ida Bloomsbury. The room was full of vendors and servants preparing for the night's event. Daisy navigated her way through the churning mass of unwanted visitors, ensuring to evade her mother's eye. As she pressed against the back wall, she glanced at her attire; Daisy was keenly aware her current state of dress would not meet her mother's expectations. Changing was not an option as her mother's summons always required immediate response or she would face dire consequences. She smoothed down her skirt and brushed the dirt off her corset as she braced herself for the harsh critique that was sure to follow. Unfortunately her attempts to remain invisible proved futile.

"Daisy, you are late," scorned the duchess without looking up from the paperwork in front of her. Daisy approached the table slowly not wanting to pull her mother's attention more than required.

"How can I be late if a specific time was not stated?" Daisy retorted. Based on the bunching of her mother's manicured eyebrows and the immediate glare thrown at Daisy, this was not the right question to ask. "My apologies, Mama. Simply a general inquiry into my tardiness so that I may not disappoint you in the future."

Duchess Bloomsbury returned to her paperwork. "There's no need for that; you are already a dire disappointment to your father and I. No amount of punctuality would lessen this displeasure." The words rolled off Daisy like water off of a duck's back. She was so desensitised to harsh words and comments that being called a disappointment could be considered quite mild.

"You summoned me," Daisy said, holding her composure. "How may I be of service?"

The duchess looked up from her papers briefly. A disgusted look came across the duchess's face that made Daisy's stomach churn. She steadied her resolve bracing for the commentary that was sure to wound Daisy's heart.

"Were you in the garden again?" the duchess asked venomously.

"No," Daisy lied, knowing full well it was the wrong thing to do. Although she tried to play her parents' games, she was never good at following their lead so that she could, at least, meet their expectations. Duchess Bloomsbury dropped her papers and slammed her hand against the table. Daisy tried not to flinch. She knew showing weakness would not benefit her. She had to remain strong.

"Don't sell me a dog, child! If you insist you were not in the garden, I shall then fire Susan for not completing her duties. After all, she is the one responsible for your attire and current…state." Daisy tried not to show her fear. Susan was the only source of happiness and love Daisy received at home. Losing Susan would destroy Daisy.

"Sorry, Mama. I did lie; however, I was in the garden by myself; Susan was unaware of my whereabouts. I thought I would enjoy the afternoon sun for a bit. Summer is nearly over." Daisy's attempt to protect Susan and provide a viable excuse for her appearance only seemed to elicit further annoyance from her mother. The duchess placed her hands on her hips and glared at Daisy for a moment. Daisy knew she was trying to figure out what to do with her. Subconsciously, she felt the scars of previous punishments ache at the thought of them being re-opened. Lucky for Daisy, a servant discreetly handed the duchess a piece of paper which pulled the duchess's attention back to the matter at hand.

"Your sister is coming home tonight. We will be holding a ball in her honour and you will be expected to attend." Daisy's composure faltered for a mere moment at the mention of her sister, but the duchess didn't notice; she was completely distracted by her paperwork. "Certainly you will bathe and wear clothes more appropriate than the filthy rags you are currently wearing. With your choice in clothing today, you seem to be a servant of a house of wealth rather than a resident of the household. You will also stay out of the garden. You are not a servant or a child, and you will not act as such. Should you continue your careless frolicking and servant-like endeavours, you will no longer be a member of this family. Am I making myself perfectly clear?"

Her mother paused, allowing the words to sink in, allowing the judgement to become clear, allowing Daisy to understand what a disappointment she really was. In a small voice, barely more than a whisper, Daisy replied "Yes, Ma'am."

"Very well. I will have Susan lay out something appropriate for you tonight. I expect you to be punctual and ready at seven o'clock. Also, Lord Corinthian will be in attendance. I expect you to make his acquaintance. Your only saving grace is your ability to provide me and your father with a grandchild. However, your options are limited as are Lord Conrinthian's due to his age. Perhaps this could be used to our advantage as the old man won't take notice of your less than satisfactory appearance." Duchess Bloomsbury looked up, an expectant look on her face. Daisy knew her next words would disappoint the duchess, but *why would it matter now?*

"Lord Corinthian… you mean the old man with white hair, yellow eyes, and a crooked nose hooked like a beak? He is ancient and hardly seems an appropriate suitor." A smirk pulled across Duchess Bloomsbury's face that indicated she expected such a retort.

"He is well connected and earning his favour may lead to a more suitable caller. However, I am assured the lord is still fruitful when it comes to providing a grandchild. To be frank, we are running out of options and time. I do not think now is the time to be picky." Duchess Bloomsbury turned her back to Daisy and walked to another corner of the room signalling that the conversation was over and Daisy was to do as asked.

Daisy left the room quickly and made her way to her chamber upstairs. The room was plain. The floor was bare, and the walls lacked decorations. Everything was a pale grey or a muted yellow. The wooden bed was simple and unadorned with aged sheets that yellowed from the sun that streamed through the windows. A tall, wing-backed chair, with a facade of regalness, sat in the corner; its simple beige fabric seemed to call out for a pattern, but to no avail. Many of the chair's buttons had fallen off as a result of years of use, leaving empty spaces in their place. Like most of the things in her room, well built was not a priority.

Her mother always said that a plain room for a plain girl was suitable. Daisy stopped and stared in the mirror by the bathroom. She pondered if she really was as plain as her mother always suggested. Her hair was dirty blonde like the colour of wet sand. Her eyes were grey and lacked voluminous eyelashes. Her lips thin, her nose like a button, and her ears slightly too small for her head. She turned and analysed her figure. Everything seemed small and flat. Had she not been wearing a corset, Daisy was sure her body would be mistaken for a man's. Perhaps she was plain. Perhaps nothing physically would attract a suitor. With a heavy sigh, Daisy walked away from the mirror and into the bathroom where Susan was just finishing running the bath water.

Susan gave a sympathetic smile towards Daisy. In reality, Susan was more her mother than Duchess Bloomsbury. Susan was her lady's maid from birth and helped Daisy navigate all of the duchess's moods. Susan was ageing now. Grey hairs sprouted amongst her black hair. Little crow's feet were just starting to show on her pale face. Yet, regardless of her withering appearance, Daisy always felt the weight lift off her whenever Susan was near. Susan moved behind Daisy and began undoing the sinched corset. Daisy glanced in the bathroom mirror watching her womanly figure disappear with each loosening strand. Her face faltered, which Susan must have noticed.

"I overheard. You needn't say anything, hun. I will ensure you meet the duchess's expectations," Susan stated. "You needn't worry. I promise that tonight will be fine."

The corset slid from Daisy's waist and Susan began pulling off the remaining layers. Eventually bared, Daisy climbed into the bath and endured the scrubbing required to be clean to her mother's requirements. The hustle and bustle of downstairs rang through the house as Daisy and Susan sat in silence throughout the entire bath. Daisy was not in the mood to speak, yet much was weighing on her that she wished to release.

"Azalea is coming home tonight," Daisy stated, finally breaking the silence. It appeared as though Susan was waiting for Daisy to speak .

"And this evening's ball is in her honour, I've been told. It will be over soon enough and your sister will leave before you know it." Susan stated and attempted a reassuring smile. However, this did not ease Daisy's stress and pain.

"It's always worse when she is home. Mama dotes on her, and Papa thinks she could do no wrong. Everything I do, everything I am, pales in comparison to her. They are so cruel to me in her presence, and I do not understand why they are so harsh toward me. When she's not home, they just seem to ignore me as though I only exist to occupy space. Even more so, they don't directly compare us. It's less painful and I can do more as I please in her absence. I love Azalea, but they treat me so much worse when she is home."

"My Dear, you are not your sister. This is true. But, you were never meant to be your sister. There are things that you have that she could only dream of."

"Of course. Because all women dream of a monochromatic palette and a flat, box-like body. I lack everything it means to be a woman. I am a faulty product that should be disposed of." Susan inhaled sharply. A look of pure fury painted her face.

"If you believe your mother's words, then that will be all you will ever be. What you need to do is leave this town and this house. Figure out what it means to be you. You will always be compared to your sister if that is all there is to compare you to." A small smile crept along Daisy's face, encouraging Susan to keep talking. "You've been living in the shadow of your sister for far too long.

Tonight, we change that. Tonight we make you turn heads. Now, let's get you out of this tub."

Susan extended her hand and pulled Daisy out of the bath. Susan directed her to the stool in front of the vanity. *What could Susan possibly do to make Daisy anything more than what she was right now? What was there to make it worthy of turning heads with such a plain canvas to start?* Susan began working on her hair. Brushes, combs, and pins seemed to fly in every direction as Susan worked to tame Daisy's mane. Eventually, Daisy's hair was smoothed into a chignon with two tight curls framing her face. Susan held out a delicate silver hair comb that was decorated with royal blue flowers.

"It was my mother's and, since I didn't have any children, I want you to have it. Wear it with pride," Susan explained as she gently fastened the comb into Daisy's hair. Susan moved over to the wardrobe and pulled out a box that was laying in the bottom. "I had this made for you. I was saving it for an important event, and I think tonight's ball counts as important."

Susan removed the lid of the box to reveal a silver, silk gown. The bodice was decorated with a delicate pattern of blue flowers that matched the comb. The intricate pattern continued to trickle down the sleeves and skirt giving the gown an elegant femininity. The structured bodice would push up her nonexistent bosums which would then be further emphasised by the dress's sweetheart neckline. Overall, it was soft and simple, yet beautiful in a way Daisy never saw herself.

"Susan, this is beautiful, but I could never wear this."

"You can and you will."

Daisy didn't argue with Susan. She knew when debating was futile. Daisy stood and moved into the middle of the room so Susan could assist her with dressing. After fastening on a corset and underskirt, the gown was slid on. The gown clung to every minor curve that the undergarments created, giving Daisy the appearance of curves and a womanly figure that was sure to capture the attention of some. At the very least, it should capture her mother's attention. She looked the part, but Daisy feared she would never act the part. At least, not to her mother's expectations.

With a sigh, Daisy put the thoughts out of her mind and turned to Susan. With tears in her eyes, Susan gleamed with pride at Daisy. It gave Daisy the extra confidence she needed to enter the ball. Looking at the clock, it was nearly seven and time to welcome guests. Daisy took a breath, turned towards the door and headed down the stairs followed closely by Susan.

Duchess Bloomsbury stood at the front door awaiting the arrival of the guests. Her husband, Duke Charles Edward Bloomsbury III, stood beside her. Together, they looked like an odd pair, different in every way. Where Charles was tall and thin, the duchess was short and plump. Her hair was long and thick while Charles was balding. Neither were particularly attractive, but the confidence Duchess Bloomsbury exuded made up for anything that lacked in her appearance. Charles' money and status in society is what made him worthy of anyone's attention. He had inherited multiple estates upon the untimely death of his parents, and uncle which made him one of the most powerful men in the area. They had been on a trade excursion when one of their boats sank killing all on board. He had not expected to inherit anything let alone so much.

The Bloomsbury's were unlike most couples; the duchess never had much for a motherly instinct and no real desire to procreate, and the duke was only interested in having a male child in order to produce an heir for his estate. Unfortunately for the Bloomsburys, they were not blessed with a male heir but, instead, twin girls. Daisy was the second born and her parents regularly made this clear to her. She was unwanted at birth and that trend did not change as she grew. Perhaps, if she was a male, it would have been different. As far as her parents were concerned, Azalea was their only hope for an heir at all. Daisy was seen as a nuisance when in the presence of her parents, or she was ignored as if she did not exist.

With the click of her shoes on the stairs, both her parents turned towards Daisy. Her father seemed genuinely surprised as his jaw physically dropped. The duchess's face gave away nothing to the unknowing viewer but to Daisy, she saw the slight curl of her lip that meant her expectations were met. The moment quickly passed as a knock on the door notified the residents of the first guests' arrival. Daisy joined her parents at the front door to greet guests.

Person after person streamed through the door, each in their best attire. Everyone seemed excited. Whether it was to attend a ball or to see Azalea, Daisy didn't quite know. She knew most people loved Azalea, but nobody quite knew Azalea like Daisy did. They were twins after all, but not identical. Duchess Bloomsbury always said it was a good thing for Azalea, but a terrible thing for Daisy. Azalea was the pretty one of course. Azalea was her parents' pride and joy, but even they didn't know Azalea as well as Daisy.

The guests mingled in the grand foyer awaiting the arrival of Azalea. Daisy moved about the crowd trying not to draw too much attention, but, oddly enough, she was failing. Her attire seemed to catch the eye of multiple young gentlemen. She blushed as one man nearly dropped his drink as she passed. It was clear that a little bit of care into one's looks could prove to be a useful tool. However, the excitement of being noticed was smothered immediately as Lord Corinthian approached Daisy. Instead, a feeling of extreme discomfort overwhelmed her being.

Lord Corinthian was a round and short man with snow white hair that nearly reached his bushy eyebrows. He wore two monocles over his piercing yellow eyes that magnified the overall size of his beady eyes. His nose protruded in a horrible fashion that made it look like a large beak. White facial hair covered most of his lower face that his skin tone was hardly discernible. He wore a white parlour jacket with a white shirt and black pants. It was an odd appearance that gave him a bird-like feel. Daisy smiled, pretending his approach was welcomed.

"Good evening, Lord Corinthian," Daisy stated in a formal, but not unfriendly tone. "So nice of you to join us this evening. I am sure my sister will be honoured that you accepted our invitation."

"Your mother said you are looking for a husband." Lord Corinthian was not one to waste conversation on simple niceties. Daisy expected a quick change in conversation to her sister, not to herself. "I never did marry for no woman ever caught my eye. I always met my… needs in other ways. However, tonight you appeared to be a woman like no other."

His yellow eyes roamed the length of Daisy's body sending chills up her spine. He walked around, viewing every angle, like a hungry lion waiting to pounce. His hand grazed her back, but Daisy tried not to cringe. His hand traced the curves of her waist, but Daisy tried not to show her discomfort with the whole situation. Daisy needed to stay focused on the task at hand. *Lord Corinthian was well connected. Lord Corinthian could get her a husband. Lord Corinthian was key to her leaving. But Lord Corinthian was an old creep. Lord Corinthian made women uncomfortable.* Daisy endeavoured to keep her mind focused, but his hands running her over her body were unnerving and highly inappropriate for an unwed young lady. Finally, she was able to break away from the conversation as the announcement of Azalea's arrival echoed through the grand foyer.

As Daisy turned to walk towards the door, Lord Corinthian grabbed her waist, pulled her back against him, and whispered in her ear, "We are not finished yet. I will have you later."

Her composure faltered at the comment, but Daisy was able to quickly move away from Lord Corinthian and towards her parents. The trio stood at the front door waiting for the completion of the quartet. All guests' eyes were on the front door, but Daisy noticed a few wandering glances in her direction. So this must be what it's like to be pretty, to be noticed. However, the pleasure of being visible vanished as the doors opened to reveal Azalea.

Chapter 2 - Homecoming

Azalea was a tall woman with natural curves that exuded feminine appeal. Her blonde hair was styled with effortless curls that draped over her shoulders like a river of liquid gold. One side was pinned back with two amethyst clips, revealing a dangling silver earring. Her eyes matched the pins as they were purple like violets. Her lips were red like currants, and her cheeks held a slight blush giving her a lively appearance. But it wasn't her face nor hair that made heads whip in her direction.

Azalea often wore revealing clothes that were far from traditional or modest. She wore a long silk gown, the colour of sage, that clung to every natural curve leaving nothing to the imagination. While she kept the corset, she did way the petticoats and ring skirts. It had a plunging neckline and straps that hung uselessly off her shoulders. Daisy was always amazed that Azalea's clothes stayed on her body considering there wasn't much holding them on. A deep slit up the front exposed her leg with every step. It was the pinnacle of femininity, but did not seem appropriate for the ball. Daisy often found herself confused regarding Azalea's wardrobe; if any other young lady had worn such an outfit, it would surely be scandalous. However, it seemed Azalea could get away with anything.

Azalea always loved the attention. She opened her arms and welcomed the gazes of strangers. Just as quickly as Daisy grabbed attention, she lost it. Daisy became invisible yet again as Azalea waltzed further into the house.

Azalea kissed both her parents, gently patted Daisy on the arm then turned to face her adoring spectators..

"Good evening everyone," her voice floated above the crowd like music: powerful, beautiful, and hard to ignore, "I appreciate your attendance at my welcoming home ball. It has been a great journey over this past year touring the world with the most prestigious school. I would now like to introduce you to my friends I collected along the way."

Azalea lifted her arm towards the doors as they opened to reveal a number of people; all were tall, fit, and the definition of beauty though slightly less stunning than Azalea. They were dressed in similarly revealing attire to Azalea, but none could quite touch her elegance or grace. Even in this hoard of genetically perfect individuals, Azalea stood out like a black cat in snow. Her guests entered the ballroom and, with that, the festivities began. Classical music emanated from the orchestra inviting guests to dance while servants meandered with various trays of hors d'oeuvres and champagne.

Daisy attempted to blend in with the crowd, hoping nothing more than to avoid Lord Corinthian for the evening. Whenever he entered a room, Daisy was quick to exit into a different section of the house. During one of her desperate attempts to avoid Lord Corinthian, Daisy stepped into a darkened sitting room. With only a few candles lit, her eyes took a few moments to adjust. As Daisy gained her sight in the dark room, she realised there were other occupants. There were several groups of young people dispersed in each of the room's shadowy corners. They

19

moved in a synchronous rhythm with low, animalistic sounds emerging from the silhouettes. Daisy was unsure about what she had just walked into; she turned to leave the room, but tripped over a discarded piece of fabric on the floor. She did not go unnoticed. Lounging upon the couch with her leg exposed through the gaping slit in her dress was Azalea who looked towards Daisy as she tripped.

"Daisy! Darling! Do come join us." Her sister shifted into a more upright position and indicated the seat next to her. The other inhabitants hardly seemed to notice Daisy as they were mostly occupied with each other in the corners and darkest parts of the room.

"I did not mean to disturb." Even Daisy could hear the discomfort in her own voice as she navigated her way around various groups of people and heaps of cloth on the floor. "I was simply looking to -" She couldn't say she was trying to avoid Lord Corinthian but her mind was distracted by the sight before her. *Were these people bared?* "To find somewhere more quiet."

"I cannot say that you've come to the right place, but I can at least offer you a seat and an ear." Daisy took the seat beside her sister and tried to avoid looking at the moving masses of people. In a whisper, Azalea said, "I know you're avoiding Lord Corinthian, and I don't blame you."

Daisy could not hide her shock. Her sister hardly ever showed sympathy towards her and certainly not in the presence of others. It wasn't that Daisy and Azalea didn't get along, they got along fine in private, but Azalea had an image to uphold in public that Daisy obviously didn't meet.

Azalea stared at Daisy with an odd look of affection and frustration.

"I am finding myself much too distracted," Azalea said quietly to Daisy. With a snap of her fingers, she grabbed the attention of the room. "Leave us immediately. Go mingle with common folk awaiting the opportunity to dabble with the prestigious."

Without hesitation, the throngs of people began to exit. Daisy watched as people picked up the discarded garments and quickly redressed. She felt her face become flush as she realised the fabric she had tripped on was clothing and the persons in the room had, in fact, been naked. She knew that it was inappropriate to be in public undressed, but Daisy couldn't imagine why their clothes were off. As the door opened and light flooded in, Daisy noticed it was all Azalea's friends that had filled the room. Not a single person was familiar to Daisy, surely implying she was not supposed to have entered. Daisy shifted uncomfortably realising that she disturbed this *private party* in the dark sitting room. When the room had emptied, and Daisy and Azalea were alone, Azalea's facade seemed to fade away. Her fake smile she donned for everyone, but Daisy, melted away leaving behind a small, genuine smile through which Daisy could see just how exhausted she was.

"I truly hate these balls. I would much rather have come home and gone to bed than have to socialise with all these buffoons." She indicated the door to the main hall with a flick of her wrist. "I've never understood the duchess's infatuation with placing me on some pedestal. It's exhausting."

"How long are you home for this time?"

"Long enough. There are matters that have to be attended to apparently. The duchess suggested there is something regarding you that needs to be addressed."

"Mama thinks I need to be married. She stated that all I am good for now is bearing a grandchild." Horror dawned across Azalea's face; obviously this was not the discussion she anticipated.

"We're hardly even of age to be married. We are just barely adults. She must be out of her mind if she thinks you should be married. She isn't pressing me to accept some pathetic hand in marriage. Is that why you are avoiding Corithian?"

"Mama thinks he is well connected and that if I win his favour, he will find me a more appropriate suitor. However, Lord Corinthian thinks he is an appropriate suitor. He makes me uncomfortable."

"He looks like an owl." Both of the girls laughed at the comment. It was easy when it was just the two of them. Azalea understood Daisy and the situation, but when there was anyone else present, Daisy faded away or was tormented relentlessly. Azalea never held much love for their parents, but she was able to play their game better than Daisy could ever dream. Daisy tried to love their parents, but it was hard when anything she did was met with insults and criticism. When it was just Daisy and Azalea, the girls could truly be themselves. With their parents, Azalea had to appear better than Daisy. This was perhaps the deepest mental wound for her as Daisy loved

Azalea and her comments in the presence of their parents cut like a knife.

"I am sorry I left you with them," Azalea sighed, and moved to place her head on Daisy's shoulder, closing her eyes. "I had to leave this place for a while. Figure out who I am. My schooling was an acceptable way to do this without inciting the wrath of our parents. I do hope you understand. Maybe one day, you will get to leave too."

"Susan said I should leave to do the same thing, but I can hardly think of a reason acceptable to our parents to permit my absence." A snore sounded from Azalea. She had fallen asleep. Slowly and softly, Daisy lowered Azalea onto the couch so she could sleep. Daisy, as quietly as possible, exited back to the ball and straight into Lord Corinthian.

Although the room was basically empty, there was no way to avoid him. The only exit was back to Azalea or behind Lord Corinthian. He was only a few steps ahead and he had already locked eyes with her. Panic rose in Daisy, but she could not think of a way out. Before long, he was in front of her with her back pressed against the door she just exited.

"There you are," he crowed. His voice was raspy and unpleasant to listen to. Daisy attempted to act neutral and unaffected. "I've been looking everywhere for you, and you've managed to evade me most of the night thus far." He placed one hand beside Daisy's head on the door making a barrier.

"I really should rejoin the ball, Sir," Daisy pleaded.

"In due time my dear." He shifted his body, trapping Daisy between the door and his arm. His free hand began to trace the side of Daisy's body. "An unspoiled thing like you shouldn't just be roaming about unaccompanied. Why don't you welcome my company?" The smell of alcohol wafted off of him as he attempted to whisper the last phrase into her ear.

"I believe there are enough unaccompanied people here that I present no problem. If you will please-"

"No!" He interrupted, slamming his hand against the wall. Daisy flinched. "No. You will give me what I want."

His hand rested on her hip and pushed himself against her. He smelled of sweat and liquor, a nauseating combination. His hand ran over her hips and tugged at her skirt. Daisy heard her skirt ripping away from the bodice and attempted not to scream. The skirt slid down and Daisy could feel a cold breeze on her hip. She scrambled to pick up the skirt, but Lord Corinthian slammed his hand against the wall causing Daisy to flinch and freeze. She wasn't entirely sure what Lord Corinthian intended, but she knew if someone saw her in such a compromising position it could ruin her and bring shame upon her family. In spite of this, she was terrified to move. She made one final attempt to escape, but he was like a brick wall. The hand on the wall slid down and grabbed Daisy behind the neck. He pulled her face towards his and forced a kiss upon Daisy.

At that moment, there was a gasp and the smashing of a dropped glass. Lord Corinthian pried himself off of Daisy to see the horror-struck Duchess Bloomsbury gaping at the scene before her. Daisy used this opportunity to pick up her ripped skirt and move away from her unwanted suitor. She approached her mother with caution, but it proved futile. Before Daisy could say or do anything, Duchess Bloomsbury brought back her hand and slapped Daisy across the face. Daisy felt her lip crack from the force of the slap; a moment later she had the unmistakable taste of blood in her mouth.

"You ruin yourself and bring dishonour to this family." Duchess Bloomsbury's nostrils flared and her lips quivered with anger. "You are to go upstairs immediately and not come out until I come for you. Do you understand?"

Daisy nodded, holding her sore cheek and sucking on her bleeding lip. She turned towards the stairs to escape to her room. As she climbed, Daisy could hear her mother apologising for her misbehaviour and Lord Corinthian agreeing that Daisy was a disappointing waste of a woman. She could no longer contain herself. Tears streamed down Daisy's face as she ran towards her bedroom. *How could her mother witness Lord Cornithian's transgressions and blame her? How could her mother be so blind as to what really happened?* Daisy knew she did nothing wrong. His behaviour was the problem, not Daisy's innocence. Daisy was the victim, not the villain. Yet, in her mother's eyes, she could only do wrong.

Slamming the bedroom door behind her, Daisy fell to the floor and cried. Years of pain finally seemed to overcome her. She curled onto her side and screamed in the empty room. It wasn't her fault. She didn't ask for this. She

25

didn't want this. The pain grew and grew. Years and years of torment accumulated to being a villain. Her sobs racked her body. She punched the floor, wanting to escape the emotional pain rampaging through her brain.

Through her cries, she heard the distinctive footsteps of her mother approaching Daisy's door. The loud thunk of the lock sliding into its place meant Daisy was trapped in her room, but that barely pierced the surface of the pain. Eventually, Daisy sobs softened until she fell asleep on the floor.

Chapter 3 - Embarkation

The sun beaming through the window was not a welcomed sight. Daisy lay on her back staring blankly at the ceiling. The sun meant morning had come which was not something Daisy was looking forward to. The morning meant her punishment was to be determined. Based on her mother's reaction, the punishment would surely be grave. Daisy felt the ridges hidden on her back from past lashes. Her mother always ensured the lash marks were hidden as scars that were visible were sure to discourage potential suitors from pursuing a courtship. She was concerned about what this infraction would warrant. Perhaps, there wouldn't be enough space left to whip that clothing covered.

Daisy rubbed her eyes to clear away the sleep and memories clouding her mind. She was not sure how long she slept. Her concept of time was foggy after the night's events. She felt exhausted, but not from lack of sleep. Her bones ached, but not from lying on the floor. Her eyes stung, but not from the sun glaring through the window. She wanted to melt into the floor and disappear, but, knowing it would never happen, she sat up.

She stretched her arms and eventually made it to her feet. She knew that her mother would not approve of her current appearance, so she dragged herself to the bathroom. With the sink running, she washed her face. Her eyes were red and puffy. Her hair was falling out of the chignon. She started to pull out the multitude of pins holding her hair in place which fell in loose waves around her face. She pinned a few pieces back to keep the hair out of her face and pushed Susan's comb into the crown of her hair. With great difficulty, she managed to slip her gown off from the night before. Lastly, she moved to her wardrobe. Like her room, most of her clothes were cotton and rarely dyed in anything expensive. She selected a plain, cream frock to wear over her corset and undergarments. It wasn't anything special, but it would certainly show that she attempted to make herself look presentable.

She sat in her chair and watched the clouds moving past the window. There wasn't much in her room to pass time as she awaited her mother's arrival. Her stomach growled with hunger as the hours waned. The sun was well past its high point before Daisy finally heard footsteps coming down the hall. She stood up and faced the door with a look of feigned bravery. However, as the footsteps moved closer, her look of bravery turned to confusion; there was more than one set of footprints. *Who else would be coming besides her mother?* The door clicked open and Duchess Bloomsbury entered with several servants.

Without even so much as a glance in Daisy's direction, the duchess began barking orders at the servants. "In the wardrobe. Grab all of her clothes and maybe throw in some of Azalea's old garments. Things that Azalea has not worn in a long time. I suppose she might need something nice," Duchess Bloomsbury announced while gesturing towards the wardrobe. "Grab her hair brush out of the bathroom and other beauty articles though she hardly seems to use them."

The servants began moving about the room grabbing various articles from different parts of the room and throwing them into the trunk that was brought in. Daisy wasn't sure what was going on, but knew not to speak until she was spoken to.

"You there. Go and grab her travelling cloak. She will be leaving promptly." Duchess Bloomsbury pointed to a young servant that raced down the hall towards the front door. Her mother finally turned to face Daisy. "You are going to Dame Agatha's School for Young Women. You are leaving in thirty minutes for the train that will be departing this evening. This is our last chance to correct this atrocious behaviour in you. Dame Agatha has deemed you a dire case and is willing to take you in even though the school year is well in progress as you need immediate intervention. I thought I could fix you, but clearly you are past my abilities now."

This news hit Daisy in waves. First, it was anger. She was being sent to finishing school obviously being deemed a lost cause not worth her mother's efforts anymore. Then, it was a relief. She was finally going to leave this place. Even if it was only for a short while, this was the opportunity Susan said she needed. Daisy could leave and figure out who she was. Maybe finishing school would be horrible, but maybe, just maybe, it would be her saviour.

"I understand, Mama." Daisy nodded her head in agreement while trying to contain the excitement brewing in her soul. She was finally leaving the house on the hill. As the servants slammed the lid on the trunk, Azalea suddenly appeared at the door. She did not seem happy. *Was it panic? Was it anger? What was Azalea so displeased about?*

"She cannot leave," Azalea blurted out. Her hand curled at her side as if trying to contain her anger. Daisy swore she saw a spark, but quickly lost that thought as she saw their mother turn on Azalea. It was clear by Duchess Bloomsbury's expression that she was not happy about the interruption.

"Azalea! You will hold your tongue. This is not for discussion as I have already told you. Your sister is leaving and Dame Agatha has already been notified of her impending arrival."

"She cannot leave. She must stay here." Daisy was confused by this change from last night. *Didn't Azalea say Daisy should leave? Wasn't that what they discussed last night in the sitting room? Why was Azalea fighting to keep Daisy here?*

"I will not tell you again, Azalea. You will shut your mouth or you will face the consequences." Duchess Bloomsbury held up her hand as Azalea attempted to negotiate. "Move this trunk to the front door. Someone will be here to escort her to the train station shortly. Daisy, I hope this works for you. It is truly your last chance. Azalea, join me in my study."

Duchess Bloomsbury grabbed Azalea by the arm and pulled her down the hallway out of view. The servant arrived with her travelling cloak. Daisy slung it over her shoulders, tied it in the front, and followed the other servants hauling her trunk down the hall to the front door.

Daisy had hoped to say goodbye to her sister and inquire into her sudden change of heart. As she approached the front door, however, she noticed that the escort was the only one waiting for her; Azalea was nowhere to be seen. The escort grabbed her trunk from the servants and guided her out the door.

As she left the house on the hill, she looked back. The stone grey exterior mirrored the cold and cruel feeling that the interior held. Daisy was finally leaving this house that hardly felt like home for a new adventure. After a short drive to the train station, Daisy grabbed her trunk and walked towards the platform. Besides a few businessmen awaiting the train to Capital, the platform was nearly empty. The escort handed her a train ticket for Grenich.

"Another escort will pick you up on the other end," he explained. "This is where I leave you. Don't miss your train."

With that, he promptly turned around and walked back towards the manor leaving Daisy alone on the station platform. She sat on her trunk in the most unlady-like fashion, but she didn't care. There was hardly anyone there, and she was unaccompanied. Completely alone. Daisy pondered this for a moment. *Had she ever been in public by herself?* Her family went on trips when they were younger, but as Azalea grew up and enrolled in her schooling, the family travelled less and less. Eventually, Daisy hardly left the house at all. Her life mostly consisted of the house and the grounds. She was now certain that she had never been in public alone before. This was her first experience of freedom. She glanced around. No one seemed to notice or even care about Daisy's presence. She was simply another person in the crowd.

The train to Grenich eventually rolled into the station. Daisy lugged her trunk towards the train where she was greeted by a porter. The porter was a young man with brown hair like chocolate and hazel eyes. He had a kind face but seemed serious about his work. As Daisy approached, he held out his hand and asked for a ticket. Daisy handed the porter the ticket. He used a metal tool and punched a small logo in the bottom corner of the ticket. He handed the ticket back to Daisy, grabbed her trunk and started making his way down the train. Daisy hurried after him, trying her best to keep up with his pace. Eventually he stopped at the cabin door, pulled it open, threw her trunk on the shelf above the chair, and left without a word.

Daisy had hoped to have a conversation with him, or anyone for that matter. She sat in the cabin hoping that some other passenger would join her. The minutes ticked on and before she knew it, the train chugged to life and began to depart the platform.

As Daisy watched the train move away from the Stratford-Glenn train station, there was a sudden commotion. A gentleman was suddenly running down the platform attempting to catch the train. Daisy watched with fascination as he reached out and grabbed on the train. He swung himself up and into the train car just ahead of Daisy's. The porter she met earlier was running down the train aisle to meet this late passenger. Daisy opened the cabin door and peered down the hallway. She could see the porter and the passenger chatting rather animatedly. Whether their conversation was going well or not, Daisy was not sure, but eventually the passenger was permitted aboard.

The passenger briefly looked away from the porter and locked eyes with Daisy. His eyes were a startling blue like the colour of the deepest waters in the ocean. Dark blue eyes that seemed to leap off his pale face. He noticed that Daisy appeared mesmerised, but he didn't seem to mind. A soft smile spread across his face. He waved to Daisy before departing in the opposite direction of her compartment.

Daisy felt heat rush to her cheeks at the simple gesture. He had noticed her. He took a moment to even wave at her before heading to his seat. How interesting it was to be travelling alone. She could stick her head in the hallway, have strangers wave at her, and no one criticised her for poor behaviour. Daisy smiled to herself at this new found freedom and pondered what else she might discover while being alone.

Time seemed to pass quickly on the train. Daisy watched the small cities of Stratford and Glenn disappear from view leaving nothing but quiet countryside. Rolling hills of green and gold shifted in the light breeze. Daisy leaned against the seat and watched the changing scenery for what felt like minutes, but must have been hours. As the train started to slow, the rolling hills gave way to the coastal town of Grenich. The waters of the ocean churned against the docks lined with small sailboats. Flocks of seabirds floated above the marina eagerly awaiting the fishermen's return with the day's catch. The view vanished as the train finally pulled into the station. Daisy had arrived in Grenich. Her opportunity had finally arrived.

Chapter 4 - The Stranger on the Train

After wrestling down her trunk from the shelf, Daisy exited onto the platform. She expected to see her escort, but besides passengers leaving the newly arrived train, the platform was empty. Before long, Daisy was the only one on the platform. She was completely alone and, while thrilling, the thought was also terrifying. Daisy knew she needed to find help. Any person that could provide directions to the school at least. She walked over to the ticket booth to look for assistance, but even that was empty. Beside the ticketbooth, she found a large map hung on the wall but years of train smoke and travellers had worn it making it illegible.

She slumped onto her trunk and glared at the laces on her carriage boots. Daisy had no idea where to go and suddenly the fear of being alone overwhelmed her. She had never been to Grenich before. She didn't know anyone here. She didn't know where she was supposed to go. She wasn't even sure how to get into town as it seemed a fairly long way to walk. Panic filled her as tears started to run down her face and splatter on her boots. She shoved the heel of her hands in her eyes trying to make herself stop crying. Daisy hadn't the slightest idea of what to do.

"Alone, are you?" Daisy looked up. The late passenger stood in front of her. Now that he was up close, Daisy noticed additional features about him. He had an angular and well-defined jaw. He was tall and slender, but his legs seemed slightly too long for his body. Raven black hair stuck out at odd angles from underneath his grey, miller hat. A peacock feather protruded from the side of his hat. The hat and feather matched the rest of his attire: a grey suit with a deep royal blue vest, a gold and green ascot cravat, and clean white shirt underneath. The buttons on the vest were off by one giving him a slightly crooked appearance. However, the mismatched buttons were not what caught Daisy off guard.

Daisy stared at the friendly face, but was confused by the wrong assumption earlier. The light must have been different, because the eyes looking down at her now were a bright, emerald green like Daisy had never seen before. His eyes sparkled in the sunlight and specks of evergreen danced through the emerald. He was stunning. His smile revealed a slightly crooked tooth and small, faint scar above his lip that somehow added to his appeal.

"I get it if you don't want to talk to strangers, but staring is not always nice either." Daisy hadn't realised how long she had been gaping at the stranger, but she did notice her jaw had slightly dropped in surprise at the man now standing in front of her.

"My apologies, Sir. I had - you, um - I was surprised." Daisy stumbled over her words, confused by her own loss for words. "I was expecting an escort to meet me, but he did not show. Now, I am here and have no idea where I am going or how to get there."

"Ah! New to Grenich then. Lovely little town. If you will allow me, I may be able to assist you in finding your lodgings." His voice was husky and melodic. Daisy didn't want him to stop talking. This was a stranger offering assistance and, against her better judgement, Daisy wanted to go with him.

"Well, it's not exactly lodgings. I've been enrolled into Dame Agatha's School for Young Women." This comment seemed to take the stranger back. His thin eyebrows disappeared under the mess of black hair spread across his forehead.

"Finishing school! For such a well mannered young lady like yourself? Hardly seems appropriate." He extended his hand to assist Daisy in standing. As her hand slid into his, she could feel herself relax. She didn't know this man apart from any other stranger, but something about him was comforting. Her concerns of earlier completely dissolved.

"My mother would strongly disagree with you." Daisy dropped her hand from his and felt some of the earlier fear resurface, but not nearly as bad this time. At the very least, she felt more certain of what she needed from the stranger. "Can you take me?"

"Of course," he stated. Daisy turned to grab her trunk. Reaching out to grab a handle and share the load of the trunk, he began walking towards the exit with Daisy in tow.

Rounding the corner of the station, Daisy could see all of Grenich below. The station was on the top of the hill that rolled down to the sea. Grenich was placed on the plateau that surrounded the river basin leading to the ocean. Daisy followed the stranger down a road that had a train bridge built over it and seemed to trail towards the town. The river split the town in two and dense forest surrounded it all. The hill was high enough to see over all the trees. Daisy had not realised how far the station was from the town site. This was going to be a longer walk than expected.

"You're from Grenich then?" Daisy questioned.

"You could say that. I come from a lot of places. Some near, some far, but I have called Grenich home for a while now. And you? Where do you call home?" the stranger responded.

"My parents live at Stratford and Glenn," Daisy explained.

"Aren't those two towns?"

"There is a hill that separates the two towns and their estate resides on top of the hill. My grandfather governed one town and my great uncle the other. My father inherited Stratford and Glenn when they both died at sea. Now, my parents live on the hill at the corner of Stratford and Glenn and govern both towns."

"But you do not live on the estate?" Daisy paused. She had not intended nor wanted to get into a deep conversation with this stranger, and yet she was willing to discuss it with him. *What was it about him that made Daisy so comfortable?*

"It is more a house than a home to me. While I am not excited to attend finishing school, I am looking forward to being away from the house on the hill." The stranger gave a knowing sideways glance, but did not pry any further.

"Well, I hope you find what you are looking for in Grenich. The town saved me years ago. Maybe it will save you."

They walked in silence for a while lugging the trunk between them. The hill descending to the river basin was steep, but flattened out as they entered the forest. It was cooler in the forest as the sun was hidden by the dense foliage. Not much light filtered through the leaves above, yet Daisy didn't mind. The darkness was an odd relief. The sun had been bright and violent, but the shadows of the forest were deep and welcoming. She breathed in the fresh air and relaxed. It was a pleasant feeling that Daisy basked in.

"So..." the stranger breathed, breaking the silence.

"Yes?" Daisy responded.

"I was getting uncomfortable with the silence. I usually walk this alone, so it's a different feeling with a companion."

"Would you rather be alone?" He seemed to ponder this question for a moment, unsure of how to answer.

"No. I don't think I would prefer that, but when you have a normal routine, change is, well, different," he shrugged. Daisy slightly giggled. "What humours you so?"

"Change is different. It's literally in the definition of change. They are one in the same."

"Yes, I suppose you would be correct." He chuckled to himself. "Like I said, I am used to walking this alone.

Your presence is befuddling but welcomed. Grenich should be just around the corner."

They turned the corner, and the small town seemed to spring up out of nowhere. As they entered the town, they passed several shops including a bakery, a bookstore, and florist. The combination of freshly baked bread and lavender wafted through streets creating a comforting and welcoming atmosphere. The street opened to a small town square. In the centre of the square, Daisy saw a beautiful, old fountain; the top of the fountain was decorated with a train with water flowing out of its chimney. A series of symbols decorated the lower bowl. As they walked past, Daisy could make out a leaf, a flame, a raindrop, and a circle. The rest of the symbols were unclear.

They made a turn down a side street and arrived at a wrought iron gate. Above the gate, Dame Agatha was written in harsh, straight letters. A stone path lined with old oak trees led to a cold, grey manor that was similar to Daisy's house on the hill. It was two stories tall, with high, arched windows and pointed roof lines. A heavy wooden door with a gold knocker adorned the front of the house. Besides the door, the manor lacked any other colour but grey. It was not inviting as they approached, but Daisy tried to keep her mind open. They came to the bottom of the stairs and placed the trunk down.

"Thank you, Sir. I'd still be sitting at the station if not for you," Daisy couldn't help but grin at him.

"A damsel in distress is always a gentleman's calling." He gently grasped Daisy's hand. In one smooth motion, he took off his hat, bowed to Daisy, and softly kissed her extended hand. Daisy felt her face flush. Certain she looked like a tomato, she covered her face with her unoccupied hand as the stranger righted himself. "I would like to see you again. May I ask your name?"

Daisy hesitated for a brief moment, unsure if it was safe to give him her name. She dismissed her worries and retracted her hands in order to feel more confident.

"My name is Daisy Mae Bloomsbury."

"Ah, *Bellis perennis*," he smirked, "a beautiful flower. A name well suited for an equally beautiful young lady. I hope to see you again soon, Miss Daisy Mae Bloomsbury." Without another word, he replaced his hat and departed down the stone path.

Chapter 5 - Dame Agatha's Schools for Young Women

Daisy watched as he disappeared down the path. *Would she ever see him again?* She certainly wanted to but was not sure if she ever would. As he passed the gate and Daisy lost sight of him, she finally decided to approach the front door. She climbed the stairs and slammed the door knocker three times before standing back to await its opening.

After a few moments, the door swung open to reveal an old lady. Her grey hair was slicked back into a tight bun with not a hair out of place. She wore a plain black dress that covered her arms and legs entirely. A high neck meant only her face and hands were exposed. Black leather shoes perfectly matched the dress. Her stern expression and wrinkled face gave her a grumpy, unpleasant appearance. Daisy imagined that she was quite beautiful when she was young, but years of managing unruly girls must have worn away at her. She glared at Daisy through her small circular glasses that perched on her thin nose. Her thin lips curled in displeasure.

"Miss Bloomsbury, I presume?" She spoke with an accent that Daisy quite liked, but her tone was not friendly. Daisy nodded her head. "A proper lady does not nod her head. She answers 'yes, ma'am' or 'no, ma'am'. Do you understand?"

"Yes, ma'am," Daisy replied, barely holding back her sarcasm.

"Very well. Leave your trunk. A servant will collect it later. Follow me." Daisy hastened to follow the lady as she made her way into the Manor. A grand staircase greeted guests upon arrival with several heavy wooden doors branching off of the main foyer. "I am Dame Agatha, and I am the head mistress of this facility. All your classes will be held in the north wing of the first floor. Meals are served in the dining room in the south wing. All sleeping quarters are on the second floor which you will be shown later. Currently, I am taking you to the assessor to evaluate how much work is required for you. This way."

Dame Agatha headed up the grand staircase, down the second floor hall to a nondescript door which led to another staircase. The second staircase was much narrower and far steeper than the first. Dust coated the railing signifying this passageway was not travelled often. At the top of the stairs, Dame Agatha turned down a small hallway. Both women had to duck slightly due to the uncomfortable angle of the roof. As they made their way down the hallway, they passed a small window overlooking the manor grounds. Daisy tried to catch a glimpse of the grounds but couldn't due to the dame's quick pace. Suddenly, Dame Agatha stopped in front of a wooden door that hung slightly off its hinges; she gently knocked on the door before turning to face Daisy. Daisy was surprised that the assessor would be housed in such decrepit accommodations.

"The assessor will collect you when she is ready. Wait here." With that, Dame Agatha walked back the way they came leaving Daisy alone in the cramped, filthy hallway.

After a moment, Daisy's curiosity got the best of her; she didn't think it was necessary that she stand in the exact spot where Dame Agatha had left her. She walked back up the hallway to the small window and looked out. From here, she was able to get her first look at the manor's grounds. They were well manicured with perfectly square bushes, flowers organised by type and colour, as well as meticulous stone paths leading away from the manor in various directions. She could see the front gate and just make out the town square down the road. Townsfolk milled about the streets. Daisy wanted to join them and not have to sit through this assessment. She placed her hand on the windowsill to try and get a better view, but the wood sill gave away, making a loud crash. Then, out of the corner of her eye, Daisy caught a glimpse of something scurrying away from her; she whirled around to see what it was.

"Cannot follow instructions." Daisy jumped at the sound of a woman's voice. "Curious. Not a good start, my dear." An ancient looking woman stood in the doorway. She made Dame Agatha look like she was in her youth. She hunched over a plain, wooden cane. A grey dress peeked out from under the tattered shawl draped over her shoulders. Her hair was white, thinning, and hung loosely around her face. She turned and began walking back into the room, indicating that Daisy should follow.

The room consisted of two wooden chairs and a chipped white table with a small tea set on it. The old lady sat at one of the chairs and gestured towards the other seat. Daisy carefully sat paying attention to the notes her mother always told her whenever Daisy sat in front of her. Ankles crossed, back straight, shoulders back, and hands lightly on her lap. The old lady eyed her. Daisy felt the assessor's eyes travelling over her face and posture, judging even the slightest detail.

"Pour the tea," the assessor stated. Daisy gently picked up the teapot and slowly poured tea into the cups on the table. She set the teapot down a bit harder than anticipated. The assessor gave nothing away, but let a small "hmm" escape. She scooped up her tea cup and inspected it with a precise eye. Minutes dragged on as she slowly turned the cup in her frail looking hands. She set the cup back on its saucer almost silently.

"Drink the tea."

"Do you have sugar, please, Ma'am?"

"No sugar. Drink the tea." Daisy delicately picked up the cup, gripping the handle with two fingers and her thumb. She brought it to her lips while watching the assessor for any indication of her expectations. Daisy tipped the liquid into her slightly parted lips. She set the cup down after swallowing. The assessor sighed and closed her eyes.

"May I speak?" Daisy inquired. The assessor opened her eyes and narrowed them at Daisy. She gave a small nod. "Freely?" The slightest hint of surprise caressed the assessor's face.

"I suppose it depends upon what you are wanting to say. A lady should be careful with inquisition. It is not always welcomed."

"I assume the core of the assessment is complete. May I ask what you are looking for?" The assessor pondered for a moment but Daisy was not sure if she was thinking about Daisy or her question. The silence grew and Daisy attempted to not squirm in anticipation.

"Your actions here dictate how much training you have had in the proper etiquette of a lady. How you sit. How you pour. How you drink. How you talk. *What you ask.* These all indicate how extensive your training has been. Usually, a student will only see me at the beginning and end of their studies here. Unless, you are like Miss Camden." Daisy didn't know who Miss Camden was, but assumed it was not a good thing to be like her.

"And what did you learn about me?"

"I do not usually discuss this with the subjects, but I am also not often asked any questions." The assessor paused, contemplating how to answer or even if she should answer. "You understand what is expected, yet you disagree with it. You do not want to conform, but you know how to. You are an interesting quandary which I do not think the dame will like. We shall see. The foundation is there, but your spirit is strong. She often breaks spirits."

The assessor stood without another word, walked to the crooked door, and indicated that Daisy should leave. Daisy followed her cue and left the room. The assessor explained that Daisy should head to the foyer for her next directions. The door clicked behind Daisy, leaving her alone in the cramped hallway. Unsure what exactly she was expected to do, Daisy began to make her way downstairs.

Each step creaked under her weight which gave an eerie tension to the air. At the bottom of the stairs, Daisy opened the door to a deserted hallway. Gas lights burned and flickered all down the hallway. She was unaware of how long she was with the assessor, but the sun had set, and strange shadows were casted by the moon that seemed to crawl across the floor. As directed, Daisy made her way back to the foyer; she hoped she would be able to find someone who could tell her what she was to do next.

As her feet touched the floor of the main level, Daisy could better hear the muffled clanking of dishes. She followed the sounds and eventually found the dining room. Fifteen girls sat around the table with Dame Agatha sitting at its head. They all sat rigid and blank, like an orchestra waiting for the conductor's signal. Dame Agatha finally noticed Daisy standing in the doorway and motioned for her to enter. The dame stood up and all of the ladies' heads turned at the same time to face Agatha.

"We have a new student joining us. Please welcome Miss Daisy Bloomsbury to our lovely school." All heads in the room snapped to Daisy. Like a well choreographed dance, a hushed and synchronised applause echoed from the dinner table. The feeling of discomfort only heightened in Daisy at this unusual interaction. Agatha indicated that Daisy should sit in the empty chair at the table. She did as told.

Dame Agatha sat, snapped her fingers, and a series of servants began rushing about with various dishes of food. Daisy couldn't help but try to see all that they were doing, and quickly noticed that all other attendants at the table stared straight ahead without glancing at anything. As food was placed on plates, Daisy watched the others in an attempt to understand what was expected. In complete synchrony, all of the students grabbed a napkin from the table, gently placed it on their laps, picked up their forks, and began eating.

Daisy felt out of place and out of sync. This was unlike anything she had seen before. Perfect synchrony amongst multiple people. She attempted to follow their lead but was always late or early in their cues or doing something completely different. They even reached for their glass of wine at the exact same moments throughout the meal despite no one uttering a single verbal cue or direction. Daisy was baffled and unable to ask for clarification or guidance. This behaviour seemed expected without proper training.

As the meal wound down, Daisy felt relief settle in. Perhaps, whatever came next, would be more free and less rehearsed. The dame stood up and all eyes directed towards her. Daisy felt a slight prickle of anxiety as the dame surveyed the scene and eventually stopped to stare at Daisy.

"I request an audience with Miss Bloomsbury and Miss Camden. The rest of you are dismissed for the evening. Sleep well," Dame Agatha announced.

All the chairs slid back in a nearly silent, fluid, single motion. Daisy's, however, scraped against the floor. Although minor, Daisy could see the other students cringe at the unpleasant grinding sound. Heat rose to Daisy's cheeks as she tried to recover, but to no avail. The ladies then quickly left the dining room. Some glared at Daisy as they passed. Others completely ignored her. One, however, sent Daisy a reassuring smile that comforted Daisy ever so slightly. Once the girls all left, Daisy, the dame, and another student that Daisy assumed was Miss Camden stood in the room.

"Miss Bloomsbury, this is Miss Rosette Camden. She is our most senior student and set to graduate relatively soon. She will be your roommate and your mentor for the probationary period of your stay. Should we see no improvement in your person, you will be deemed incorrigible, and returned to your family." Dame Agatha acted like it was a statement hardly worth exploration and ploughed on despite Daisy's surprised expression. "Miss Camden, please escort Miss Bloomsbury to your room. Good night ladies."

Rosette turned to leave the room and Daisy followed. As they walked down the hall towards the foyer, Daisy glanced sideways at Rosette. She had deep coloured skin like someone that had spent many hours in the sun. Long, thick, copper curls loosely framed her face and fell down her back. Hazel eyes, light pink lips, high

49

cheekbones, and a slender jaw gave her a regal and beautiful appearance. Daisy imagined that she would appeal to most men and yet, she was here at finishing school. Perhaps, finishing school was not solely meant for hopeless cases and disappointments. Perhaps, some parents send their young women for other purposes. As they began to climb the stairs, Daisy decided to take a chance and speak to her escort.

"How long have you been here?" Daisy inquired. Rosette's face showed no expression nor indication that she had heard Daisy. "How long have you been studying at Dame Agatha's?" Daisy tried again. Rosette stopped abruptly and turned to face Daisy.

"A young lady does not make idle discussions in the hallways, Miss." There was a slight drawl to her voice when she said 'miss'. Rosette continued climbing to the top of stairs, turning left on the landing, and continuing down the hall. The shadows had shrunk since Daisy was last in the hallway. The gas lamps burned brighter casting a warm glow to the area. Eventually, Rosette stopped in front of a door nearly at the end of the hallway and opened it.

Behind the door, sat a small room split in mirrored halves. Each half contained a tiny wooden bed with white linens. At the end of the bed sat their trunks, both now empty. A wardrobe, vanity, and stool completed each side. A tall, arched window split the room in half. The only difference between the sides was the right side contained a door which led to a simple bathroom. Rosette entered and moved towards the left side of the room.

"Your side is to the right. The maids hung your clothes in the wardrobe prior to dinner." Daisy went towards the wardrobe, opened it, and glanced at the various dresses hanging on the rod. Majority of the dresses were the plain gowns she was used to, but there were a few pops of colour from Azalea's wardrobe added to the array. Rosette moved to close the door and with a loud thunk locked it. She stood at the door for a few moments, and Daisy wondered what she was doing.

"It appears everyone is sleeping. The manor appears quiet." Rosette's posture suddenly relaxed. She strutted to the bed and threw herself upon it in the most unlady-like manner possible. "I apologise for the formality of this. Outside of this room, you must act the part or be punished, and the punishment is much worse than acting out the expected mannerisms. You can call me Rosie when we are alone, by the way. Miss Camden sounds horrible."

Daisy smiled. This change in behaviour made her feel more comfortable and welcomed. Clearly, this was more acting than anything else, and Daisy was sure she could do her part.

"I've only ever been called Daisy, so you may call me that. So…" Daisy paused, "how long have you been here?"

"It has been a horrible and arduous four years. She says I am close to graduating, but every time I do the assessment, I cannot pass."

"Why can't you pass?"

"Try not to use contractions. Those will get you punished," Rosie informed Daisy as though this was a natural habit for her. She sat up and looked at Daisy. "I cannot pass because the one thing that I cannot do is lie to myself. I value myself more than that. Act like a stiff hag? That I can do. But lie to myself? I will not ever do that."

"What are you lying about?" Rosie eyed Daisy suspiciously. Daisy assumed that Rosie was determining the level of trust Daisy had earned.

"Another day perhaps. Now, it is time for bed." Rosette stood up from the bed, grabbed a sleeping gown from her wardrobe, and closed the door to the bathroom behind her. Daisy stood alone in the silent, lifeless room. The bed beckoned her closer; travelling was wearing, and she knew the next day would also be exhausting. As she laid down on the bed, intending to wait for Rosette to exit the bathroom, her head hit the pillow and the exhaustion in her bones overwhelmed her.

At some point during the night, Daisy woke up to the click of their door. She looked around and noticed Rosie had left. Thinking nothing of it, Daisy quickly changed into more comfortable clothes and went back to bed.

Chapter 6 - Adjustments and Corrections

The morning was announced with the tinny ring of a bell sounding down the hallway. Rosette immediately rose and started to get ready. Daisy was unsure when she had returned to the room but followed Rosie's lead in getting ready. She picked one of the plain, cream frocks from the wardrobe and got dressed. She brushed her mousey hair back into a bun and slipped a small, flower barrette in it. Lastly, she slipped on a pair satin house boots. Rosette also appeared to be ready to go, but stood by the door, waiting. Daisy went to stand beside her.

"There will be a second bell," Rosie explained in a hushed voice. "That is when we enter the hallway for inspection. If our attire meets the Dame's expectations we are permitted to go to breakfast. If not, you will change your outfit until it does. She doesn't tell you what she is looking for, but eventually you will figure it out. There is no hard rule as it varies from person to person. I wish you luck and hope you will join me at breakfast soon."

Shortly thereafter, a second bell rang through the manor. Doors, including theirs, swung open and ladies in sets of two flooded into the hallway. Standing on either side of the door, the ladies waited for their turn. Daisy could feel her anxiety building. It was like waiting for her mother's harsh criticisms everyday, but somehow worse. She was terrified that she would not meet the expectations of the dame and be repeatedly sent to change. Her stomach growled in protest. She did not realise how hungry she was until the thought of not eating presented itself.

Daisy watched out the side of her eye as the dame waltzed down the hall. The first few girls were acceptable and followed each other down to breakfast. Dame Agatha paused at the next girl. Her face reflected no emotion, yet Daisy was sure that Dame Agatha was not pleased with what was before her.

"You are not wearing the appropriate corset, are you Ellie?" The girl, assumed to be Ellie, shook with fear as she stared back at the Dame. "Turn around." Ellie did. The Dame undid the back of her dress in the hallway and glared at the lack of undergarments"

"My corset wouldn't fit this morning, Ma'am," Ellie pleaded.

"Then you have gained too much weight and could do without breakfast anyways. You will join the other students at the first lesson."

Without a glance back, Dame Agatha continued making her way down the line. Some girls made it through, others had to make changes. Those requiring changes were quick to do so and came back to the hallway for reassessment. Finally, Dame Agatha came to her and Rosette. Agatha glanced at Rosette and dismissed her with a subtle wave of her hand. Agatha then turned her attention to Daisy.

The weight of Agatha's eyes were heavy as she examined every inch of Daisy. Unsure of what was delaying Agatha, Daisy started going through a mental checklist of her attire. Corset, petticoat, tights, shoes, and frock were all accounted for. She didn't have much variation in colour to change into something different. Her hair was tidy and pulled back. Daisy wasn't sure what could be displeasing the Dame.

Suddenly, Daisy felt a sharp pain in her cheek and saw stars in front of her eyes. She reoriented herself and gently grabbed her cheek. Before Daisy had time to fully understand what had occured, she felt the same pain in her other cheek.

"Get colour in those cheeks or expect regular adjustments. Today, you are dismissed. However, this best be corrected by tomorrow."

Daisy caressed her burning face as she made her way down the hall. *Had the dame truly just slapped her twice to bring colour to her cheeks?* Daisy's head swam. *What was this place? What had Daisy been thrown into?*

She made her way to the dining room, face burning with pain, and met Rosette at the table. Each lady in attendance had different food and acted in much more relaxed fashion then they had the previous night at dinner. There was idle chit chat and hardly anything was synchronised. This made Daisy feel more comfortable but the surprise of the last five minutes had not yet worn off. Rosette eyed Daisy over her porridge and tea.

"Let me guess," Rosie started and the room fell quiet as she spoke. "Not enough colour in your cheeks?" A few snickers echoed through the room. Daisy felt like she was being left out of some joke and did not appreciate being the object of humour.

"She slapped me. Twice," Daisy retorted.

"Better than some of the girls' first experiences. I promise you."

"She cut my hair in the middle of the hallway," offered one lady with short red hair.

"She tightened my corset so much I passed out," another slender and tall girl with brown skin stated. It was the same girl that gave Daisy a reassuring smile the night before. She must have been a recent addition and the pain of being new was still fresh.

"She ripped my dress clean off me," Rosie finished. Everyone stared at Rosie with a mix of fascination and horror. "She apparently thought it was stolen. Not entirely sure where that came from, but she ripped it off and I stood in the middle of the hallway in my knickers. I'd take a slap to the face over standing in my undergarments in a hallway."

Another girl entered the dining room obviously passing her second examination. She appeared frazzled, but otherwise unharmed. "The dame will be arriving shortly," she explained and took a seat at the table.

This announcement appeared to sap the joy and friendliness out of the room. Suddenly, everyone was sitting properly, slowly eating their food, and attempting to match other people's movements. Daisy followed suit, mimicking actions and behaviour, endeavouring to understand the unusual patterns. Another lady entered shortly followed by the dame. Agatha sat at the head of the table and began eating without another word. Daisy noticed that no one spoke and simply stared at the person across from them. It was uncomfortable to lack any social aspect of a meal. Even though her family was not amicable in most cases, Daisy could at least listen to her mother and father discuss the estate, or local politics, or anything really. It made meals not feel lonely. A slight tinge of homesickness bubbled in her stomach but quickly subsided as the dame began to speak.

"As usual, we will be hosting the Winter Solstice Ball for all of the town's people at the end of the season. It is expected that you will be on display for potential suitors." The dame paused and almost seemed to glare at Rosette over her next words. "Wealthy, *male* suitors. Although all will be in attendance, you are expected to focus mostly on appropriate matches while maintaining the perfect decorum of a lady. Most of you were sent here to find suitors or be made into an eligible bride. We have had a sharp increase in the number of students starting this season. As such, this season's lessons will focus mostly on preparing for the ball including group etiquette, partnered dancing, and consuming sustenance in the presence of others. Classes begin immediately following breakfast. Students will be pulled out individually for attire assessments and dress fittings. You are excused."

Dame Agatha stood from the table and strode out the open door. Shortly after, each girl also rose from the table and filed out the door. They seem to split in two directions as the group was separated into two classes.

Rosette explained that Daisy would be staying with her for the time being. As such, Daisy followed Rosie to their first class.

Their first class was a thrilling lecture on the proper uses of different forks. Although there would be no formal meal at the ball, the ladies were still required to understand the different forks and their purposes. Daisy kept confusing the table and dinner forks. They all looked the same. Some were big, some were small, but didn't they all serve the same purpose? Allowing one to stab food to transport to their mouth?

After examining various forks for what felt like hours, there was a series of dishes brought out that utilised the different forks. As the instructor droned on about matching the forks to the appropriate dish, Daisy glanced outside.

There were several gardeners standing outside of the window looking confused. Daisy noticed several white and yellow flowers had sprouted across the lawn seemingly overnight. They were not in the manicured flower beds, nor did they seem to match any of the flowers beside them. Daisy tried to contain a giggle as she noticed a gardener struggling to pick one of the flowers from the ground. When he promptly fell over from his attempt, Daisy made a slight snort which Rosette noticed. She also glanced out the window. Another gardener was pulling with all his might to extract this flower and failing horribly. A third gardener soon joined them with pruning shears that also seemed unable to cut through the flowers. Rosie made a slight, stifled laugh which Daisy noticed. Their brief moment of joy was destroyed as Daisy heard her name called from behind them.

Standing in the doorway to the classroom was the dame and a small man with black hair that was starting to whiten. He seemed nervous and almost hid behind the dame. Daisy understood it was her time for wardrobe assessment and dress fitting. She politely excused herself from the table and joined the dame at the door. Daisy was escorted back to her room where a draped box and mirrors were placed in the centre of the room.

"Sir Fedewick is the manor's tailor," Dame Agatha explained. "He will assess your attire and determine what will be most appropriate for the ball. Please open your wardrobe for his perusal."

Daisy did as instructed and stepped back for the tailor to examine the wardrobe. He shuffled things around and eventually pulled out a royal blue, faille dress and garnet red, silk dress. Daisy knew these dresses were some of the old dresses from her sister that her mother tossed in her trunk. Daisy doubted they would fit her properly. Azalea had a much fuller, womanly figure than Daisy. She fell flat in most places, but did not feel obligated to inform the other people in the room of the situation.

"I believe either of these will be the most appropriate for the ball based on her wardrobe." Sir Fedewick had a high, nasally voice that sounded like someone was holding his nose while he spoke. "The majority of her wardrobe is plain and lacks anything that will catch a suitor's eye. They will require extensive alterations, however."

"Very well. Miss Bloomsbury please try on the blue dress first. Your eyes are relatively grey, but hopefully the dress will pull some blues into your eyes." The dame appeared displeased with Daisy's selection of dresses, but conceded to the tailor's professional opinion.

Daisy pulled off her current frock and stood in her undergarments. She felt exposed and vulnerable as the other people in the room analysed her uncovered body. Before Daisy could put on the other dress, the dame tightened her corset, re-adjusted her petticoats and stockings, and made Daisy take off her shoes. Cinched, positioned, and barefoot, Daisy stepped into the faille dress.

The dress fit better than Daisy expected. The plunging neckline exposed her corset which Daisy knew was unacceptable. Azalea's figure allowed her to wear clothes like this without a corset. There was a piece of fabric wrapped around her waist, making her waist appear even smaller. A full length skirt and long sleeves gave the dress a sense of elegance. It lacked the normal patterns and frills, but Daisy actually preferred that. A slit up the front of the dress slightly exposed her leg as she walked towards the box in the middle of the room and stood atop it.

The tailor and the dame surveyed Daisy, taking in every inch of the dress. The dame occasionally poked or pulled at different parts of the dress, assessing the quality and fit. The tailor stood nervously beside her and fiddled with the tape measure in his hands.

"We will have to build in the corset. She does not have enough figure to hold the dress and the corset showing through the neckline is not expectable," Dame Agatha critiqued.

"Alternatively," the tailor squeaked, his anxiety palpable. "We could put in a complimentary colour panel to raise the neckline, remove the current waist wrap, and add a matching sash."

Agatha glared at the tailor, considering his offer. She didn't seem pleased with the suggestion, but Daisy wanted to say she was more comfortable with the second option. Azalea was the showy one; Daisy was always more reserved and was not ready to expose herself like this to the world yet. Especially after what happened with Lord Cornithian, Daisy wanted to blend in more than stand out.

"I suppose that is an option," Agatha conceded. "Besides, she should not be a primary attraction yet as she is not ready for a suitor. Please stitch up the leg slit as well. Miss Bloomsbury, change back into your attire and return to your class."

Daisy did as instructed and made her way back to class. The instructor was just finishing comparing a dessert fork and a pastry fork. Rosette looked completely absent and jolted at Daisy's reappearance beside her. Rosie seemed pleased to have Daisy sitting beside her again. The lecture was completed with a boring finale of pastry forks and the ladies were dismissed.

Daisy and Rosie proceeded into the hall for a short break between lectures. The break was considered a refreshment period where the ladies were able to digest the information from the lesson before proceeding to the next.

Rosie led Daisy outside for a refreshing jaunt in the sunny afternoon air. Daisy was excited to get the chance to go outside as she was curious about the flowers that challenged the gardeners. The girls made their way over to the flowers and found that the gardeners had abandoned them, whether in frustration or just temporarily in order to acquire new tools, Daisy was unsure.

As they approached the flowers, Daisy couldn't help but smile. Spreading across the lawn was a series of white and yellow daisies. It was not common to see daisies back at home as they weren't natural to the area. But here, they seemed to grow plentifully and uncontrollably. Daisy bent down and delicately plucked a flower out of the ground with very little effort. Rosie snickered at the ease in which Daisy picked the flower in comparison to the gardeners' struggle.

Rosie then attempted to pick a daisy, but, alike the gardeners, she was unable. She pulled with all her might, but the flower would not budge. Soon, her hands gave out and she promptly fell over in a mess of skirts. After helping Rosie back to her feet, Daisy moved over to the flower Rosie was struggling with and pulled the flower out of the ground as if it was sitting in a vase. Colour flushed Rosie's face as Daisy handed the flower to her.

"I swear you have some way with these flowers. No one can pick them but you," Rosie said perplexed.

Daisy and Rosie laughed at the concept. It seemed like a silly thought and yet, oddly true. Daisy had no issue picking daisy after daisy. Rosie, on the other hand, fell over trying to pull a daisy from the ground.

Daisy looked around, wondering when the gardeners would return. Suddenly out of the corner of her eye, she noticed a man with messy black hair disappearing into the forest at the edge of the property. He seemed familiar, but Daisy couldn't place him. The thought left her mind as quickly as it had entered.

"Can I ask you something, Rosie?" Daisy said. Rosie nodded her head. "Where did you go last night?"

Rosie's face paled, and Daisy became uncomfortable. Clearly, Daisy wasn't supposed to know Rosie left.

"When you have been here as long as I have, you gain certain - privileges. Little freedoms if you will," Rosie stated.

"So, where did you go then?" Daisy inquired. Rosie pursed her lips and shook her head. She did not appear to want to discuss her adventure, and Daisy did not have the courage to press her further. Rosie turned away from Daisy as if she was hiding something.

After a few moments, Rosie broke the awkward silence, "We best be returning to class.We will not learn about the various uses of spoons any other way." Reluctantly, Daisy followed her lead.

The afternoon lecture was a thrilling mix of spoon and glassware use. Daisy felt nearly equipped to deal with a place setting consisting of ten forks, eight spoons, and twelve glasses. Knives, on the other hand, still were perplexing. She knew she would eventually learn, but her brain was already so full of flatware that she wasn't sure how much more she could withstand.

The evening was a relaxing session of reading common literature. When dismissal for the evening came, Daisy was oddly excited for bed. Rosie and her exited quickly after dinner and made their way to the solace of their room. When they opened the door, they were greeted by the light scent of flowers. The window was open and sitting in its sill was a bouquet of daisies in a carved stone vase. The flowers almost appeared to be the same daisies from the garden.

"When did those get there?" Rosie asked.

"I was hoping you would know," Daisy responded. She approached the flowers carefully. There was a small card in the flowers.

"What does it say?"

"Enjoy. From A."

"Who is A?"

"No idea."

Chapter 7 - Invitations

As the season waned and the ball quickly approached, an air of excitement and anxiety filled the manor. Many of the ladies nearing completion were hoping to catch the attention of a suitor. The other girls were excited to socialise with those outside the manor. It became quite clear to Daisy that students of the manor did not interact much with the town's people or other outsiders. It seemed the manor kept much to itself. The only people to leave often were the servants to grab supplies and Rosie who sneaked out several nights a week. When Rosie would come back, her clothes were often rumpled and her hair a bit messy, but she would quickly crawl into bed; Daisy never had the nerve to ask her about it. Daisy always wanted to follow her, but the day's lessons proved more exhausting than Daisy expected, leaving her without the energy to pursue Rosie.

The majority of the season's lessons were overwhelmingly boring; however, some aspects were slightly helpful. The class on posture and foot positioning was a particularly dull class. The only class Daisy found interesting was dance. She had seen her sister dance so many times, but never really experienced the beauty in the movements herself. Azalea was elegant and graceful like a swan and always captured an audience's attention even in crowded ballrooms. Although she was still learning, Daisy could comfortably dance a waltz, polka, two step, and schottische. She was no expert and certainly found keeping time a challenge, but she enjoyed the task nonetheless.

Rosie's companionship continued to be useful for Daisy. She helped Daisy pass most of the morning inspections and filled in the gaps of Daisy's education. As it turned out, Daisy hardly knew anything about being a proper lady. She thought she was well trained, but Dame Agatha and her instructors regularly poked gaping holes in Daisy's education. Without Rosie, Daisy would have flopped already and been sent home as a lost cause. Throughout their companionship, a friendship between the two girls blossomed. They were nearly inseparable. They did nearly all their lessons together and were often partnered during special tasks. It was a relief to Daisy to have someone that treated her well and actually seemed to like spending time with her.

Rosie became even more important to Daisy when a letter arrived one day in late September. Daisy was called to the dame's office and a piece of parchment lay on her desk. The dame instructed Daisy to sit. A concerned look on the dame's face made Daisy incredibly uncomfortable. Slowly, the dame slid the parchment across the table to Daisy. Expecting a letter, Daisy was baffled to see a mourning card placed in front of her. Staring back at Daisy from the mourning card was a picture of Azalea.

"How did you get this?" Daisy fumed. It must not be true. Azalea could not have died.

"It came with a letter this morning from your parents," the dame responded. Daisy tried to hold back tears but was failing.

"Why did they not send for me?" Daisy managed to mutter through the tears. "I should have been there."

"According to the letter, your parents thought your schooling was more important than your attendance and did not think your presence was required."

"May I see the letter?" Dame Agatha paused. She seemed to ponder if this was the best option before sliding another piece of paper across the desk. Daisy picked up the piece of paper and instantly recognized the loopy, slanted writing of her mother's penmanship.

Dear Dame Agatha,

Enclosed, you will find a mourning card for our beloved daughter, Azalea. She died unexpectedly on August 31 after a terrible carriage accident. As such, it would appear that Daisy is our last chance at an heir. We expect that you will focus on getting her ready to marry. We do not wish to see nor hear of her until she is betrothed. If you should fail and she is unable to secure an acceptable match, her claim to the Bloomsbury name will be renounced.

Duchess Bloomsbury

Daisy had arrived at the manor only a few days after her sister's passing, surely her parents would have had enough time to send for her. However, it appeared her parent's wanted nothing to do with her now that Azalea was dead. Perhaps Azalea was the only reason Daisy hadn't already been disowned. Now that Daisy was their only hope for an heir, she proved somewhat useful, but no less a disappointment. Her options were becoming even more limited now. She was ruined and nearing rejection by her parents. The only family that cared for her was dead. Daisy had very little left to hold on to.

Daisy ran from the Dame's office and straight to her room. She collapsed on her bed and cried. Shortly after Daisy entered, Rosie appeared in the room. Rosie immediately came to Daisy's aide. Daisy curled against Rosie and cried for what felt like hours. The sun was setting before Daisy finally stopped crying. Rosie assisted Daisy down to the dining hall where dinner was just finishing. Dame Agatha must have informed the other students of Daisy's loss for no one questioned Daisy's appearance or absence. Daisy sat at the table surrounded by people but felt completely alone. Many of the other students sent sympathetic glances towards Daisy, but otherwise left her alone. She did not want to talk to anyone anyways. Food was placed before her, but she could not manage to eat. Everyone was dismissed after dinner, and, exhausted by the emotional trauma of the day's news, Daisy promptly fell asleep.

In the months that followed, very little pierced through Daisy's sorrow. The only thing Daisy enjoyed was the random gifts that kept showing up in her and Rosie's room. They were small pieces of joy that could momentarily distract Daisy from the pain of her sister's death and her parent's dismissal. One day, there was a beautiful wooden box; in it Daisy found a small hair comb decorated with daisies. Daisy wore it for the next week. There were lots of little gifts always on the window sill and always signed by A. The gifts' intended recipient remained unclear until a poem was left on the sill. As Daisy read the poem, she felt herself blush, and, despite Rosie's inquiries,

Daisy refused to let her read it. It appeared that Daisy had a secret admirer.

It was the day before the ball. The manor was teeming with a palpable excitement that even Daisy was feeling. Although the pain of her sister's death had not subsided, the ball seemed to provide a perfect distraction. The ladies were getting ready to go into town and deliver invitations. Daisy thought it odd. At home, her servants did this. Yet, Dame Agatha insisted that the ladies present themselves to the public and personally invite each resident. The dame never explained why and Daisy had quickly learned not to question her. The girls were to be paired and sent with wicker baskets containing rolls of parchment to specific streets. Luckily enough, Daisy was paired with Rosie.

Daisy and Rosie made their way down the front path, arms linked with their baskets in the other hand. Both were excited to be leaving the manor even if it was just to hand out invitations. Unlike the other pairs, Rosie and Daisy were not assigned a street. They were instructed to stand in the town square and hand out rolls to passerbys. This was a preferable option to Daisy. She had hoped that she might run into the stranger from the train. His voice and image often appeared in the back of her mind; these sounds and images were little rays of light that managed to shine through her dark sorrow. Daisy would often focus on him just as a distraction. Perhaps it was because he was the only other person outside of the manor she knew, or perhaps it was because she found him extremely handsome. She worried he might not remember her for it had been several months since he walked her to the manor. Either way, she desperately hoped to see him again.

They arrived at the town square which was nearly empty. It was early morning and it appeared that most of the townsfolk were still resting as hardly a rodent even stirred. Rosie took off to talk to the baker on the corner. After living in Grenich for four years, Rosette seemed to know most of the merchants around the town square. This did not appeal to Daisy. She did not enjoy idle conversation and small talk. Instead, Daisy made her way towards the large fountain in the centre of the square.

She vaguely remembered the fountain from the first time she passed the square. It was made completely out of stone. The train at the top of the three tiered fountain shot water from its chimney. Water overflowed from each bowl down to the next. Various symbols adorned each layer. The top tier was decorated with clouds, swirls, flames, and what appeared to be smoke. The middle tier had leaves, mountains, wolves, and rough circles. The final bowl, which was the largest, had various water symbols, but every once in a while a person's silhouette broke up the pattern.

As Daisy got even closer to the fountain, more details became clear. At one point in time, the fountain must have been stunning, but the years had not been kind. Daisy noticed on the bottom bowl paint that had been chipped away from years of weather. The fountain now looked like plain stone with flecks of coloured dirt. Even more saddening was the shape of the train. Some of the wheels on the train had broken away. The engine was off centre. Based on the jagged base Daisy could see, she assumed that there was once train cars in addition to the engine. Now, the engine stood alone and broken atop a deteriorating fountain. In her investigation of the fountain, Daisy had not realised that someone else had joined her. It wasn't until he spoke did Daisy realise she ran into exactly who she was hoping to run into.

"There's a story to this fountain, you know." The stranger stood beside her. His hair tousled and ebony in the sun. He admired the fountain and continued to speak. "People say that long ago, there was a battle between two factions: the Oppressors and the Subjugates. Of course, the Oppressors did not name themselves that, but history is often written by the victors. Anyways, the Oppressors had ruled for a great length of time, but were cruel and evil. They sought out those that were different and burned them at the stake in public forums. Those that were burned were named the Subjugates."

"Eventually, the Subjugates tried to fight back, but were losing horribly. They fought as best they could, but they lacked the manpower and abilities to make a stand which proved to be deadly. There was another group of people, however, that were immensely powerful, but tried to stay out of the war. They did not relish the idea of conflict and tried to live peacefully. They mostly used their powers to benefit humankind, not fight for it. They were able to conduct the forces of nature around them. Earth, fire, air, water, and mind. The Subjugates were able to align with these people to push back the Oppressors. However, in doing so, they took many losses. Eventually, the Subjugates won thanks to this group of people."

"But why the train?"

"The people that changed the tide of the war were said to come from the trains. Trains were uncommon at the time. Legend says that after the war, they became the conductors of the trains and used their way with the elemental forces to power and control the trains. Some people still say that train conductors are the group from the story, but there is really no proof of this. Today, the group has become known to some as the Conductors due to their job and their abilities to conduct elemental forces. Maybe also because of the train thing, but really, trains were so minor. I think it is mostly because they conduct the forces."

"It is a truly fascinating story. I can only imagine what a time like that would have been like."

"I see they have been teaching you formality, my lady." He removed his hat and bowed to Daisy. She had not meant to be so formal, yet she could not help it. "It's a perfect shame to ruin a mind, such as yours, with the frivolity of ladyship. Might I intrigue you in an afternoon of freedom?"

He extended a hand in her direction. Daisy stood stunned, contemplating the stranger's offer. She hardly knew this man. She glanced down at the basket full of invitations. She had duties to attend to. She looked towards Rosie who was still chatting with the Baker, clearly ignoring their assigned task. Were any of the other ladies attending to their responsibilities? Or was this the opportunity to break rules and experience that which the manor deprived them of?

"I have invitations to give out,"Daisy finally managed to say. "The manor is hosting the Winter Solstice Ball tomorrow, and all Grenich residents are invited."

"Ah," he stated, but his voice did not seem disappointed. "In that case, I will just take an invite." He reached into the basket and grabbed out an invite. "And one for Tom, my co-worker. And one for Pim who rents a room in the same Inn as me. And one for..." he continued saying names and pulling invites until the basket was empty and his hands were full of parchment. Daisy couldn't help but laugh at his ingenious way of removing a barrier.

"Just a moment then." Daisy excused herself and went over to Rosie who had just finished talking with the baker. Rosie smiled as Daisy approached.

"Your basket is empty," Rosie noticed.

"Quite right." Daisy lowered her voice so that only Rosie could hear. "I have what may be a potential suitor vying for my attention this afternoon." Daisy gestured towards the stranger standing at the fountain. Rosie looked at him and he gave a slight, awkward wave.

"Can he be trusted?"

"If he was going to harm me, he had plenty of opportunities already to do so. I think he is rather harmless."

"Well, I must say, I am glad you are willing to bend the rules. I was concerned you might have gone completely lady like on me." Rosie smiled with a soft laugh that reassured Daisy. "I've seen him in town before and he has never taken much interest in other people. However, I know hardly anything about him." Her look suddenly turned stern and almost motherly. "Do be careful, Daisy. I would never forgive myself if something happened to you."

"Of course, Rosie. I will ensure I am back before we are due to return to the manor. Please cover for me if required."

"Obviously," Rosie smiled and Daisy departed. The stranger beamed with excitement as she approached him. He stuck out his arm for Daisy to grab; she obliged.

He pulled her out of the square towards the waterfront. He took a turn at the docks and headed down the beach. Winter was setting in. Some ice chunks dotted the beach. The trees had lost their leaves and some snow pillowed on bare bushes. The town square still seemed so fall like, but on the ocean, winter was more prevalent.

"How did you like the gifts?" he asked.

"What gifts?" Daisy pondered.

"Um, the flowers and the hair comb and all the other little things. I, uh, had them delivered to the manor."

"Oh, so you are my secret admirer then?!?" Daisy felt an odd sense of relief at knowing who it was, but also slightly uncomfortable that this stranger was giving her so much attention and so many gifts.

"I guess that is one way to put it. It's hard to get into the manor or to talk with its residents, but I enjoyed our conversation on the way to the manor. I just wanted to stay in contact. Though, the conversation was rather one-sided I might add."

"I did not know who was sending them in order to respond," Daisy dictated. He looked at his feet and smiled.

"Yes, perhaps a small oversight on my part."

A cool sea breeze snapped Daisy's attention back to the sea and away from the stranger. The cold breeze hitting her skin was a welcomed feeling. Daisy had not realised how hot she was until the breeze hit her face. Thus far, the fall had been mild with very few signs of winter. She breathed in the salt air and momentarily closed her eyes. When she opened them again, a blanket and a basket sat before them. They appeared as if out of nowhere. Perhaps Daisy had not seen the basket as they were approaching, but she was positive the beach had been bare and he had not been carrying anything. She couldn't understand it, but maybe the stranger could provide more insight.

"Were you planning on bringing someone here today?" Daisy teased.

"More like I had hoped to bring someone here today. Otherwise, I was going to enjoy a peaceful lunch by the sea with the most handsome man in all of Grenich!" Daisy raised her eyebrows at him. "Well, me of course."

Daisy giggled at his comment. His confidence was attractive. He dropped her arm and bent down beside the basket. He pulled out a cushion and handed it to Daisy. Grabbing the cushion, she took a seat on the blanket opposite to him. He was rummaging around in the basket and pulling out its contents in a seemingly random order.

"May I ask you a question?" Daisy inquired.

"Only if you drop the formality." He looked up at Daisy through long lashes with a smirk across his face.

"Sorry. Dame Agatha does make it a habit," Daisy explained endeavouring to drop the annoying tendencies that were being brainwashed into her. "I've met you several times now, but I don't know what to call you. What is your name?"

He scowled, but Daisy was unsure if it was because of the basket contents or her question. He finally stopped fussing with the basket and looked directly at Daisy. His eyes were tense and most definitely blue. Blue like indigo actually. A shocking and beautiful colour that confused Daisy. Weren't his eyes green before? But there was no mistaking his eyes now. They were such a bright and startling shade of blue that entranced Daisy in their depths.

"What do you wish to call me?" The question befuddled Daisy. Most people go by their names so who would ask such a question?

"What would I call you besides your name? I know nothing of you and call you a stranger in my head. I would like to know your name. You know mine." He returned to pulling things out of the basket. Moments passed and Daisy felt like she somehow insulted him. She had no idea what could have insulted him, but she was certain she did something wrong.

"I've gone by many things and will likely go by many more." He finally sat down across from Daisy on his own cushion and took a large bite of an apple he had pulled out. He frowned at his apple. "Currently, my friends call me Ambrose, Ames for short, but it is not a name I particularly enjoy."

His words confused her yet again. He was an interesting man, yet the majority of what he said made little sense to Daisy. She was trying to make sense of his words when she realised it had been many moments since he had spoken. She looked up and saw that he was watching her intently.

"It's a unique name," she said, unsure of what else to say.

"It was not my choice, that I can assure you."

"I don't think any of us choose our names. Our parents do that."

"You'd have to have parents in order for that to be true." His voice was flat and not hinting at what he meant by this statement. He looked down at his shoes avoiding eye contact. The only thing Daisy could think of was that he was an orphan; Daisy could understand this pain.

"I recently lost my sister," Daisy stated in an attempt to empathise with him. "Losing those we hold dearest can be difficult. I cannot imagine the pain of losing those that we know should be important to us before we can even remember their names."

He stared at her in complete awe. It was like whatever he was burying was lifted from his soul. He reached out his hand in a comforting manner for Daisy to grab. She accepted and immediately felt some of the pain of her loss dissipate. She could feel a slight spark of happiness from the gesture. Clearly, he was the distraction she needed in order to escape from the fog of grief.

"You can call me whatever you desire," he finally said which broke whatever moment they were having. Their hands disconnected and Daisy busied herself with straightening her skirts.

"I would like you to call whatever you wish to be called," Daisy responded. He looked up at her. His face seemed perplexed and relieved at the same time.

"Abe. I think Abe is a better shortened version of Ambrose." He handed her an apple. She smiled at him and tried to bite into the apple in a lady-like manner. Most meals at the manor were strictly consumed by using utensils. Daisy was unsure about how to eat the apple, but reminded herself he did not seem to want the formality of a lady.

They sat for a while in near silence. The only sound present was the sea lapping at the shore and the quiet munching on an assortment of foods. He handed her bread, cheeses, various fruits, and eventually a piece of chocolate. He had poured a glass of wine, but wanting to keep her wits, Daisy declined the beverage. Abe now lounged on the blanket with the cushion propping up his head. His gaze was focused on the sky.

"How are you liking Grenich so far? You've been here a while now."

"I haven't seen much outside the manor. Today is the first day we've been permitted out and it's just to complete errands for the school really. We were not meant to socialise more than necessary." His head flopped to one side in order to look directly at Daisy.

"I apologise for pulling you from your duties, but I wanted to see you again. You intrigue me."

Before she could stop herself, Daisy blurted, "and why is that?"

He propped himself up on his elbows, really focusing on Daisy. This amount of direct attention made her uncomfortable. She picked at her dress trying to avoid his heavy stare.

"Do you believe the story I told you?" The change in topic took Daisy by surprise.

"Most folk's tales have some line of truth to them, so I assume somewhere in there is truth."

"I didn't ask if you thought it was true. I asked if you believed in it. Santa Claus isn't true, but people believe in him nonetheless." Daisy contemplated him for a second.

"Yes. I do believe it."

"And that is why I find you interesting." He laid back down and returned his focus to the sky. It appeared like Abe thought this explanation enough, but Daisy hadn't gained any additional insight. As if sensing her lack of understanding, he spoke again.

"On the train, you were the only one that stuck your head into the hallway. You are curious. When you realised your escort didn't show at the station, you endeavoured to find assistance or direction. You are resourceful. When we walked to the manor, you didn't expect me to haul the trunk alone but, instead, helped me. You are independent. I met you admiring a broken down fountain today. You are able to see beauty in the broken. You listened to a story and believed in the impossible. You were brave enough to leave the safety of the town to come with me, but smart enough to not accept my wine and only eat after you watched me consume the same food. You are an enigma in this monotonous world, and I have enjoyed the moments I have managed to have with you."

Daisy was stunned and was sure her face showed it. However, Abe seemed more interested in the sky than looking at Daisy.

"You can hardly know that from just meeting me. You barely know me."

"I may not know you, but I see you, and I think that can be more important sometimes. I do hope you will give me the opportunity to get to know you, however."

In the quiet that followed, Daisy could just make out the chiming of the clock in the town square. It was nearly time to return to the manor. She stood up from the blanket and brushed off her dress. Abe stared up at her from the ground. His hair spread out around him like a halo of night. With it pulled back from his face it was noticeable how long his eyelashes were. He was not particularly tall when he stood, but he was stretched out on the blanket giving him a lengthy appearance.

"I am expected back at the manor shortly. I really must return or I will be -" she cut herself short from saying punished. She knew that he would not like to hear of her being punished, but she didn't know how she knew that. "Or I will be late and that is frowned upon in the manor."

Abe stood up. He was taller than her, and she had to tilt her head up to look into his eyes. He was beautiful in a way. All harsh lines and dark colours against white skin and bright blue eyes.

Blue eyes? Or green eyes? She stared at his eyes trying to focus on their colour, sinking it into her mind. Why did she have such a tough time remembering his eye colour? His hair was black. His skin was white. But his eyes. Were they blue or green? They constantly seemed to change. Maybe it was the lighting. Maybe they were green in some lights and blue in others. Currently, in the flat light of an early winter day, they were a deep midnight blue. How could they ever be green when they were such a vibrant blue?

"We seem to keep running into the problem of staring at each other," he teased, pulling Daisy out of her revere.

"My apologies. Your eyes are entrancing at times and confusing at others."

"Confusing? How so?"

"This may seem rude, but what colour are your eyes?" Daisy needed to know the answer.

"Ah, yes." He laughed half-heartedly and began packing up the basket. "They are green and blue. Depends on my mood and the lighting. They change from time to time. I understand the confusion."

He smiled at her, picked up the basket, and extended his arm to walk her back to town. The walk back was relatively quiet. Only the sound of Daisy's shoes on the sand and brick broke the silence. It wasn't until they neared the square that noise started to echo from every which way. Daisy noticed Rosie sitting on the fountain, her basket empty. She waved as they approached. Rosie came running over to them and introduced herself to Abe. While he was polite, he did not seem interested in conversing with Rosie and quickly pulled Daisy out of ear shot.

"I must bid you goodbye here," he stated. A grin spread across his face. He bowed to Daisy, gently kissed her hand then stood awaiting her farewell.

"Will you be joining us at the manor tomorrow?" Daisy inquired.

"I suppose I have acquired several invitations." He chuckled at his own joke and Daisy couldn't help but smile. "Yes, I do believe we will be there."

"We? Who will be joining you?"

"My family of sorts. I do live in Grenich." Daisy felt her heart sink. Perhaps she was reading his signals wrong and he was just being friendly. If he had a family, perhaps he had a partner already. Surely, she would find out tomorrow, but her heart hurt with the idea of him belonging to someone else.

"I look forward to becoming acquainted with them."

"Until then, good day, my lady."

He gave one more slight bow and disappeared in the crowd. She watched him go until she lost him amongst the rushing people.

Chapter 8 - Daisy

His head felt light and fuzzy. He could hardly focus and nearly ran into several people on his way home. He felt like he just drank an entire keg of mead to himself, but without the regret or sickness. He was giddy and felt like a child.

She could see him.

Not that she knew what she knew. She hadn't the foggiest idea what any of it meant, but she could see him and that meant opportunity. There hadn't been many through all his years that could see him. He allowed the occasional person to see him, but she saw through his defences. She saw before he let her see. She was fascinating. She was unlike anyone he had met before, but he couldn't fully understand why. *What was it about her?* It wasn't normal for people to see through the veil. Maybe she had the innate ability. *When was the last time that someone had the innate ability?*

He wandered through his memories, trying to remember the last person that had innate abilities. None of his current studies displayed such characteristics. He allowed them to learn although they weren't predisposed. They had become skilled enough, but he couldn't remember anyone in recent years with such abilities.

Lost in thought, he barely noticed when he arrived at the train station. His feet had carried him there without conscious awareness; he stood in front of the plain brick wall beside the ticket booth. Abe glanced in the ticket booth to make sure no one was there before walking through the brick wall into the chamber hidden behind.

The room behind the wall was always interesting and constantly changing. This time, a series of hammocks were slung between walls. The two hallways off the main room were hidden behind heavy curtains of maroon fabric. Various pillows and blankets of the wildest colours covered nearly every inch of the place. There was a fire stoked in the fireplace on the far wall. Smoke drifted through the air carrying hints of jasmine and cedar. Overall, it was a warm and cosy aura that helped to clear Abe's mind of the strange girl.

Lounging about the room were his studies. Arlo laid in a hammock, sleeping with his face covered by a topless top hat. Brighid and Evander sat amongst a thousand pillows on the floor gently passing an orb of fire between them. Lastly, Alina stood by the fire making the flames dance.

Even in the dim, flickering light, he could see the startling mark of the Conductor's: mismatched eyes. Arlo's hat covered green and red eyes. Brighid was brown and blue while Evander was blue and purple. Alina's were always the most brilliant with a wine red and eggplant purple iris. They were a mixed bunch which was unusual for studies. Usually similar Conductor's grouped together, but Abe enjoyed a challenge and knew he was able to teach every force.

They hadn't noticed Abe's arrival yet and he cherished the moment before they would. Abe liked surveying his studies when they weren't aware. It gave a more clear concept of their progress. He took a deep breath and moved further into the room. The clicking of his shoes on the stone announced his arrival. The ball of fire fell to the floor causing all of the pillows to ignite. Evander snapped his fingers and splashed the pillows with water to put out the fire. Clearly, Abe's arrival was distracting.

"Damn it, Ames!" Brighid shouted. Brighid was young and sometimes her behaviour reflected her lack of life experience. "We were doing so well before you showed up."

"I saw," Abe stated. "You've made significant progress."

Brighid smiled brightly at him. Her eyes twinkled in the dim light. She clearly had been working hard on mastering the fire ball whereas Evander seemed bored with the task but assisted nonetheless.

Alina turned slightly and nodded to acknowledge Abe's arrival. She seemed irritated, but she was typically challenging to read. Nearly impossible at a distance. He navigated his way through the maze of hammocks and pillows to where Alina stood. She seemed completely focused on analysing her nails and purposely ignoring Abe.

"Her non-primary is coming along well," Abe said, breaking the ice between them. Alina looked up from her nails and flipped her hair in an irritated fashion. "You can't seriously be mad at me still?"

"I can be and I am," Alina spat. "You shouldn't have left this morning. You are supposed to teach these studies you've selected. I am here to assist you, but not do it for you."

"You chose a long time ago to join me. You knew what that meant. Quit acting like you don't want to teach them."

Alina crossed her arms. She lifted her chin and raised her nose clearly wanting to disagree with Abe but knowing she couldn't.

"What are you carrying?" Alina asked regarding the various pieces of parchment he carried.

"Ah, yes. I suppose I should address everyone." Abe clapped his hands and gathered everyone's attention. Evander smacked Arlo to wake him up. "Tomorrow evening we will be going on a field trip. We have been invited to a ball at the manor."

There were several groans and moans. No one seemed particularly pleased with this announcement. Abe needed to sell this, so he could see more of Daisy without abandoning his studies.

"As a Conductor, we still must blend in with the common people. It is important to socialise and talk with average people. We've been extended this invite, and we would be fools to not take it. As such, you will be required to dress appropriately. Brighid, Alina will assist you with a dress. Before you protest, yes you must wear a dress with shoes and the proper undergarments." Brighid, who had raised her hand in protest, let it drop in a pout.

"I'm used to pants," she grumbled. Her arms were crossed and her bottom lip protruded. Clearly the idea of proper attire and a ball were dissatisfying to her.

"Evander and Arlo, you may pick through my closet or muster your own attire, but your hats must have tops, and your ties must be clean."

"It had a top,"Arlo protested. "I don't know where it went, but it did have a top. It used to be a nice hat."

Although Abe had an office, he rarely used it, so he stored most of his belongings in the main room. Arlo hopped down from the hammock and made his way over to the trunk in the corner where Abe stored most of his clothes and began rummaging through it. He threw clothes in various directions with complete disregard for care of the clothes.

"And this is why your hats have no tops. Please be more careful."

As the various parties milled about the room discussing the ball and the requirements set out by Abe, he couldn't help but grin. It wasn't often they got out. He thought they'd be more excited, but instead they complained like children. They were becoming accustomed to hermitting and Abe knew this would not be beneficial in the long run. He had been around long enough to understand that humans required socialisation. No matter how independent or introverted, people needed people. It was Abe's responsibility to care for them. Regardless of how much they complained, he would have them all attend the ball.

He needed to attend the ball. He needed to see Daisy. He needed to learn more about her. The ball was an opportunity that he could not pass up.

***

Daisy and Rosie arrived back at the manor to a flurry of activity. Servants hauled flowers, decorations and candles to different parts of the manor in preparation for the Winter Solstice Ball. Dame Agatha stood in the centre directing the traffic. The door shut behind Daisy and Rosette which immediately caught the dame's attention.

"Did you distribute all of your invitations?" Dame Agatha questioned as she assessed a flower arrangement.

"Yes, Ma'am," they responded in unison.

"Very good. The tailor is in your room to complete your final fittings. Go now and when you are done please return here for your next assignment."

They immediately departed for their room. When they entered, both of their dresses were on mannequins.

Daisy's blue dress had a green panel added to raise the neckline. A matching emerald sash was tied around the waist. The colours were stunning jewel tones which were very contrasting to Rosie's peach dress. Rosie's straps came slightly off the shoulder emphasising the sweetheart neckline. Sir Fedewick instructed them to get changed which they quickly did. They helped each other with their chemises and corsets. Each dress consisted of multiple layers and various undergarments making them nearly impossible to get into without the assistance of another.

As Rosie stood on the pedestal with the tailor fussing over every minor detail, Daisy wandered over the flowers on the window sill. Even after all this time, the flowers had not wilted. They were just as fresh as the first day they arrived. They were lovely, but it still seemed unusual. Daisy hadn't thought about how long the flowers had lasted or how they remained fresh, but she didn't care. They were beautiful. She read the card again. When she held it up the window, she realised there was text on the other side.

Bellis perenis. Just as beautiful as you are.

Daisy felt herself blush. Abe certainly was a charmer. Perhaps not a proper suitor, but he knew what to say and when to say it. She imagined that Dame Agatha would be displeased with this expression of interest, yet the flowers had somehow gotten here. In fact, multiple gifts had gotten there. They would have had to go through the dame to get into the manor, so she mustn't have disapproved that much.

"Did you identify A?" Rosie inquired. Her arms were raised as the tailor analysed the side seam of her gown.

"Yes. His name is Abe."

"Will he be attending the ball tomorrow evening?"

"He said he plans to attend with his family."

"He has family? I have never seen him with other people."

"I suppose you will meet them tomorrow night then. I am sure they will be just as pleasant as he is."

The tailor made an odd sound and scrambled away from Rosie to rummage through his kit. He pulled a small needle, promptly poked Rosie in the side, and decided her dress was complete. It was Daisy's turn. Daisy stood on the pedestal. The tailor quickly walked around glancing at Daisy's dress.

"You are done," the tailor announced.

"You've hardly looked at it," Daisy exclaimed.

"I said, you are done. Now get off my stool so I may move on."

Daisy was confused, but obliged. The little man picked up his stool and scurried out of the room. They watched him go then dressed in their regular attire.

"So," Rosie said. "What exactly is Abe intending with you?"

"What do you mean?" Daisy questioned as she fixed her hair in the mirror.

"He seems interested in you."

"I am honestly not sure. He says I intrigue him. What that means, I do not know."

"I look forward to interrogating him tomorrow."

"Rosie!"

"Someone has to. You are not, therefore I must." Daisy smiled. Rosie often reminded her of Susan. She had a protective and caring nature. Daisy hadn't realised how important Rosie had become until that moment. Not only was Rosie her only friend at the manor, but she also felt like a sister. Daisy actually felt closer to Rosie than she did her own sister. Rosie was always kind and supportive. Azalea was only gentle with Daisy when they were alone. Rosie was the exact support and care she needed.

They quickly changed and departed their room for the next assignment. Rosie and Daisy were assigned to the thrilling task of stacking glasses for a champagne tower. It was tedious work that hardly seemed appropriate for young ladies. They ended up having to climb ladders to reach the top row. After completing four separate towers, and nearly toppling one, Daisy and Rosie were dismissed for the night.

"There will be no dinner tonight," the dame called after Rosie and Daisy as they climbed the stairs to their room. "The room is being decorated so there is no table available at this time. A servant will bring you food to your room."

"Yes, Ma'am," they responded. Daisy found the unison had become nearly second nature after her time at the manor. It still felt uncomfortable to Daisy, but it was easier to do now.

They opened the door to their room and a metal cart sat in the middle with two gold cloches. Rosie wasted no time in revealing dinner. On the plate sat a roasted turbot over gnocchi and morels. A green pesto flourish finished the dish. Daisy had not realised how little she ate that day until the food was presented. In their solitude, they abandoned their manners and devoured the food.

"Are you looking for a suitor tomorrow?" Daisy questioned.

"I hardly think I will find one," Rosie scoffed. "I've been attending these soirees for four years and have yet to meet a single interesting person that I would be allowed to consider a suitor."

"Below your status?"

"Um, you could say that. Although my status is not particularly high. My family doesn't own a manor like yours. I don't have servants that wait on me besides our cook and one maid that cleans the entire house. We aren't poor by any means, but I would say we are one of the lower class houses." Rosie played with remaining food on her plate seemingly having lost her appetite.

"Oh," Daisy paused. "Then I must ask, why are you here?"

"The same reason as you really. To be made the perfect wife for a *male* suitor." Rosie rolled her eyes.

"Do you not wish to be married?" Rosie stood up, placed her plate back under the cloche, and began pacing the room slowly.

"I do, just not in the way they want me to be." Daisy looked curiously at Rosie. There was something Rosie was not telling her. "It's nothing important. Don't worry about me."

She stopped in front of Daisy and brushed a piece of hair back behind Daisy's ear. Their eyes locked and in Rosie's eyes Daisy could see sadness and pain but also love and hope. Rosie's hand rested for a mere moment on her cheek before pulling it away. Rosie whisked herself away towards her wardrobe.

"We should get ready for bed. Tomorrow will be a long day." Rosie immediately changed into her nightgown, and Daisy followed her lead. The room was oddly silent after that. Daisy felt like she somehow offended Rosie but was unsure how. This seemed to be a growing trend for Daisy that she did not particularly like.

"Goodnight, Rosie," Daisy said as she crawled into bed. Rosie laid in hers and, within moments, was lightly snoring.

The moon was just visible through the window; it was a very bright full moon. Daisy stared at it in wonder. It was truly amazing. A giant white orb surrounded by the blackest black with twinkling specks. She watched the moon in silence until sleep finally overcame her.

Chapter 9 - The Ball

The next morning dawned with bright streaks of orange, pink, and red blazing across the sky. Daisy had hardly slept that night and found herself awake before the bells had even rang. The ball was the first true spark of excitement Daisy had felt since she found out about her sister's death. Daisy could hardly wait for the evening's event. She quietly crawled out of bed, ensuring she did not wake Rosie, and started refreshing herself in the lavatory.

When the bells rang, Daisy felt clean after days of being unable to properly wash. Their lessons occupied most of the day and were quite exhausting. By the time they returned to their room each night, they were barely able to change into nightgowns before falling asleep. Washing seemed hardly useful, but luckily the tasks were not overly physical requiring regular washing afterwards.

Exiting the washroom, Daisy saw that Rosie was completely ready to go. Not only that, but Rosie has selected Daisy's outfit for the day and laid it out on the bed. Daisy was grateful and changed into the assigned outfit.

"Could you help me with this?" Daisy asked, indicating the back buttons that Daisy could not reach. Rosie paused, uncertainty plain on her face.

"Yes, of course." Rosie shook her head, as if clearing cobwebs from her mind, and moved to assist Daisy. Rosie's hands were warm and gentle against Daisy's skin. Daisy hadn't realised she was cold, until Rosie's hands skillfully buttoned up her dress, skimming her skin with each movement.

The second bell indicated they were to move into the hallway for inspection. Daisy pinched her cheeks for colour as Rosie opened the door. Sitting in front of the door was a metal cart similar to the one from dinner the night before. Daisy glanced out the hallways and saw that every room had a cart outside of it. On the top of the cart sat two silver cloches. On the shelf underneath, sat a series of books, quills, and parchment. A small card was placed in-between the two cloches. Rosie grabbed the card.

"To prepare for the ball, all students will remain in their rooms," Rosie read aloud. Many of the rooms close by also listened. "There is literature to prepare talking points for tonight as well as sustenance for the day. When the orchestra arrives, all students will be expected in the main dining hall. Signed Dame Agatha."

"Are you serious? We are stuck in the room for the day?" asked one of the girls down the hallway.

"It appears so, yes." Rosie grabbed the cart and wheeled it into their room. Daisy was not particularly interested in eating yet, but she knew whatever the food was would be better warm than cold. Rosie removed the cloches revealing the sustenance for the day: eggs benedict with truffles and fresh basil. Rosie grabbed a plate and sat at her vanity with her back to Daisy. Clearly, their conversation from last night carried into today. It made Daisy uncomfortable. She did not want Rosie upset with her, but she figured it was best to give her space and time.

Daisy grabbed a plate and the book, *How to Converse Properly in Crowded Settings*. She sat at her vanity and read the book while absentmindedly eating the food. Hours passed and the booked lulled. Body language was the most important part of group conversations. Apparently, the direction of one's feet indicated the level of interest in a conversation. It was an informative read, but Daisy found herself struggling to stay awake. She found herself wanting to talk to Rosie, but, as Daisy had learned from her book, Rosie was not interested in speaking to her. The ringing of a bell indicated the orchestra had arrived and the ladies were expected to be ready promptly.

Rosie stood from her vanity and immediately began to dress. The sound of broken music as the orchestra warmed up mixed with murmured excitement that echoed through the halls. The boring tasks of the day only heightened the tension. Isolation proved to be exhausting and the thought of open socialisation was thrilling. While the intent for many was to meet a potential suitor, Daisy only had one thought on her mind.

Abe.

He had hardly left her mind since yesterday. He was witty and kind. He was handsome and manicured. He was interesting and exciting. He was everything Daisy wasn't looking for, but oddly wanted. Since their time on the beach, she was excited for any opportunity with him.

There was a sudden knock on the door. Daisy went to answer the door as Rosie put the finishing touches on her look. Behind the door stood a servant who held a black box.

"The dame requests that all attendees wear these." The servant opened the box to reveal two masks. One of the masks was green with blue detailing. The other was white with peach detailing. It was obvious which mask belonged to who. Daisy grabbed the masks and dismissed the servant. Returning to the room, she handed Rosie her mask.

"Interesting choice for the dame," Rosie said. Daisy was relieved to hear Rosie speak again. "In the four years I have been here, we have never had a masquerade. Did you actually read an invite?"

"No, I never thought to read one."

"Nor did I. How very interesting. Will you help me put it on?" Daisy assisted Rosie in repositioning her hair so that the mask sat comfortably. Luckily, Daisy decided to keep her hair in tight curls with just the sides pinned back, making the mask an easy addition.

Dressed and masked, Daisy and Rosie were ready for the ball. Whatever was bothering Rosie earlier appeared to vanish with the expected start of the ball. They departed their room and headed for the main dining hall. They were the first to arrive besides the dame who stood ready to inspect each arriving girl. The dame's eyes immediately fell on Daisy when they entered the room.

"You both look quite well put. Please stand over there." The dame indicated the far wall with a quick flick of her hand.

Slowly, the remainder of the students entered. A few were sent back for modifications, but the majority of ladies met expectations. The room was full of dresses in various colours and fabrics. Some of the girls nearing completion wore dresses that highlighted their feminine figure. Other ladies, like Daisy, were more reserved and modest.

"Our Winter Solstice Ball is about to commence," the dame announced. "Ladies that are ready for suitors will be introduced with a grand entrance into the foyer from upstairs. The remainder will be mingling with arriving guests. Once the introductions are complete, you will all be expected in the grand ballroom for dancing and socialising. I expect absences to be limited. Aim to socialise with as many people as possible as a good host is attentive. Now, to your places. Guests should be arriving shortly."

Daisy followed the ladies not ready for suitors into the foyer; Rosie continued upstairs to await the introductions. While Daisy's parents had made it quite clear she was to find a husband as soon as possible, the dame did not think she was quite ready yet. Daisy wished that they didn't have to separate, but Daisy was new, and Rosie was close to leaving. Daisy stood in the foyer with other ladies. Directly off the foyer was the grand ballroom. The ballroom was usually a plain looking room where lessons were held, but tonight, it had been transformed into a magical space that beckoned its guests to dance.

There were several bare trees with white bark meticulously placed around the room. There were crystals and small tea lights in glass orbs hanging from every tree. The crystals scattered the light from tea lights casting rainbows across the room. Round tables, decorated in silver and blues, had large vases of the white flowers sitting in the centre. The middle of the room was left open for dancing and the orchestra sat at the far end. The champagne towers Daisy and Rosie built flanked the orchestra. The room was elegant, elaborate, and enchanting; it was more than Daisy would have ever expected.

The orchestra began playing a soft tune meant to signal the arrival of the first guests. Soon, the ballroom was a crowded sea of all sorts of people dressed in elaborate masks, gowns, and tuxedos; they milled about the room awaiting a signal from the dame. The ladies of the manor did as they were instructed and socialised with the guests as they arrived. Daisy had been told to stay with a small, brunette girl named Clara. Daisy was often paired with her if Rosie was unavailable or absent. Clara exuded ladyness; her mannerisms and etiquette were exceptionally fine tuned. She was also beautiful with fine features giving her an almost doll-like appearance. Daisy knew when she was paired with Clara she would fade into the background just as she had with Azalea. Oddly enough, Daisy preferred this as it gave her time to look for Abe and his family without being considered rude.

The orchestra stopped playing and a tall, thin man stood in front of the band. He directed everyone to the foyer for the grand entrance. Slowly the guests made it to the foyer. There was hardly room to move with everyone packed so tightly in the small space. Daisy found it suffocating and was eager to move away from the area. Everyone congregated around the bottom of the stairs and directed their attention towards the dame.

The dame stood three stairs up from the bottom which placed her just slightly above everyone. She stood with her hands interlocked in front of her like she was singing in a choir. It was the first time Daisy had seen her wear something other than black. She wore a grey dress with black, lace detailing and long sleeves that slightly puffed out from the shoulder. It was a simple yet formal dress. She raised her hand and a silence fell over the crowd.

"Thank you for attending our event tonight," Dame Agatha announced in her most formal voice. "The manor is excited to host such a momentous evening as this. I would now like to direct your attention to the top of the stairs as I welcome our most eligible ladies to the ball."

One by one, the suitor-eligible girls made their way down the stairs. They moved like swans gliding across the water. As each girl reached the dame, she announced their name before they joined the crowd. Rosie was at the very end of the line. As she descended the stairway, she locked eyes with Daisy and smiled. Instead of mingling into the crowd as most of the girls did, Rosie immediately went to stand beside Daisy.

"Please enjoy your evening." With that, the dame dismissed the crowd and people dispersed in multiple directions.

"That was horrible," Rosie whispered to Daisy. "I hate being stared at like a cow at an auction."

"You'd make a very pretty cow," Daisy joked. Rosie returned the sentiment with a friendly jab to the ribs. "What? It's true!"

"Your contractions, my dear." Rosie winked and began to make her way towards the ballroom. Daisy followed. She made sure to keep her eyes out for any sign of Abe.

As they entered the ballroom, the dance floor was in full swing. Couples moved together in time with the music in an unusually complex dance that Daisy did not know. She watched idly for a moment as Rosie grabbed drinks for the two of them.

There was one couple that seemed particularly well versed in the dance. Their movements mirrored each other perfectly. Daisy could barely take her eyes off of them. The gentleman wore a black, double breasted vest with gold detailing that sparkled in the candlelight. A gold mask with a thick black band hid most of his face and hair. His ruffled shirt sleeves contrasted with his pressed, black pants. His lack of a jacket made him stand out amongst the other suitors, but he seemed comfortable and confident.

His partner wore a dusty rose dress with a large, frilled skirt underneath it. It was a style mirrored by many of the other guests. She was plain, but her movements made her stand out amongst most of the women. She clearly knew how to move well and knew exactly how to use her body to attract the attention of others.

Daisy noticed that Rosie was also watching the couple. While it was the man that intrigued Daisy, Rosie seemed to pay more attention to his partner. *Maybe it was the dress that Rosie liked?* Daisy thought that it might be considered pretty by some.

The crowd around them seemed to speak in whispers about the dancing couple. Even though plenty of others were dancing, this particular couple seemed to be stirring some gossip. In a small town like Grenich, everyone knew everyone, but, as Daisy idly listened to the murmurs around her, it became clear this couple was not familiar to most. Some gossipers said they had seen the man around town a few times, but the woman seemed completely shrouded in mystery.

As the dance ended and the couples bowed in thanks, the mystery gentleman's gaze fell on Daisy. He smiled with great excitement and waved at her. She looked around her expecting the stranger to be waving at someone else, but there was no one but Rosie beside her who also seemed confused at the gesture. The man and his partner made their way toward Daisy and Rosie. He bowed in front of Daisy and kissed her hand gently. The sentiment was familiar. It wasn't until he righted and Daisy saw his bright eyes did Daisy know who was behind the mask.

Abe.

Abe's partner seemed rather displeased with him, but she did not say anything.

"Miss Bloomsbury. It is lovely to see you again," Abe stated. His partner suddenly snapped her head towards Abe and looked incredulously at him. Daisy did not understand the reaction.

"As it is to see you, Sir Ambrose," Daisy responded. The formality felt uncomfortable and yet required considering the environment. His partner seemed incredibly irritated and left in a huff of skirts. Abe watched her leave before returning his attention to Daisy. Rosie rolled her eyes and departed in the direction of Abe's partner.

"You will have to excuse Alina. She was not thrilled with having to attend this evening. Did you enjoy the dance?" He asked, though there was a slight mocking tone to his voice.

"I did not know you could dance like that," Daisy responded and felt heat rush to her cheeks. She noticed several ladies talking behind their hands to each other, but looking at Abe. This made the heat feel like flames as she realised she, too, had become the object of gossip.

"The way to man's heart is through his stomach, but the way to a woman's heart is dance. Shall we?" He extended his arm as an invitation to dance. Daisy was nervous with the idea of dancing. She felt uncertain of her skills and even more uncertain about dancing with Abe. He seemed so experienced.

"I am not sure. I have not learned many dances yet," Daisy explained in hopes of avoiding dancing altogether. She had never been a good dancer. Her mother even hired a private dance instructor for her and her sister when they were younger. Unlike Azalea who effortlessly learned new dance moves, Daisy seemed to have two left feet. Where Azalea had been graceful, Daisy was clumsy and uncoordinated.

"Worry not. I will ensure you exceed expectations. It is all in your partner anyway." He indicated his arm again and Daisy obliged. Her hand slid around his elbow and she could sense a feeling of ease enveloping her. The fear of making a fool of herself nearly disappeared. They moved to the centre of the dance floor as the down beat for the next song began. Abe guided her into position as his arm gently caressed her lower back sending shivers up her spine.

"Are you alright, m'lady?" Abe breathed into her ear. He must have noticed her shiver. He gazed deeply into her eyes with a concern Daisy did not think she had earned yet.

"Splendid, actually." A grin spread across his face and Daisy found herself relaxing into his arms.

Her feet began moving in perfect synchrony with his. The music seemed to sweep her away. It felt like she was out of her body watching her and Abe dance across the floor. She could feel him guiding her in the most subtle of ways and found herself completing dance steps she had no idea how to do. For one move, their hands detached. Suddenly, Daisy felt like she was being slammed back into her body; she felt awkward, disoriented. Then she felt Abe grasp her hand and the feelings of lightness and ease resumed. It was as if her connection with Abe caused those feelings of contentment and effortlessness.

For a while, Daisy didn't want to let go of Abe and the only socially acceptable way to do that was to keep dancing. As the night wore on, Daisy grew weary of dancing; however, her desire to stay with Abe trumped her fatigue. Even though Daisy knew that dancing with one suitor was typically frowned upon unless there was consideration of an engagement, she didn't care. She was already being gossiped about so what more could they say? Besides, hardly any other suitors looked at her. Many other girls glared at her and whispered. Not only was Abe a mysterious and refreshing stranger, but he was clearly considered an eligible bachelor that Daisy didn't meet the suitability requirements for. Daisy tried to ignore the murmurs and glares. She was focused on Abe and his movements. All she wanted to do was to keep dancing with him. Finally, after several dances, a waltz started to play.

"I know how to do this one!" Daisy exclaimed. Some of the other dancers around her snickered at Daisy's remark, but she was barely aware of their presence. Abe's smile lit up his face as he indicated to Daisy to lead the way. He seemed overjoyed at Daisy's expression.

This time, when they took up a dancing position, Daisy didn't feel the same lightness. She didn't have an out of body experience, but she still enjoyed the dance. She was able to follow his steps though not as perfectly as previously. Abe seemed to allow Daisy more freedom in this dance although she was not sure what was different. Nonetheless, she enjoyed the dance.

As the song neared its end, Daisy noticed Rosie standing at the edge of the dance floor looking rather disappointed. Daisy felt obligated to see her friend. Abe almost seemed to sense it and immediately let go of Daisy at the end of the song. He bowed deeply.

"I require a short break. Would you like to meet my family?" Abe inquired. Daisy smiled and nodded her head. "Let us see if we can find any of them."

107

They moved to the side of the dance floor. Daisy heard many whispers as they moved. As they reached the edge of the dance floor, Daisy noticed the assessor intensely watching them. She seemed oddly pleased with Daisy and Abe's connection. The assessor slightly nodded as a final indication of approval before disappearing into the crowd. Daisy felt an odd sense of relief overcome her with the thought of someone's approval.

"Ah! Yes. Right there. You see the young girl with the blonde hair and the yellow dress?" Abe pointed to a couple in the middle of the floor. They were not dancing the same as most of the people, but seemed to be having a great time. "That would be Arlo and Brighid. Evander appears to be sulking in the corner over there."

"They all seem very nice," Daisy responded. She honestly wasn't sure what to say. She expected to speak with them, not just have them pointed out.

"If you will excuse me, my lady, I require a refreshment. May I rejoin you shortly?"

"If you can find me." Daisy winked and walked away, leaving Abe looking slightly confused in the wake of ladies suddenly converging on the unattended suitor. Daisy briefly looked over to where the majority of the refreshments were and noticed Alina, Abe's dance partner, standing by the table. Daisy tried to think nothing of it. She was somehow his family after all.

Instead of waiting on Abe, Daisy worked her way towards Rosie. When Daisy arrived at Rosie's side, she appeared deep in thought. Rosie hardly even noticed Daisy as she approached. Daisy gently bumped Rosie with her hip and snapped Rosie back to her surroundings.

"Welcome back to earth," Daisy jested. "You will find that you are in the middle of a ball with several hundred people."

"Oh, you are so funny," Rosie retorted dripping with sarcasm.

"What has vexed you, Rosie? You seem lost in your thoughts."

"I watch the ones I want to dance with infatuated with another that I cannot understand." Daisy looked at Rosie confused, but encouragingly. "Would you like to step outside with me for a moment?"

Daisy looked around, trying to locate Abe in the throng of moving bodies. She couldn't seem to find him. "I would love that."

Chapter 10 - Eavesdropping

When the girls exited the front door to escape the ball, they could hear elevated voices fighting somewhere in the field. They were loud enough to be heard over the music escaping from the manor. Rosie seemed to be thinking the same thing as Daisy and started to drift towards the voices, curiosity overwhelming them both. They rounded the corner of the manor to where a small patio sat. There were lanterns lighting the square and illuminating the two occupants. Quickly, Rosie and Daisy ducked behind the corner so they could listen to the argument without intruding.

"You keep running off to her!" One voice exclaimed that sounded female. "You've barely interacted with her over these past months, but you keep running to her and ignoring the rest of us. What is it about her?"

"Why does it matter?" Another voice responded, but it wasn't just any voice. It was Abe. Daisy felt something claw at her stomach, but she was curious. She knew so little about Abe and this seemed like an opportunity to learn much about him without interrogating him.

"You risked exposure repeatedly with these flowers and gifts and Gods only know what else. You danced the entire night with her and I can only imagine what exactly you were doing. What is your objective?! You are putting us all at risk. You brought us to this event for her, not for a learning experience. This is a great risk for what benefit?"

"She is fascinating." Daisy could hear the sense of awe in Abe's voice. It was the way Daisy thought most women wanted to be talked about. "I can feel an energy from her, and it is incredible and so very different from anything I have felt before."

There was a pause in the argument as Abe's words settled. Daisy could feel his intrigue in the way he spoke of this mystery woman. Clearly, whoever he was talking about was someone truly incredible. She imagined that the woman arguing with him also identified this and mustn't have appreciated his tone.

"Do you love her?" She questioned with a slight hint of pain and accusation.

"What does that have to do with anything?" His volume was raised with great insult at his partner's comment.

"It has to do with everything. You know the risks. What if the Grand Master finds out? You brought us all to a ball which is a great amount of exposure."

"She hasn't found out yet. I don't think that will change by interacting with one more person. Besides, tonight was a masquerade. We were not easily identifiable."

"How do you know? When was the last time you saw the Grand Master? What if she *is* the Grand Master?"

"I last saw her when you did. When she was in her last body. I don't even know what she looks like now." Rosie raised an eyebrow at Daisy. This sentence confused both of them. "But I know she isn't the Grand Master. I can feel her energy and it doesn't match."

"Are you sure you want another study? It has nothing to do with anything else?"

There was a great pause in their argument. The only sound was muffled music escaping from the manor. It was finally broken by a heavy sigh from Abe. When he spoke next, his voice was softer and lost its angry tone.

"We cannot be together and you know that. We tried, but it didn't work, so move on." There were footsteps, ruffling of fabric then quiet. Daisy peaked her head around the corner to see the two figures kissing. The girl had her hands wound tightly around Abe's neck. His hands were pushing against her hips and away from him, but her grip and kiss held. The lady's head obstructed Daisy's full view of Abe, but she didn't need to see him to know it was him. His voice had become etched in her memory. As they broke apart from their embrace, Daisy tucked back behind the corner to avoid being seen. This behaviour would be deemed unacceptable by most members of upper society. Daisy wasn't even sure what to think. *Did this mean they were married or going to be married? Was she ruined just like Daisy was?*

"Tell me you don't love her," the girl whispered. It was just barely audible.

"I barely know her." There was a sadness in his voice.

"Do you love me anymore?"

He paused. "I care about you deeply as I always have."

"That is not the same as love. Did you ever love me?"

There was an exasperated sigh then Daisy and Rosie could hear quick footsteps leaving the square and heading in their general direction. They pressed themselves against the wall trying not to be seen by the oncomer. The girl ran past Daisy and Rosie, not noticing them. It was the girl that had been dancing with Abe at the beginning of the ball. Alina. Clearly, she wasn't just some attendant nor was she just family. There was something more to Abe and Alina's relationship that Daisy just couldn't understand fully.

Panic crept up Daisy's throat. He had or maybe was in a relationship with this woman and he dismissed her so easily. Daisy grabbed Rosie's hand and began ushering them both away from the square and back to the manor. When they re-entered the manor, breathing heavily, Daisy directed Rosie into a secluded corner and finally stopped to explain to Rosie why the sudden need to leave. When she finished explaining, Rosie seemed completely unconcerned.

"You must be a wooden spoon then," Rosie responded, leaving plenty of space between each word for dramatic effect. "They were talking about you. He may be in love with you. You fascinate him. You are the mystery woman."

"But they were a couple at some point. She is clearly in love with him still," Daisy pleaded. She wanted her concern to be shared, not dismissed.

"Hun, you have found yourself a suitor without even trying. I have been stuck here for four years because I cannot find a suitor. He seems nice and you get along well enough. Why are you so adverse?"

"What if they were not talking about me? What if there is another lady?"

"You can speculate all you want, or you can experience and learn what this all means for yourself." Rosie gently placed her hands on Daisy's shoulders, pushing Daisy around to face Abe who was wading through the crowds towards them.

He was truly gorgeous. Even behind his black mask, his eyes shone bright blue. He walked with confidence and caught everyone's eye as he moved. Whether from attraction or intrigue, Daisy wasn't sure. He was the centre of attention yet seemed to ignore everyone around him. He had tamed his messy black hair somehow. The mere sight of him took Daisy's breath away and yet, an uneasy feeling had settled upon her.

Abe was practically a stranger. She had been in Grenich for barely a season and pure accident led her to meet Abe. Ever since then, it was a whirlwind of gifts, and courting, and learning. She didn't even know it was Abe courting her at first. Daisy was starting to feel overwhelmed. She could feel her legs getting heavy, her palms were sweaty, and her heart pounded harder with each step Abe took towards her. It was like time slowed, and Daisy could feel her anxiety building. Nothing about this was normal. Nothing about this was comfortable. She turned to run away, to hide, to avoid Abe, but Rosie's hand held strong.

"Daisy, do not let your head ruin a moment," Rosie whispered in her ear. Abe had nearly made it through the crowd.

"That is easy for you to say. I am panicking," Daisy squealed.

"Break a few rules. Go and *enjoy* him."

"Breaking rules is what got me here. I already ruined my name. Going with him will not assist me."

"Ah, but that is exactly why you should go with him. You have nothing left to lose." Rosie pushed Daisy and she fell forward directly into Abe's arms. He pulled her to her feet. They were very close now. Daisy could feel his breath on her cheek; the scent of lavender and cedarwood overwhelmed her senses. She tried not to shiver or pull away from him. She needed to hold her ground.

"Mind if I steal her for a dance?" Abe asked Rosie, but did not look away from Daisy. His mask highlighted his eyes even more and entranced Daisy.

"Not at all, but do return her eventually," Rosie said. Abe smiled and pulled Daisy back to the dance floor.

As the music sang through the room, Daisy found herself relaxing into the movements. She really did enjoy dancing, and Abe was an excellent partner, but she could not shake this feeling of concern. They completed several dances and the feeling still would not subside. She was enjoying herself greatly, but trepidation sat in her chest. *What would Abe do to her if he casted Alina aside so easily?*

"Would you join me in the garden for a moment?" Abe asked. Daisy nodded as she was unsure she could speak. Abe grinned and escorted her off the dance floor.

Most people ignored them as they made their way outside. The cold, winter night air was refreshing. Many guests had also moved outside. Daisy had not realised how stifling inside was until they moved further away from the manor. Out in the middle of the garden was a gazebo covered in ivy surrounded by rose bushes. There had been heavy snow the night before causing the ivy to lose its leaves and thick snow to blanket the rose bushes. The moon was bright and lit up the gazebo well. Abe moved away from Daisy and stood in the centre of the gazebo. He turned slowly, taking in the view, before stopping and staring at Daisy. He extended his hand and invited her into the gazebo. Daisy obliged.

Inside the gazebo, little fireflies flew around. Abe leaned against the railing on one side as Daisy turned in circles in the centre of the gazebo, amazed by the fireflies. It was unlike anything she had seen before. These dazzling bugs were blue and red and green and purple and bronze. They seemed to dance across the sky rather than aimlessly fly. They were extraordinary. Abe seemed just as amazed but not by the fireflies. As Daisy turned in circles, she kept

116

catching Abe watching her. There was a look of admiration on his face that was oddly comforting. Daisy eventually stopped gawking at the bugs and turned her attention to Abe.

"They are unlike anything I have seen before," Daisy explained. Abe stood and moved to stand directly in front of Daisy.

"I quite agree." Something in his tone indicated to Daisy that he was not talking about the bugs. Her cheeks flushed and she averted her eyes from Abe. "Though, I do not think they are the most phenomenal thing here tonight."

Daisy looked up into Abe's eyes. His hand lightly interlaced with hers. Daisy felt the same lightness like when they were dancing come over her. All her worries suddenly disappeared. It was like he picked up her fears and moved them aside. She relaxed, completely forgetting the conversation she had overheard earlier.

"I didn't get the chance to meet your family yet. You only pointed them out," Daisy stated, trying to find some conversation.

"Is that really what you want to talk about right now?" He asked while moving a piece of hair out of her face and tucking it behind her ear.

"No."

"What do you want to talk about?" She took a step closer to him. He placed his hand on her waist but ensured to keep distance between them.

"I am not sure."

"There is nothing in particular you wish to discuss?" Something was gnawing at the back of her mind, but she could not place it. *What was it that had her so concerned? What did she want to talk to him about? It was important, she was very concerned, and yet, it was gone now.*

"I cannot remember what I wanted to talk to you about."

"Should it come back, do let me know."

At that moment, a window in the manor opened and the music playing became clearer in the quiet night air. Abe placed her hands around his neck and began to gently sway to the beat. She could feel his hair tickling her hands, soft and fine like silk. He leaned forward and pressed his forehead to hers.

"This is not a style of dance I am familiar with," Daisy whispered, not wanting to break the moment.

"It's not a common style, but it works well when there are just two people." His voice was soft, almost like he was half asleep. "It's something I learned a long time ago when music was more simple."

"You talk like you are hundreds of years old."

"Well, I am." Daisy lightly giggled at his joke, but his stern face cut her short. Whatever moment they were having seemed to disappear. He dropped her waist and stepped back from her. "I am not joking."

"You do not look much older than me." Daisy attempted to recover from whatever she said that switched the mood so suddenly.

"I may not look older, but I am. Significantly actually. I thought maybe you would have an open enough mind to understand the abnormalities of the world." Daisy was thoroughly confused now. This was not what she was expecting to happen outside. She was not planning on insulting Abe somehow and yet, she did. She did want to understand and thought her mind was open enough to understand.

"Then how old are you?" He looked confused and slightly... angry? Daisy was not sure what emotions he was actually feeling. He turned his back to her and placed his hands on the railing.

"I am not sure, to be honest. I cannot remember when time started to keep count of how old I am. Immemorial, perhaps, is the best way to explain it." His words seemed like utter nonsense to her. Like many of things he talked about, nothing seemed to quite fit, but still somehow made sense in the grand scheme. Daisy was unsure what else to say or do.

"We should get back to the manor. I am not supposed to be alone with an undefined suitor. Unless you are proposing to me, I suggest we get back." Daisy smiled trying to support the joke, but a serious manner had completely overcome Abe.

"Before I return you, can I show you something?" Daisy hesitated. There was a ball going on with hundreds

119

of people and Daisy was breaking every societal rule by being alone with a man that was not family. Everything about the situation was wrong and uncomfortable. She knew that she needed to get back to the manor, to the ball, to Rosie, but Abe's pleading eyes softened her concern. "I will ensure you are back before long. They won't even notice you are gone. I promise."

"Oh, alright, but if I am much later, Rosie will beat you," Daisy joked. She was trying to ease her own discomfort more than anything. He smiled, offered his hand and led Daisy away from the gazebo and the manor.

There was a small path that went into the forest that edged the manor grounds. They followed the trail for a while. Birds chirped in the trees as the bare branches swayed in the cool, winter breeze. Luckily, winter had not fully sunk its claws in the area and the evening wasn't overly cold. The moon was bright and lit the path. Stars poked through the densely entwined tree branches.

Eventually they reached a clearing where five large stone pillars stood in a circle. Abe led her to the centre of the circle and the world fell silent. He dropped her hand and came to stop a few feet in front of her. She looked at the stones and noticed similar symbols to the fountain carved into the rocks.

"Do you remember the story I told you about the Conductors yesterday?" Abe asked.

"Yes, it was quite interesting," Daisy replied.

"It is said that this area was used by the first Conductors to learn the elemental forces. These stones represent the five forces. Air, the ability to conduct wind and sound. Fire, the ability to conduct flames and heat. Water, the ability to conduct fluid and frozen liquids. Earth, the ability to conduct ground and plants. And mind, the ability to conduct man and animal." As he explained the forces, he pointed to the corresponding stone. His passion for the story was evident and Daisy couldn't help but also feel excited. "Learning the forces allowed one to control the environment around them. What would be seen as magic by the outside world was purely a connection to the underlying energies of the world. It's a powerful and ancient place. I often come here to think."

"Think about what?" Daisy asked as she spun in a slow circle trying to take everything in. The details of the stones were stunning. Careful precision was evident in every scratch on the rocks.

"Life and what it means. What I want to do with mine and how my actions impact others and those around me. I have to make a lot of decisions that greatly impact the lives of others. The smallest of decisions for me can completely change the direction of everything. Like bringing you here tonight."

"Why would bringing me here change the direction of everything? That seems like a rather dramatic statement."

Daisy, however, did not hear his response. She approached the water rock and gently placed her hand against it. A sudden cacophony overcame Daisy deafening any response Abe may have said. The pattering of rain during a storm. The smashing of waves on the shore. The rush of rapids in a river. The smashing flood of a waterfall. The cracking of ice on a frozen lake. All muddled together yet distinguishable.

Daisy fell back from the rock, as if pushed, and was caught by a set of arms. Looking down at her were the concerned eyes of Abe. He helped her back to her feet, but kept one hand on her upper arm as if prepared to catch her again. Daisy's head throbbed as though a thousand nails had just been pounded into it. She closed her eyes and rubbed her temple in hope to relieve some of the pain.

"Are you alright? It looks like you might have hit your head," Abe asked worriedly.

"I am fine. Must have drank too much wine today. Just a headache." She wanted to explain what had occurred, but the words evaded her. *Would Abe think her crazy?* "I really need to get back to the manor now. Please take me."

Abe nodded his head. Daisy kept her eyes closed to ease the pain growing in her head. Abe wrapped one arm around her and guided her through the forest. She let her head fall against Abe's shoulder as he navigated her back towards the manor. Each step felt like a knife driving into her skull. The pain was nearly unbearable. Yet, Abe provided support and comfort as Daisy stumbled her way back.

Eventually, Daisy felt her foot land on the stone patio beside the manor. Waves of music from the ball swelled around her. Daisy could hear running feet approaching her and Abe. A warm and firm hand grasped her upper arm.

"What the blazes happened to her?" Daisy instantly recognized the voice of Rosie.

"I'm f-" Daisy tried to speak but the pain was too much. "I em fi-," she tried again.

"She fell and hit her head badly," Abe lied. "She should be fine but this wound needs to be cleaned and she needs rest."

Daisy couldn't remember a wound.She couldn't remember much. Perhaps Abe didn't catch her and she did hit the ground? No. She was positive he caught her. Another throb of pain pushed the remaining thoughts out of her head.

"My Lord. That is quite the gash. Where did you take her?"

"We just went for a walk on the grounds and she caught her foot on something and fell." *Was there genuine concern in Abe's voice?* He seemed nearly panicked at the thought of Daisy injured.

"Can you help me get her inside?"

"Of course."

The three of them hobbled down the path leading around the edge of the building and towards the front door of the manor. The pain was getting worse and Daisy felt her consciousness slipping. Her feet dragged against the ground.

"Stay with us Daisy." *Who was it that spoke? Abe or Rosie?*

"Come on. Just a little bit further"

"Daisy, you need to keep walking"

"Daisy."

"Daisy?"

"Daisy!"

Chapter 11 - Blackness

Daisy stood in a room of black. She couldn't tell where the floor ended and the walls started. She couldn't even tell if there was a ceiling. Her feet were bare and she wore a white nightgown. Her hair was wet and clung to her face. All she could see was black. She stepped forward and heard the unmistakable splash of water; however, she could not see it nor feel it against her skin. She began to run into the blackness; the sounds of slapping water and her breathing echoed in the emptiness. She ran and ran looking for anything besides black. Nothing appeared. Nothing.

"Daisy!" disembodied voices echoed all around her, stopping her in her tracks. Panic swelled in Daisy. *What was going on? Where was she?*

"Daisy!" the voices called again. Her body shook as she glanced around. She couldn't see anyone. She couldn't tell where the voices were coming from. She spun in circles trying to find the voices, trying to see anything in the darkness.

"Daisy." She clenched her hands around her ears. She didn't want to hear the voices. She didn't want to go towards the voices. She wanted the voices to go away.

"Daisy!" She screamed trying to drown out the echoes, but her scream was carried away and muddled with the voices. The voices called, and her screams echoed underneath: piercing and terrified.

"Daisy!" they called; she screamed. She fell to her knees and made a large splash. Her nightgown was wet; she was wet. Suddenly she could feel the water and it was welcomed. She stretched out her fingers and could feel the water run between them. The water relaxed her. She breathed and sank deeper into the water. She lifted her hands above her head and commanded the water up, up to her head. It enveloped her and carried her away from the voices. The water did as it was told.

She was swimming. Swimming through blackness, but the voices didn't sound under the water. She felt the water around her and commanded it to move her, to push her to safety. The water did as it was told. She glided through the water at a pace faster than she could ever swim. She moved freely, and she felt free. Eventually she slowed. The water stopped pushing her. She commanded the water to take her to the surface. The water did as it was told.

Her head broke the surface, and she inhaled fresh gulps of air. She stepped out of the water, like stepping out of a hole, and now stood on top of the water like before.

The sound of her name pierced the silence, but it was different now. It was one voice. It was Abe's voice. She turned around and there he stood. He was wearing a white shirt that was unbuttoned exposing his abdomen. Raven black pants matched his dishevelled hair. He extended his arms, and she ran to him. She flung herself into his arms and felt safe. The voices couldn't get her now.

"Daisy," he breathed into her hair. She pulled back and looked at his face. She inhaled sharply. Looking back at her were two eyes: one as green as grass and the other as blue as the ocean. He placed a hand on her cheek, and Daisy relaxed into it. The shock and fear of his different coloured eyes disappeared with each stroke of his thumb on her cheek.

"You are safe," he assured her. "I've got you. Nothing bad will happen to you while I am here."

She believed him. She trusted him. She knew he would save her. She pressed her head against his chest and felt his arms tighten around her. *She was safe. She was safe. She was safe.* She cried into his chest. Her whole body shuddered with the heaves of her sobs. *What was happening to her?*

At that moment, she felt like the floor beneath her was pulled out from under her, and she plunged into icy cold water. Her breath left her lungs immediately and darkness painted the corners of her vision. She attempted to swim, but the water felt like syrup, too sticky and thick to move. Each movement felt like ten thousand pounds weighed her down. She struggled to breathe, the darkness slowly creeping further to the centre of her vision, blacking everything out. She felt her life slowly slipping away.

"Focus," she heard Abe whispering from somewhere beyond her, "Tell it what you want it to do. Focus."

She closed her eyes and tried to focus. *But focus on what? Tell what to do what?* Air. She needed air. Suddenly she could feel bubbles on her face. She opened her eyes. Millions of bubbles were swarming around her head, colliding into each other and forming larger bubbles until one massive bubble surrounded her entirely. Outside the bubble, she watched the water swirl and dance in currents.

She could feel the cold radiating through the bubble, but it held. Not freezing, not shattering, just floating in the churning, black water.

She took a deep breath in, relieved that she survived. She hugged her knees with dread-filled anticipation of what was coming next. She knew something would come. *Why did she know things without actually knowing them? What was her brain hiding? What was this torment?*

With her next breath, the bubble popped and she found herself tumbling but not through water. She was falling through the air. A white light in the blackness appeared, and she was quickly spiralling towards it. She was expecting to splatter on the ground, but as the light approached, she felt a warm sensation then a slight thunk as she hit the ground. When she opened her eyes she found herself in a room without walls surrounded by a sea of blackness. To her left, stood a single door. As her eyes began to focus she was able to make out the shapes of furniture. As she moved closer, she recognized the unmistakable decor as that which belonged to her mother's office.

The door opened and Azalea walked through with their parents in tow. There was a great feeling of joy as Daisy watched her sister alive and well. Azalea moved about the room in the same way she always did. She always exuded such confidence. Daisy tried not to run towards her sister or cry at the sight of her alive. She just wanted to enjoy the moment; she knew it was impossible that Azalea was alive, well, and at home with their parents. She knew this was a cruel dream.

Azalea sat behind the desk and instructed her parents to sit opposite her. While their parents often followed Azalea's request, there was something different about their demeanour. They almost seemed like puppets, and Azalea was the puppeteer. Azalea however, seemed bored. Whatever joy Daisy experienced was quickly snuffed out when Azalea flicked her hand and watched as their parents choked each other. Daisy could hear them struggling to breath and watched in horror as neither stopped their assaults. In contrast, Azalea watched with apathy as if the sight of her parents killing each was nothing more than paint drying. Daisy gasped no longer being able to stay silent as the joy of seeing her sister dissipated into the horror of her not doing anything. Azalea's head snapped to where Daisy sat on the floor. Instantly, Daisy noticed that Azalea's eyes had changed. Unlike their usual purple, she now had one eye coloured a deep chocolate brown. The purple eye flared as both of Azalea's eyes locked on Daisy. Azalea snapped her fingers, and their parents went limp in their chairs.

"What are you doing here?" Azalea asked accusingly. "You aren't supposed to know about the elements. This shouldn't be possible."

Azalea stood from the desk and started towards Daisy. Daisy feared what would happen when Azalea got to her. There was a fury in Azalea that Daisy had never seen before. The woman approaching seemed nothing like her sister. Everything about her was wrong.

"You're being tested," Azalea sneered. "I can see your mind, and you are being tested, but *how*? How did you learn?"

Daisy tried to stand, to move away from Azalea, but she felt stuck to the floor. She felt as though she was chained and locked in place; she couldn't even lift her arm.

"You try to move away from me. You try to help them. Why would you want to help them? They tormented you. Tortured you. They ignored you when I wasn't home and they treated you worse than an obstreperous mule when I was present. They were horrible to you, and yet you want to help them. You have power now. Why not just kill them? Why not free yourself from their grasp? Why not accept your power and move onto something great?"

Daisy wanted nothing more than for Azalea to stop talking. She wanted Azalea to go away. Something inside of Daisy snapped, and she felt a sudden release. Her arm was free. She raised her hand and commanded Azalea to stop. Azalea froze mid step. Everything in the room stilled. It wasn't just Azalea that stopped. It was like time stopped. Daisy cocked her head and the thought of restarting, of trying this whole thing again, entered her mind.

There was a flash of silvery white light and suddenly Azalea was back behind the desk. Their parents sat upright in their chairs. Daisy ran towards them and commanded Azalea to stop, to not hurt her parents. Azalea stopped and her eyes glazed over. Daisy could feel Azalea's mind. She could feel Azalea's pain, anger, and fear as if it was her own. These feelings overwhelmed Daisy and she released her connection. Azalea snapped her fingers, and Daisy was back in the blackness. She felt exhausted and stretched thin as though she was being pulled in multiple directions, nearing a breaking point. She waivered on her feet. She needed to stay upright. She needed to focus. She needed to survive.

Heat came next. Sweltering, burning heat. It started at her feet as if she was standing on fire. She looked down and saw nothing. She tried to move, but with each step the temperature grew. All of a sudden, flames erupted all around her. Hot, orange trendles licked her skin with searing pain. She cried out and clutched the injured spot only to feel another lash of pain, another slash of heat. Her lungs burned from the fire. She scratched at her throat begging for air to enter her lungs. Tears swelled as the smoke stung her eyes. She looked around for an escape. For some way to get out of the flames.

Just past the flames, Daisy could see an outline of a person. No, not an outline. It was Rosie. She seemed to be dancing in the flames, undeterred by the pain encompassing every part of her. She moved fluidly and gently between the flames like a boat gliding across a calm lake. Her hair was down and loose and flicked around with each movement. Daisy tried to call to her, but her voice died in the roar of the flames. Another lash of pain on her back brought her attention back to Rosie's actions. Her movements and dancing were soothing in the excruciating pain. Daisy started to move along with her, following Rosie's movements, trying to think of anything but the pain. As Daisy swayed to a silent beat in time with Rosie, her mind started to focus.

"Focus, Daisy," Abe's bodiless voice whispered amongst the crackling fire, "Focus."

She closed her eyes and swayed slightly. She extended her hands into the flames and felt the raw power behind them. Her head tilted upwards, and she took a deep breath in. She felt the flames surrounding her but there was no pain. She was in control now. She opened her eyes and saw the fire had compressed to fit in the palm of her hand. She turned her head curiously at the dancing fire in her palm. It was hers now. She owned it. She closed her hand around the fire and snuffed it out, leaving her alone again in the blackness.

She didn't feel fear this time. She felt calm. She felt comfortable and at peace. She knew she wasn't done yet, but what came next she did not fear. She was sure she could handle it. She didn't even hesitate as she suddenly stood at the edge of a canyon. A raging river roared far below her. She looked behind her and saw several people running towards her. Her parents, Susan, Dame Agatha, her classmates, and even the assessor were charging towards her like an angry mob. She was going to die. She would either jump off the cliff, or she would be pushed off the cliff.

Or she could cross the river.

There was a cliff on the other side and the other side would be safe. Time was running out. The crowd was getting closer. She looked around for a rope or something she could throw to the other side, but there was nothing. She needed to get across. She bent down and placed her hand against the dirt.

There was a buzzing sensation in her hands. The dirt was alive, and she knew she could use it. She searched her mind for something to help her across. Her fingers curled in the dirt, and she ordered it to grow, to fill the gap, to allow her to cross. Sprouts of plants began to extend from the cliffside and weave themselves into a bridge. They grew slowly together, closing the gap inch by inch. This was going to work. She would be able to cross.

In her focus on growing the bridge, she forgot about the crowd quickly closing in on her. The bridge was nearly done but not quickly enough. Her hands were ripped from the ground as two strong arms lifted her up, and threw her off the cliff. She was falling. Plummeting. She was going to die.

Chapter 12 - A Lover's Quarrel

"What the hell did you do to her?" Rosie shouted at Abe. Daisy had collapsed at the patio just around the corner from the front doors. Blood trickled down her face from a gash on her head. Rosie ran to help Abe hold Daisy up. Rosie's hand briefly touched Abe's, sending shock of pure fear and love through him. He quickly withdrew his hand and tried to refocus his attention on Daisy.

"Nothing. I did nothing," Abe explained for what felt like the one-hundredth time. "She fell and smacked her head. I swear. I don't know what happened."

"Daisy, stay with us," Rosie shook Daisy desperately searching for any sign of life. "Can you carry her the rest of the way?"

"Yes, of course." Abe placed an arm under her knees and the other around her shoulders. He picked her up, and her head lopped lifelessly to the side. Abe bumped her a little so Daisy's head flopped against his chest.

"Daisy," he breathed into her ear. He was worried about her, but he knew she was alive. He could still feel her energy. She just needed to make it through this. She just had to choose to survive. Abe was positive she could make it through the trials.

Rosie ran ahead and opened the front door to the manor. Music spilled out. The joyful tune seemed in stark contrast to the fear crawling through Abe. He followed Rosie as she weaved through the few stragglers in the foyer and stopped at the foot of the stairs.

"Upstairs, last door on the left, bed on the right. I will get help." Abe followed Rosie's instructions and carried Daisy to the last room.

"You are safe," he whispered to Daisy although it was more to reassure himself than anything else. "I've got you. Nothing bad will happen to you while I am here."

He laid her down on the bed and grabbed a handkerchief from his pocket to press to the wound on her forehead. A sudden image of Daisy in a white gown in a room of black flooded his mind's eye. He knew she was surrounded by water. He could hear her crying and feel her fear, but she got through the first test. She could do this. She could survive.

"Move out of the way," the dame barked at Abe as she shoved him back from Daisy. He had recognized her from earlier but the pure panicked expression contorted her face making her seem many years older. As Abe's hand left Daisy, he saw her fall into cold water. *Was she going to make it?*

"Miss Camden, what happened to her?" the dame demanded. Rosie was being pushed towards the door as several people bustled around the room.

"She fell and hit her head on the ground," Rosie answered. She was not good at hiding her panic. Her face was gleaming with sweat, and her body slightly shook. Abe wanted to comfort her but wasn't sure how or if it would be appropriate.

"And who is this stranger? Why is he in your room? Why was he left unattended with Daisy?" Abe and Rosette stared blankly at each other. They had, but a moment to try and figure something out; a mutual lie without speaking a single word. Rosie knew that Abe and Daisy had been seeing each other out of regular form which would not be acceptable in most cases. Something had to cover the unacceptable behaviour while still being reasonable enough for future conduct.

"I am her -" Abe fumbled. "Cousin, twice removed, relatively distant, but familiar." Rosie subtly glared at Abe, but that was the lie he decided upon.

"Daisy told me he lived nearby. She ran into him when we were handing out invitations," Rosie added.

"Fine. Leave now. He can wait in the hall."

"I'd rather stay." The dame's head whipped around. Her eyebrows nearly hit her hairline. Her face was as red as an apple. Clearly, Abe should not have spoken.

"I do not know you. You are a stranger in a sea of familiar faces. I am not even sure how or why you are here, but you should be appreciative that I am even allowing you to stay in the manor at all. I could have you immediately escorted out, which I should, but I will not at this time. Furthermore, Sir, a gentleman should never be in an unwedded lady's chamber," she fumed. She stood mere inches from his face. She was a small woman, but her fury was mighty. "Nor should he make demands in another's home. You will wait in the hall. Now."

Rosie grabbed his arm and dragged Abe from the room. Abe wanted to fight it, but he couldn't risk further exposure of himself or his magic. He glanced back as the door shut and saw Daisy vibrating on the bed. Something was not going well. She had to pass. She had to get through. She had to. She had to. She had to!

Abe paced the hall just outside the door. He usually did not feel this nervous, let alone actual fear. Rosie leaned against the wall. Her head was tilted back and her eyes were closed. She seemed more calm than Abe. *What had he done? Did he just kill Daisy?* He just wanted to see if she could feel the forces. She wasn't supposed to be tested. The forces weren't supposed to pick her, and yet, they did.

"So," Rosie broke the silence. She was staring at Abe now. "Cousin, eh?"

Abe smiled and shook his head. "I needed a reason to stay. Family, but not too closely related, seemed like the best way to do it. You know, like a cousin twice removed."

"Needed to stay?" Rosie inquired.

"Yes." He stopped pacing and looked at the door. There were no signs of anything that was occurring inside the room. "I am responsible for this, and I want to ensure she is okay."

"Is that the only reason?" Abe flicked his gaze over to Rosie. He knew she was suggesting something else, but he wasn't sure what his answer was to it.

"At this moment," he hesitated, "that is the only reason I am here."

Rosie didn't seem satisfied with that answer. "She would be disappointed in that response."

"Oh, does she tell you everything then?" he snapped. His anxiety was reaching a peak, and he couldn't help himself. He huffed in frustration and ran his hand over his face, "Sorry. I don't mean to be rude." Rosie seemed unoffended, but nearly impressed.

"I've become quite close to her over the past couple months, and I am certainly closer to her than you." Her tone was sassy and unladylike. Abe appreciated it. He smirked, and she seemed to relax incrementally. "When she overheard your, erm...conversation this evening she certainly disclosed much to me about her interests in you. And your conversation seemed to suggest you were quite interested in her."

"And what conversation are you referring to?" Abe could feel his temper flaring. He was stressed enough already and Rosie's interrogation did not aid his mood.

"Perhaps when you wish to argue with a past lover, you should do it more privately and not outside a ball." Rosie's tone was snide and knowing. Abe hated it. They were privy to a conversation they only understood half of. "From saying that Daisy was fascinating, you have certainly changed your pace."

"It's not like that. You only know half of what we were discussing."

"Then enlighten me, Sir. My dear friend is intrigued by you and if you are not feeling the same, I highly suggest you leave." Rosie pointed towards the main staircase. Her tone was final and unwavering. She was clearly serious about the situation.

"Alina is an ex-lover of mine, yes, but it happened a long time ago. After I rescued her from a terrible situation, she saw me as a hero. Later, she helped me get through an incredibly tragic event, but I didn't love her and she didn't love me. It was more the emotions of the moment that spurred a relationship which was not sustainable. There is familiarity there, but not passion, not love. That's all in the past now."

"Fine. I think that raises more questions than provides answers, but I will accept your answer for now," Rosie huffed. Her hands were on her hips as she glared down her nose at Abe. "What about Daisy?"

Abe rocked on his heels. He kept getting asked this question and was truly not sure how to answer it. He felt she had power and that intrigued him. He enjoyed her company and certainly wanted to spend more time with her. She was honest and innocent. He was far from both. She was everything he wasn't, and he felt balanced with her. After the last time he fell in love, he feared ever feeling that again. It had been so long he wasn't even sure he knew what love was.

"I am not sure yet what I feel about her," Abe began, allowing himself to speak freely and feel what needed to be felt. "I want to get to know her more and tonight's accident certainly does not help. She is intriguing and kind and honest and beautiful and everything that I didn't realise I needed."

139

"I understand what you are saying," Rosie replied, "She is naive, but the kindest person you will meet. She looks plain, but up close there is beauty in her details. She seems quiet, but she is clever and brilliant. She is full of surprises and always seems to know what you need. She is something extraordinary, and I don't think most people even see her let alone get to know her."

Her voice had softened while she spoke, taking on a nearly loving tone. She almost seemed to escape into her own mind as she discussed what she found so amazing about Daisy. Finally, Abe understood an earlier reaction from Rosie. That moment of fear and love was not just because of their friendship.

"You're a sapphist." Abe hadn't meant to say it, and Rosette clearly hadn't expected it either.

"That is a horrible thing to suggest," Rosie seemed taken aback and surprised, but not necessarily hurt. Almost like there was some relief to hearing someone say it aloud.

"It is only horrible if you think being a sapphist is something to be ashamed of." She pursed her lip and furrowed her brow. She fell quiet for a moment and almost appeared to be fighting herself.

"They won't allow it. I haven't told anyone, but it's why they won't let me leave the school. The dame supports me and has let me sneak out for years to see Maria at the bar. But my family. My family won't accept it. They keep saying I can't fulfil my wifely duties, that I am wrong and broken. It was either finishing school or conversion therapy. I had to choose between two horrible fates, so learning wifely duties seemed the better option. But what if this isn't what I want. I don't think I am broken. I don't think there is anything wrong with me." She whispered the last part mostly to herself, and Abe was kind enough not to pay too much attention to it. Her eyes were filled with tears. "How did you know?"

"I touched your hand when we were bringing Daisy in, and I read your mind." There was a brief moment of confused silence before Rosie let out a sweet, soft laugh.

"What a terrible joke," she deflected. It seemed to ease the tension that Rosie was feeling which helped Abe relax. He shrugged. Joke or not, it came down to whatever the person believed, and Abe did not feel obligated to enlighten her more.

They eventually existed in an anxious silence as they waited. There didn't seem the need to talk about anything else. Abe didn't particularly want to talk more, and Rosie seemed to have talked too much already. Abe slid down the wall and sat on the floor with his head resting in his hands. He hated this. If he was in there, in the room with Daisy, he could have helped. He could have ensured she survived. Instead, he sat in a hallway waiting for regular doctors to fix something they did not, could not, understand.

The music had long since died when the door finally opened and people streamed out of the room. The last person to exit was the dame who quietly closed the door. Both, Rosie and Abe, scrambled to their feet and presented themselves to the dame.

"Before either of you say anything, I need more information," she stated. "I am Dame Agatha and I am the lady of the manor. Who are you *actually*?" Her gaze fell to Abe.

"My name is Ambrose, but I go by Abe or Ames, preferably Abe. I've lived in Grenich for sometime now, but I don't mingle much which may be why you haven't seen me before. I, um, study plants so I keep to myself and the forest mostly. And, as I said before, I am her cousin. Twice removed." He made sure to emphasise the last part. "I didn't know she was being schooled here, but I was pleasantly surprised to see her in the town square. Our families became estranged when we were younger, but she has hardly changed since we were children."

The dame eyed Abe suspiciously as if assessing if he was honest and trustworthy, or if he should be thrown out immediately. It appeared that some of earlier fury had died down, but Abe still felt uncomfortable. After a moment, she nodded slightly. The explanation seemed to satisfy the dame's question. She did not seem pleased with the answer but believed it nonetheless.

"And what exactly happened? You said she fell and hit her head, but the doctor said this was a fairly substantial injury."

"She was walking backwards when her heel got stuck in a crack in the patio square outside. She toppled over and her head hit on the stones. The rocks were quite rough which is what gave her the laceration," Rosie stated. If Abe hadn't known the true story, he would have believed

Rosette's telling. Dame Agatha also seemed content with the story.

"She has stabilised and is now resting. I would usually recommend that you leave her alone, but judging by the looks of you two, you would ignore the request regardless of what I say. As such, please be quiet. We are not sure when she will wake." The dame turned towards Rosie. "When she wakes, please come and get me. Otherwise, he is not to be left alone in a lady's chamber again."

With that, Dame Agatha left down the hallway. Rosie and Abe paused for a moment to watch her leave before rushing the door to see Daisy. The room was dim. A few candles burned; the curtains were mostly drawn except for a small crack showing the early colours of dawn tracing across the sky. Even in the dim light, the scene before them was gruesome. Several bandages sat in a bin beside the bed covered in a significant amount of blood. Two bowls of water sat beside the bed, one was deep red from the rinsing of instruments. A white bandage was wrapped several times around Daisy's head where the cut had been. Her dress was rusted on one shoulder and her hair stuck to her face and pillow from sweat. Her whitened skin gave her a ghostly appearance.

Rosie gasped as her eyes fell on the scene. Abe, however, hardly cared to look around. He ran to her bedside and grabbed her hand. It was cold and clammy, but he barely noticed. He needed to know if she succeeded, if she was alive or lost. He closed his eyes and focused on her pulse in his hand. Slowing his breathing, he cleared his mind and felt the tingling sensation of a proper connection. His consciousness dissolved into hers, and he could see her falling over a cliff, plummeting. She was about to fail.

"Daisy!" he exclaimed. His connection suddenly snapped. His eyes opened and looking back at him were two eyes: one silver, one gold. Daisy had woken up.

Chapter 13 - An Awakening

Daisy ached all over as she attempted to push herself into an upright position. Rosie sat on her own bed staring at Daisy across the room. Abe knelt beside Daisy, clutching her hand in his. Concern was apparent on both their faces. Daisy winced as she finally managed to get into a sitting position. Her head spun, and she tried not to vomit. *What had happened to her?*

The music from the ball had long since faded, and the sky broke with colours of the morning sun. Clearly, a significant amount of time had passed, but Daisy hadn't the slightest idea what day it was. She noticed she was still wearing her gown from the ball. Some blood had stained the neckline and sleeve of the dress, but otherwise, the dress did not appear crumpled like she had been laying in it for several days.

Rosie stood up and walked over to the bed beside Abe. They were both concerned for Daisy. She had never known this kind of care before, and it made her slightly uncomfortable. Clearly, she had been well cared for after whatever happened. In all honesty though, she just wanted to wash and change and go back to sleep.

"How are you feeling?" Rosie asked.

"Exhausted," Daisy replied. Abe seemed to relax slightly.

"You must have had quite the fall. They had a doctor in here for several hours working on you. I am guessing the bleeding would not stop." Rosie stated and flicked her hand to indicate the bloody bandages beside the bed. The sight of the bandages made Daisy's stomach roll.

"I am not sure. I don't remember much of anything to be honest," Daisy responded. Her voice felt rough in her throat.

"What do you remember, Dais?" Abe interrupted. Daisy was confused by the shortening of her name, but she liked it. It was a nice alternative to the names she was accustomed to being called.

"I remember… dancing and music. I remember feeling jealous of something and hurt about something else, but no specific images come to mind. How long was I out of it?" Daisy pleaded as she hoped it had not been too long.

"A couple hours." Abe and Rosie responded simultaneously.

"The dame was not sure when you would wake. I am supposed to notify her as soon as you do," Rosie stated.

"Abe, could you go? I would love to get washed and out of these bloodied rags, but I will need Rosie's help, I think." Abe seemed displeased with the request. He did not appear to want to leave her side.

"Erm - yes, I suppose I can do that," Abe hesitantly responded.

"You don't need to stay. You could go home," Daisy explained. Abe stood and directed his eyes towards his shoes. He seemed uncertain and uncomfortable.

"If I leave..." he looked up and his eyes locked with Daisy's. She took a sudden intake of breath as his eyes surprised her. One was blue and one was green. She tried to act not adverse to it. "Will I be allowed back? Will I see you again?"

Daisy could feel his fear. He was truly worried that if he left, she would be shut away from him in the manor. She had only been here a few months, but Rosie and Abe felt more like family to her than her own flesh and blood.

"I will ensure we see each other again," Daisy smiled, and Abe nodded his head sharply before exiting the room.

Daisy gingerly swung her feet off the bed and stood unsteadily. Rosie grabbed Daisy's arm to help with balance. Slowly, they worked their way towards the bathroom. Rosie drew a bath as Daisy carefully removed the blood stained clothes. Her once beautiful dress was now caked with blood that flaked off as she peeled the gown off her skin. She discarded the dress in a heap and stared at herself in the mirror.

Her face was pale and large bags shadowed her eyes. Her lips were a very light pink, so light that you almost couldn't tell them apart from her skin. There was slight bruising peeking out from under the bandages. Daisy slowly and tenderly unwrapped the wound on her head. Her pale brown hair had turned into a dark rusted brown due to the blood that had been caked in it. She braced herself against the sink and tried not to faint at the sight of her own blood. It wasn't the first time she had tended to her own wounds or saw her own blood, but it was never easy. She always felt queasy with the sight of her own blood.

Rosie appeared in the mirror behind Daisy. She smiled at Daisy before indicating the bath. Slowly, Daisy made her way towards the bath and was assisted into it. She sat in the water. Hot water was a commodity in the manor and obviously the ball had expended it. Daisy shivered in the water but welcomed the notion of feeling alive. Rosie gently poured water over Daisy's head and massaged out the dried blood. Eventually, the water ran clear and the majority of the blood was rinsed out.

Daisy delicately touched her head where the wound was. Just under her hairline was a small cut that felt like a crescent shape. She put her hand down which came away clean. Daisy was worried the cleaning would have pulled off any scabbing leading to more bleeding but that did not seem to happen. She breathed a sigh of relief.

The water temperature was starting to get to Daisy. Her body ached already, but the cold made it worse. A sudden flicker of pure blackness entered Daisy's mind, but disappeared as quickly as it came. Daisy started thinking of warm things like a fire, sunny summer afternoons, and fresh tea straight out of the pot. She idly moved her hands across the surface of the water and with each swish she could have sworn the water got warmer. However, that was an insane thought. No one could make water warmer. No one could change temperature. She shook her head to clear it of the strange thoughts and asked Rosie to help her out of the tub.

Just as the girls managed to get Daisy into a nightgown, the door to their room swung open. They exited the bathroom, Rosie nearly carrying Daisy, and saw the dame with another gentleman standing in the room. He held a large leather bag with a cross stitched to the side. Daisy assumed he was a medical doctor of some sort. Rosie guided Daisy to the bed and helped her lay down. The gentleman immediately rushed to inspect her.

"How do you feel?" he asked while staring intently into her eyes, looking past their surface for signs of injury.

"I am very tired and my whole body hurts," Daisy responded, but she felt like it was minimising what she actually felt. To Daisy, it seemed like her entire being was drained from her body then shoved back in with a bit of extra stuff added. Her body felt small and cramped, like it didn't fit. But it also felt very weak, like she had just walked for miles uphill. How could you explain this amount of pain and exhaustion when it was nothing more than a head wound.

"You appear to have had quite the fall. Can you tell me your name?"

"Daisy."

"Your full name.

"Daisy Mae Bloomsbury."

"Good. And what day is it today?"

"Erm... I hit my head on December the twenty-first. They said I was out for a couple hours, but I am not sure exactly how long I was out to know the date." Daisy looked out the window through the crack in the curtain and saw the sun just creeping over the horizon. Obviously, a new day had come, and Daisy did not realise it until then.

"Very good. And can you tell me the names of the people in the room?"

"Rosie, sorry, no. Miss Camden and Dame Agatha. I don't know your name."

"Contractions, dear," Dame Agatha called from behind the doctor which earned her a stern glance from him.

"Yes, sorry. I do not know your name, Sir."

"I am Doctor Goodwin. Thank you for asking." He turned away from Daisy and looked at the dame. "Her linguistic and memory pathways seem undamaged. Her motor skills do not appear majorly impaired, but obviously she has had a major fall. There are no other apparent injuries to her body. All I can recommend is significant rest and lots of fluids."

He stood up and promptly walked out of the room without waiting for the dame or any sort of dismissal. She seemed lost in her own thoughts and hardly paid any attention to the doctor leaving until the door slammed loudly behind her. She startled then narrowed her gaze on Daisy.

"Get some rest. When you are feeling better, come find me and we will assess your status at this school. Miss Camden, you will have the day off from your studies to care for Miss Bloomsbury and report anything that occurs directly to me. You will be expected in classes tomorrow," the dame said stiffly, almost like it was scripted. She turned and left, leaving Rosie and Daisy alone in the quiet room.

Daisy curled up on the bed and wrapped herself in blankets. She was freezing and exhausted. She felt drained and sore. Nothing made sense and yet everything made sense at the same time. Something had changed, was changing, but Daisy wasn't sure what. She could only hope it was for the better.

Chapter 14 - Days Gone By

After informing the dame and being quickly escorted out of the manor, Abe slowly made his way back to the train station; he was full of emotions. He felt nervous leaving Daisy as so much was unknown. He wasn't even able to concretely confirm that Daisy was a Conductor. Sure, her eyes had changed, but that was only one sign. However, Daisy didn't give him much choice in staying, and the dame very quickly removed him from the premises.

He felt angry about being dismissed when he so badly needed to stay, to help, to ensure Daisy was safe. It also made him feel useless. These humans thought themselves more capable than him and kept moving him away.

Then there was the guilt. He didn't want to test Daisy yet. That wasn't his intent at all, but the forces picked her. The forces decided to test her without any of the usual prescreening. Abe had exposed her too soon and that was eating away at him. It felt like a beast sitting in his chest trying to claw its way out of the cage. He truly had no idea what to do, but to return tomorrow and hope he could see Daisy again.

He walked through the streets of Grenich aimlessly, sitting his feelings, before finally making his way back to the train station. There weren't any trains booked for that day, so the station was deserted. Abe liked sitting in the empty station sometimes. It was generally peaceful when no one else was there. Things often got noisy with the Conductors and peace was a rare commodity.

He walked through the wall to an empty main room. He expected to at least see Alina, but perhaps they stayed at the ball longer than he realised. Judging by the silence, they were either asleep, out of the station, or… dead…

A fear grasped Abe's heart that he hadn't felt in a long time. There were multiple reasons why Abe rarely had the Condoctors interact with the public, but he put those reasons aside for the ball with Daisy. He feared he made a grave mistake. Abe quickly made his way down the hallway and opened the first door to Brighid's room. Light streamed in through the opening to expose a mess of pillows and blankets on a large, four post bed. Abe ran across the room in two bounds and started throwing pillows across the room. Abe tried to slow his heart, to contain the building panic, but he could feel his stomach churning. The bed was empty.

He knew that Brighid often shared a bed with Alina when she couldn't sleep. After watching her parents get murdered when she was young, Brighid often suffered from night terrors. Alina was able to sooth Brighid's mind. Abe hoped, beyond all hope, that Brighid was asleep with Alina.

He sprinted down the hall to Alina's door and threw the door open. There was a loud bang as the door smashed the wall. A small yelp immediately calmed Abe's racing mind. He knew that whimper. He knew that sound like the sound of his own breathing. Abe let out a deep breath and looked at the bed. Alina was leaning against the plain headboard with her arms wrapped around Brighid. Both were wide eyed and staring at Abe.

"What are you doing, Ames?" Brighid questioned in a half-awake, sleepy tone. She yawned and cuddled back into Alina. Alina, however, stared at him knowingly. She knew the fear that had gripped him and lightly nodded to acknowledge it.

"It's okay, Brighid. Go back to sleep," Alina stated. She tenderly laid Brighid on the bed and stood up. Before Alina had even reached Abe, Brighid was softly snoring. Abe stood for a moment watching the gentle rise and fall of Brighid's chest. Her snores were soothing. With each wheezing sound, Abe felt his chest ease, his stomach stop rolling, and his breath steady. Brighid was safe. All of his studies, his family, were safe. Nothing had happened.

Alina moved out into the hallway and Abe took one step back. He watched Brighid sleeping until the very last second of the door closing. Abe let out a deep sigh. Alina extended her arms and welcomed Abe into a hug. Reluctant

153

at first, Abe eventually caved into Alina's arms. His head rested on her shoulders even though he was significantly taller than her. With her warm grasp, he felt a strong sense of relief overwhelm him and tears started pouring down his cheeks. She slowly rubbed his back like a mother calming a sick child. He felt immense relief, but he couldn't contain himself, couldn't bring himself back to a logical state. The fear had been so great that even the relief of knowing they were okay was not enough to fully calm him.

"I thought… I thought it happened again," Abe cried.

"I know. I saw the look on your face, and I knew," Alina responded. "Let's move to your office so we don't disturb them. They all need their rest."

Abe nodded against Alina's shoulder. She moved away from Abe and started down the hall. Abe trudged behind her, not really wanting to move, but knowing Alina was right. He shouldn't disturb the others. They needed sleep even more than he did.

When the door to his office clicked shut behind him, he collapsed on the floor. He felt completely drained like his very soul had been taken. His studies meant everything to him. They were the closest thing he ever had to family. He and Alina were practically raising Brighid. Although Arlo and Evander came to them much older than Brighid, they still required much guidance and care. As most Conductors, each one of his studies were damaged in some capacity. Conductors couldn't really maintain a normal family. As such, many had lost their family in some way before becoming a Conductor. Some were worse than others. Because of this loss and their history, each of his studies required something different in their teachings and in their care.

Brighid was a gentle soul that needed extra care and attention. Alina found Brighid shortly after her parents' murders. Alina and Abe were passing through a small town when they came across Brighid who was aimlessly roaming the streets. Abe knew as soon as Alina saw Brighid, dirty and cold, that they would be taking on a new study. It wasn't even a question. Ever since then, Alina was fiercely protective of Brighid and always ensured Brighid received attention and love. Alina was more Brighid's teacher than Abe, which Abe didn't mind. Arlo and Evander were a lot of work on their own.

Evander required a strict hand. He was brilliant, but his mind was often his greatest weakness as well. He required much stimulation. He needed to be kept busy and challenged, or he would find ways to amuse himself. He excelled in nearly everything he did and got bored easily. Abe always had to stay two steps ahead of him which was nearly impossible. Furthermore, Evander knew when Abe wasn't prepared and knew exactly how to use this to his advantage. He often made himself seem better than everyone which Abe found infuriating, but his confidence was admirable. He was a difficult student, but Abe enjoyed the occasional challenge. Unlike Arlo and Brighid, Evander didn't lose his family; he left his family by choice. When asked about it, Evander would explain they were never close anyways. He was a middle child of twelve children, so he felt ignored. In order to feel important, he would seek out theories and myths to find the truth underlying them.

As such, Evander had found out about the Conductors on his own and started seeking them out. Somehow, through either sheer determination or luck, he found Abe and Alina. Abe didn't want to take Evander in, but he knew he had to or someone else would. That scared Abe even more. Evander held great potential for good or evil, and Abe wanted to make sure Evander was on the right side.

In contrast, Arlo did the bare minimum. He was lazy and disorganised. His conduction was often careless, but he still achieved results. That was a part of the problem. Arlo saw results with his bare minimum attempts and rarely saw reason to do more. Abe had to push him more than the others or Arlo would do nothing. He held great potential but needed great coercion into doing anything. Alternatively, Arlo could easily be tricked into doing things if he thought it would allow him to continue being lazy or if it meant seeing Brighid happy. Although he would never admit it, Abe could see that Brighid was like a little sister to Arlo. Before Arlo was a Conductor, he lived with his younger sister and mother. His dad was drunk and was often gambling away what little money they had. As a result, Arlo hardly saw his father. When his sister got sick with consumption, Arlo stepped up in his father's absence. He started working so his family could afford his sister's care. As she got sicker, his mother started to withdraw; she became a shell of herself. When his sister died, his mother withdrew further until she decided that taking her own life was preferable to living without her daughter. After his unfathomable losses, Arlo lost all motivation. Abe often saw a younger version of himself in Arlo; his unmotivated, disinterested, and anguished nature spoke to Abe. He knew that he needed to intervene in order to save Arlo from himself. However, this was no easy task as Arlo didn't seem to want Abe's help; he seemed more than content to wallow in his self-loathing.

Abe seemed to attract the broken and downtrodden like a magnet. Brighid, Evander, and Arlo all had significant trauma and Alina was no different. After trying to drown his own sorrows in a bottle, he accidentally stumbled into a brothel and that's where he met Alina. Her parents had sold her years before as they simply couldn't afford to feed her and her brother as well as her three other siblings. While Alina's business in the brothel was purely to satisfy the physical needs and desires of those who visited the establishment, Abe found a different sort of companion in her that night, a friend. After sobering up, Abe bought Alina out of her indenture and offered her her freedom or the opportunity to join the Conductors. Ever since then, they had become inseparable. She had many opportunities to leave, but she never did. She always stuck around and had become his rock. Tonight was no exception.

Alina kneeled beside Abe. Her hand gently grazed his arm in a comforting manner. She sat on the floor, idly stroking his arm until Abe could compose himself. Eventually, his fear subsided and he could convince himself that everyone was safe; no one was in danger.

Over the years, Alina came to know Abe well, and she knew that after one of his anxious episodes he would often find solace and comfort in the pages of a book. As such, she had already grabbed his favourite book. After some time, he stood and crawled into his bed. Alina then read to him like she often did to Brighid. Abe listened to Alina's calm and soothing rendition of his beloved tale until he slowly drifted off to sleep.

It was not a restful sleep. He felt even more tired when he awoke, and his body hurt all over. He needed more rest, but his sleep was full of haunted memories that he did not wish to revisit again. Instead, he got up and made his way down the hall. He could hear laughter and joy coming from the kitchen which lifted his spirits ever so slightly. As he entered the room, he saw Brighid laughing at Arlo. Although Arlo never tried very hard, he always managed to make Brighid laugh. Evander rolled his eyes, but Abe saw the smirk hidden behind his hand. Evander always tried to hide his fondness for Arlo and Brighid. Abe always encouraged his studies to form strong and lasting friendships, so he never understood why Evander acted so distant and indifferent towards them.

"Ames!" Brighid exclaimed when she noticed Abe enter the room. She raced over to him and wrapped him in a tight hug. "Last night was surprisingly fun. Thank you for the opportunity."

Abe savoured the hug for a moment. He relished knowing she was safe and alive, for the knew moments like these were fleeting. For now, however, she was safe.

"It was fine, I suppose," Evander said disinterestedly while playing with a glass of water on the table.

"It seems that you enjoyed *one* particular aspect of the night, Ambrose," Arlo joked. Alina immediately straightened. Though her back was to him, Abe knew exactly what expression her face was making. Disgust. Anger. Maybe even jealousy. However, at this moment, her feelings weren't his focus. Abe just wanted to focus on everyone being together. He wanted to disappear in their jokes and snide remarks to each other. He just wanted to feel their company and be completely enveloped in it. These people were his world and he didn't know what he would do without them.

"Perhaps if you had partaken in the dancing, you also would have enjoyed the evening," Abe retorted. Arlo shrugged. "I do hope everyone at least learned something while at the ball. It's important to be able to interact with non-conductors. "

"I learned that regular people are still boring and vazey. I hardly found anyone stimulating. The punch provided more entertainment than the poor company," Evander remarked rather snidely. Abe ran his hand over his face in exasperation, but was saved from having to lecture him again regarding proper decorum as Alina placed food on the table pulling everyone's attention away from Evander's less-than-pleasant attitude.

There was a brief moment of silence as everyone filled their stomachs. Abe hadn't realised how famished he was until Alina's cooking was placed in front of him. While they continued to idly discuss the previous night's festivities, they all devoured the puddings, pies, and kedgeree. Brighid loved seeing everyone in dresses so much so that she stated she was considering switching back from pants since she felt so beautiful in a dress. Evander continued to find anything to complain about. Arlo apparently found a gambling table and managed to win an extensive amount of coin. Abe was certain Dame Agatha had not approved this gambling ring and was even more certain Arlo had somehow set it up.

Then, Abe's mind returned to Daisy at Dame Agatha's manor. He had been temporarily distracted and nearly forgot the peril Daisy was in. He suddenly stood from the table and moved towards the door when he was suddenly blocked by Alina. Her teeth were clenched and her nostrils slightly flared. She was infuriated with Abe, and he knew it.

"Where are you going?" she demanded.

"I believe you know," Abe responded, trying to be calm. He really didn't have the patience or time to deal with Alina's jealousy.

"You just saw her last night. Isn't that enough?" Alina spat. Abe could sense her anger building. She was trying to keep her voice down so the others wouldn't hear, but Abe wasn't sure how long that would last. "We are having breakfast as a family. We are all here enjoying each other's company. Why is that not enough for you?"

Abe paused for a moment taken aback by Alina's comment before replying. "I have to make sure she is okay. There was a bit of an accident last night."

"An accident? Like what? You didn't ruin that poor girl, did you?" Alina raised her eyes in an expectant manner. It would not have been the first time Abe was accused of such events though they hardly ever proved true.

"Hardly. I took her to the stones." Alina's anger broke slightly as pure surprise painted her face.

"You did what?" This time, Alina wasn't quiet. All of the studies turned towards them. Abe could feel their eyes on the back of his head.

"Alina," Abe said forcefully, "I will discuss this with you later. I need to leave. *Now*."

Abe pushed Alina out of his way trying to exit the train station as quickly as possible. Alina followed him most of the way down the hall, yelling at him to stop. Abe ignored her and promptly left the train station without a word. He found himself nearly running towards the manor, not wanting to waste anymore time. There were always other ways of transport as a Conductor, but Abe needed the distraction of a mundane task more than anything.

As he arrived at the manor, he could see several people moving in the main hall through the windows. They appeared to be dismantling the previous night's affair. Abe knocked on the door and awaited a response. Although Abe could see multiple people, hardly anyone seemed interested in answering the door. He knocked a second time and stepped back from the door. Eventually, a servant answered the door. She smiled and bowed at Abe who returned the sentiment.

"I was wondering if I could seek an audience with Miss Bloomsbury," Abe requested in the most formal tone he could muster. It felt uncomfortable, and Abe didn't like it.

"Sorry, Sir. The dame has closed the manor to all visitors after last night. Perhaps, tomorrow she will feel differently." Without waiting for Abe's response, she promptly closed the door on him. If he had the opportunity to touch her, he may have been able to change the servants mind, but the situation did not lend the opportunity. Conductors with mind as a primary were not as limited as Abe, but Abe was exceptionally poor at the mind force and found that physical touch aided his abilities. Because of this limitation, he only used the mind element when it was necessary or convenient. Instead of trying again, Abe headed back to the train station.

As he arrived at the train station, he expected everyone to be in the main room, but he found it deserted. Abe sighed with relief as an empty main room meant Alina's inevitable interrogation would be delayed. However, as he made his way to his room with the intent to freshen up, he was greeted by a rather irritated looking Alina perched on his desk.

"You are back," Alina stated.

"And you are in my room," Abe retorted and took to finding something to change into.

"You took her to the stones?" Alina demanded.

"May I change before the interrogation begins?" Abe begged. Alina's glare clearly indicated an immediate answer was required. "Yes, I did. I was checking to see if she could sense the forces as we've done with many studies before."

"But you did not discuss this with me."

"I need not discuss everything with you, Alina." She inhaled sharply, and Abe knew he insulted her. They had been through much and often acted like partners in any situation related to their studies. "Alina. Please, we need not argue about this."

"What happened?" Clearly, Alina was not ready to let the conversation lie. Abe sighed. He knew she would not rest, but he had no real interest in discussing it with her at this time.

"The forces selected her," Abe explained, which corresponded to a gasp from Alina. Abe rolled his eyes. "She was tested and, I believe, she passed, but I was unable to see her today to verify this. There were missing pieces to suggest she was fully accepted. Her eyes were undecided at awakening. Neither matched a primary."

Alina began pacing the room deep in thought. Abe took this distraction as a moment to change his shirt and quickly did so. It wasn't like Alina hadn't seen him naked before, but he didn't want to invite her longing gazes and awkward moments. Alina hardly seemed to notice. Instead of awaiting more questions from Alina, Abe left his study and finally found his studies sitting in the main room ready to learn. At least teaching would be an idle distraction from Daisy.

The next day, Abe walked to the manor and was turned away again by another servant. He asked to speak to Dame Agatha before Daisy, but that didn't generate results either. The following day held the same outcome. Each time, Abe attempted to make some brief physical contact to sway things in his favour but nothing seemed to work.

By the fourth day, Alina had given up on lecturing him. He left in the morning, but was turned away again. Instead of heading back to the train station, Abe found himself wasting the remainder of the day with Madam Hooch. He briefly ran into Rosie at the bar, but she seemed quite distracted and uncomfortable at seeing Abe. Furthermore, Abe was much too drunk to fully understand anything Rosie was saying. He knew she assured him that Daisy was fine, but Abe couldn't remember anything else they discussed. He went to bed that night drunk, but feeling slightly more at ease with the idea that Daisy was alright.

As he awoke for the fifth day and his fifth attempt, he knew that today he would see her. He wasn't going to take no for an answer. Rosie's reassurance of the previous night was not nearly enough for Abe. He needed to see for himself that she was okay. Somehow, someway, Abe was going to ensure he saw Daisy.

Chapter 15 - A New Dawn

At some point, Daisy had fallen asleep. When she awoke, the sun was in full light and streamed warmly through the crack in the curtains. Some of the pain had subsided, but she was still dead tired. Sitting up, she looked around for Rosie who appeared absent from the room. Daisy decided to stand up and open the window. This proved to be more challenging than expected. She was still wobbly on her feet, but she managed to get to the window. As she flung open the blinds, she screamed in surprise. Standing on the other side of the second story window was Abe.

He clung to the window, clearly struggling to remain on the small ledge. His uncomfortable grimace turned into a slight smile when he noticed Daisy gazing at him. He tried to wave at her but slipped, nearly falling off the ledge. Daisy threw open the window, and Abe gladly crawled through.

"What are you doing?!" Daisy exclaimed.

"They weren't telling me anything so I figured I would get my own answers," he answered looking rather sheepish.

He now sat straddling the window sill, able to jump out at a moment's notice. His eyes fell on Daisy and his eyebrows shot up. Daisy glanced down and noticed she was wearing only a night gown. Daisy walked away from Abe towards her wardrobe to find something to wear.

"I suppose that is one way to get answers, but it cannot have been that long since you last saw me," Daisy said as she pulled out a loose frock that she could slip over the nightgown. It would at least cover more of her body than her current attire.

"Dais," Abe's voice softened. Daisy closed the wardrobe, more appropriately dressed, and made direct eye contact with Abe. He seemed slightly disappointed, but his concern was more apparent. "Dais, it's been five days."

"What do you mean it has been five days?" Daisy thought it had been a couple hours at most.

"Today is the twenty sixth. I haven't seen you since you woke up after the ball."

Daisy tried to rack her brain about what had occured over the past five days. Did she just sleep for five days? What had happened?

"You don't remember," Abe said, his surprise evident.

"Not really. I remember having a bath and thinking the water was getting warmer." She chuckled at the thought. "Then I crawled into bed and fell asleep. Have I been sleeping for the past five days?"

"I haven't the slightest clue. Like I said, they wouldn't tell me anything. I ran into Rosie one evening at the bar, but she was whisked away before I could ask her anything. I didn't know what was going on, but I had to make sure you were okay."

"Why is that? You barely know me." Abe suddenly stood and moved swiftly to stand in front of Daisy. He gently placed his hands on her upper arms, asking for permission with his eyes. He moved slightly closer; their chests almost touched. Daisy could smell the strong scent of lavender and cedarwood: earthy, fresh, and calming.

"Because I care about you," he spoke softly and sweetly. He looked down at her and his long lashes casted strange shadows across his cheeks. Daisy urged herself not to blush. "I care about you, Daisy, and all this has done is show me how much you mean to me. I don't understand it. It honestly makes barely any sense, and yet it makes all the sense in the world. There is just something about you."

Daisy fully understood what he meant. Her experience with him was confusing and unusual, but welcome and calming. She wanted more and kept aching for that next opportunity. It all made sense, but also made no sense at all. Without thinking, Daisy felt herself curl into Abe's chest. His arms wrapped around her. She could feel everywhere his body touched hers. It was like fire coursing through her veins as he pulled her closer. She felt herself surrender to the feeling. However, as quickly as it started, it departed.

The door opened and behind it stood Rosie looking surprised and impressed at the scene in front of her. She quietly closed the door, not breaking eye contact with Abe and Daisy. Abe's arms left Daisy leaving her feeling cold and empty. Rosie moved more into the room. She placed her hands on her hips like a disappointed mother about to scold her children.

"Abe, you are not supposed to be here," she held up a hand to stop him from interrupting. "Just stating the obvious. I really don't care what you choose to do. What I do care about is that Daisy has woken up."

"Just a few moments ago. Abe was standing on the window sill," Daisy replied meekly.

"You mean he climbed the outside of the building and scaled to our window to see if you were alright?" They both nodded, unsure what to say. "I am impressed."

Rosie dropped her hands and walked over to her bed where she threw herself down in the most unladylike fashion. Daisy felt herself relax. Clearly, Rosie wasn't here to scold them. Abe also seemed to relax but still appeared ready to jump out the window at a moment's notice.

"What happened to me? Abe was saying that I woke up five days ago, but I don't remember anything since then," Daisy stated. Rosie seemed slightly uncomfortable from the question.

"You don't remember anything?" Rosie asked while idly twiddling her thumbs in a slightly embarrassed fashion.

"Not really," Daisy responded.

"I suppose that makes sense. You appeared to be asleep, but a lot of… weird stuff happened. I kept it a secret from the dame. I do not think she would have liked what was happening." Her voice got softer with every word. By the end she was nearly whispering while adamantly avoiding looking at Abe or Daisy.

"What happened Rosie?" Rosie shook her head. "Rosette! You will tell me what happened!"

Daisy was unsure where this force and power came from. She felt confident, but it also scared her. Clearly, this behaviour was unexpected as both Abe and Rosie snapped their heads toward Daisy and gazed, awe-struck.

"I don't even know how to explain it," Rosie stammered.

"Well, try," Daisy said. She was starting to lose her patience.

"When you fell back asleep, the room got hot. Like really hot. Like I ended up sleeping -" She stopped and glared at Abe. Abe put his hands up as if he was being accused and trying to prove his innocence. "Nevermind. It was so hot, but as soon as you stepped out in the hallway it felt totally normal. It's like it was contained to this room and I couldn't figure out why. There was no fire or anything that would produce heat. I kept touching your forehead to feel a fever, but never noticed one. It made no sense."

"The next day, I left you sleeping and went down to lessons as instructed. I told the dame you were resting. When I came back from the lessons that afternoon, everything was wet. It was like someone dumped buckets of water over the room or like the window was left open during a storm. Again, I couldn't find the source of all this water. I cleaned it up as best as I could without raising suspicion and then went to bed."

169

"The following night, I woke up at midnight to you… you doing something. I couldn't quite see because it was dark, but it looked as if you were floating? Maybe it was a dream, but I was positive you were hovering above your bed."

"After that, I made sure to tell the dame that you were doing well, but I didn't think you could attend your studies yet as you were still so tired. She insisted on seeing you, so I brought her up here. I was so worried she would call my bluff and send for a doctor. When we entered the room though, it was like her whole personality changed. She was sweet and happy and nice. She looked around, gave me a compliment about my dress and promptly left without further inspection. She was nice to me in the open. I didn't know what to do with her. I was so lost but relieved that she didn't inspect you more."

"Then yesterday, I came in and those flowers that Abe gave you, well they had been looking a little rough, but yesterday they looked as if they were brand new. They had also multiplied and changed colours. They were beautiful. I thought Abe gave you more flowers somehow, but I wasn't sure. I had never seen daisies like this. Everything was strange and now I feel like I have gone insane as I describe all of this to you. Nothing has made sense over the last few days, but I just kept hoping you were okay. I kept checking on you. Please tell me you are okay. Please tell me I am not insane."

Rosie looked between Daisy and Abe, pleading for someone to disagree with her. Daisy was also confused, but

Abe seemed deep in thought. His hand stroked his chin and his brow furrowed.

"These all happened roughly one day apart?" Abe asked.

"Yes," Rosie replied.

"And they were contained to this room? No one else saw anything?"

"The only other person that came in here was the dame, and I already told you what happened to her."

"Five days, five events, five elements," he said quietly to himself. He suddenly sprung into action and started throwing stuff from Daisy's wardrobe into her trunk at the end of her bed.

"You are not crazy Rosie, but I must take Daisy immediately. She cannot stay here any longer," he asserted.

"What are you talking about?" Rosie and Daisy exclaimed at the same time. He stopped stuffing clothes in the trunk and braced his arms against the edge. Abe appeared defeated.

"I am about to make sense of everything, but Rosie, you must swear to secrecy. You cannot tell anyone what you are about to see or you will put us all in danger. Do you understand?" Rosie looked terrified, but nodded. "Very well, the Conductor's are real. It is not a story, and I am one of them."

"You cannot b-" but Daisy was cut short as an orb of water suddenly hovered above Abe's hand. He threw it from one hand to the other like a ball. Then, he snapped his fingers and the ball of water disappeared as quickly as it had appeared.

Daisy assumed her expression was similar to Rosie's: wide eyes, open mouth, slightly pale complexion. Both were completely surprised and hadn't the slightest idea what to say or do. Daisy's brain was running at a million miles an hour. *What else could he do? What else was he capable of? What else hadn't he told her?*

"You can do magic," Rosie finally stammered.

"I can conduct elemental forces," he explained as he continued packing Daisy's things. "Anyone can learn to conduct but it takes a certain level of natural abilities for the forces to fully accept you. The forces will test you and if you are chosen, you receive the mark of the Conductors."

"And what exactly is the mark?" Rosie inquired.

"Different coloured eyes," Daisy said quietly, realisation dawning on her. Abe had a green and a blue eye because he was a Conductor.

"Correct," Abe replied. "Heterochromia is the technical term."

"But what does this have to do with Daisy?" Abe stopped moving and looked at Rosie.

"I want you to look at her." He narrowed his eyes at Rosie, almost challenging her to disobey him. "Tell me, what colour are her eyes?"

"I don't need to look at her to tell you her eyes are a pewter grey."

"Are they?" Rosie rolled her eyes, but moved her gaze to Daisy. She was quiet for a moment before she let go a small gasp. "Quite right. They now look gold, don't they?"

"But her eyes are grey."

"Her one eye is silver, the other is now gold."

Daisy felt panic rising in her chest. She ran to the nearest reflective surface and stared at her reflection. Her same round face, small lips, and weak jaw greeted her, like old friends. However, new to her face was one gold eye that looked like liquid sunshine shimmering even in the reflection. It felt out of place on her. It was something beautiful on her plain figure. Daisy ran her hands all over her face, trying to convince herself it was real, that her eyes did in fact change.

"Okay, so her eyes changed. What does that have to do with anything?" Abe slammed the lid of the trunk shut after packing the majority of Daisy's things.

"She is not safe, nor is anyone around her safe until she can learn to control the elements. It can be unpredictable and dangerous at the beginning. She must leave and come with me so I can teach her properly. So she can learn properly."

"Learn what?"

Daisy had enough of being talked about while standing in the room. It was like Abe and Rosie were making decisions for her and Daisy wasn't going to let that happen. She stepped in between Rosie and Abe, cutting off their line of sight to each other. They both watched Daisy as she surveyed the scene in front of her. Abe appeared furious and stressed whereas Rosie's face was full of fear and concern. Daisy understood what Rosie was feeling, but realisation dawned on her.

"To conduct elemental forces." There wasn't any doubt in Daisy's voice. She understood now. It was clear as day. There wasn't any other choice. "I am a Conductor now, and I must go with Abe."

Chapter 16 - The Fifth Element

Abe grabbed Daisy's trunk and threw it out the window. He then stuck his head out and surveyed the area before extending his hand to Daisy, indicating it was time to leave. He needed Daisy to hurry, but she seemed uncertain. She quickly ran over to Rosie and gave her a hug.

"I will come back eventually. I promise," Daisy said to Rosie.

"Dais. We really need to go," Abe expressed, trying to keep the panic out of his voice. She had already exposed too much of the forces to Rosie without meaning to. Daisy's strength of conduction would only grow from here. He needed to get her away and learn to control the conduction before something bad happened.

"I'm coming," Daisy announced.

She squeezed Rosie's hand before turning and running to Abe. Her hand slid into his. It was warm and soft and welcoming. He smiled before defenestrating himself and pulling Daisy along with him. Daisy screamed slightly, but Abe knew she was in no danger. He could control air like he could blink. It was second nature to him. They gently glided to the ground. Daisy seemed awed which lifted Abe's spirits. The last fews days had been exhausting and draining for him. Not knowing what was going on with Daisy was anxiety producing and made his head ache. He felt more calm now that Daisy was with him, but before he could relax, he had to get her back to the station.

It was not often that a new Conductor was made. Even Brighid, who was his youngest study, had been made over twenty years ago. It took time to learn how to conduct the elemental forces, to do *magic*, but by learning, life became extended, time slowed, years wore like months. He was excited for someone new, but also nervous as the first few weeks were critical.

"Where are we off to?" Daisy asked, interrupting his thoughts and refocusing his attention.

"Quite right," Abe said, coming back to the mission at hand: get her safe first, figure out the rest later. "The train station actually. We are called Conductors for more than one reason."

Daisy giggled at his joke. She always seemed so innocent and naive, so far from what Abe was. He smiled back at her, appreciating her youth. He picked up the trunk and began walking towards the woods. He knew they couldn't leave by the front gate or they would be spotted. They would have to work their way through the woods and around the town without being seen. If they were seen... Abe didn't want to even think about what could happen.

He started off and Daisy followed without questioning. She trusted him so openly and he felt his heart constrict. *What had he done to such a beautiful, young soul?* She idly hummed a song as they walked. Abe was sure she wasn't even aware she was doing it, but he found the song soothing and familiar.

"What are you singing?" Abe inquired, slightly breathless. The trunk weighed more than expected. Daisy seemed to notice his struggle and instantly grabbed a handle of the trunk to share the load.

"It's a song my sister used to sing to me through the walls of the house when I was locked in my room. I sometimes hum it when I am feeling nervous." A sadness overcame her and Abe suddenly remembered that she recently lost her sister.

"How does it go?" Abe said in hopes to ease some of the pain he was sure Daisy was feeling.

"I am never quite sure. She always sang it through the walls so it was muffled. I often asked her the words but she would never sing it for me in person. Hence why I hum the tune. I miss her. Things like this tune help me keep her close."

"I know how you feel." Abe smiled at Daisy to try and comfort her. "If you ever learn it, do let me know. I am sure it is a beautiful song."

Daisy suddenly stopped. A concerned expression painted her face and Abe felt a sense of unease growing inside him.

"What's wrong?" Abe asked.

"What about the rest of my family?" Daisy questioned.

"What about your family?" He was genuinely confused by the question and her level of concern.

"Well, they are going to be told I am missing from the manor. They will worry, I think. They already lost my sister. They shouldn't have to lose both of us. Shouldn't I tell them something? Give them some sort of reason for me leaving so they don't lose me and my sister." Her eyes were large and pleading. Abe's heart hurt. He wanted to help her, but truly wasn't sure how to help her.

"Don't worry. I will deal with it. We need to keep moving." Abe needed time to think of a plan. He pulled on her arm and she reluctantly began to move. She seemed lost in thought and Abe wasn't sure what to do or say.

She was taking it fairly well in Abe's opinion. He hadn't meant to expose her to the forces, untested, then leave her without the needed support. He meant to show her the stones as the first test of her ability. He never thought that the forces would choose to fully test her then. It was uncommon. Experiencing the forces for the first time could crack the brain, fracture the personality, and corrupt the soul. He had seen it happen many times before. He had been around many studies and watched as they slowly decayed and died. It was truly a horrible sight.

Yet, Daisy seemed relatively unharmed. She had gone through the test and experienced the forces alone, unsupported. Somehow, she fared well and her mental capacity seemed completely intact. Abe was relieved that, overall, Daisy appeared normal or at least as normal as he knew her. She was still amazing to him and perhaps even more fascinating now. *How did she manage so well being completely unsupported and untested?*

Daisy gasped beside him. She pointed upwards and Abe saw that it was starting to snow. The air had been chilling over the last bit, and now the snow fluttered about them in giant flakes. Daisy seemed amazed by the snow as if it was her first time in the snow. She stuck her bare hands out and caught a snowflake which promptly melted on her hand. Several snowflakes had landed on her eyelashes, making her eyes appear even larger. Against the growing white, the colour of her eyes popped even more. She was even more stunning against the snow.

"You act like you've never seen snow before." Abe enjoyed observing her innocent wonder, but he continued walking to encourage them forward.

"I have, but only through the window. We weren't really permitted outside at the manor much. At home, however... as soon as it snowed, Mama wouldn't let us outside anymore," Daisy stated. She had turned her face up towards the sky letting snowflakes land on her cheeks. Her eyes were closed and Abe was guiding her by tugging on the trunk that linked them.

"You've never played in the snow before?"

"There was one time, when we were quite young, that my sister and I snuck out after the first snow. There was barely any snow on the ground, but we played in it under the midnight moon. We were so cold and soaking wet when we came back in. It was one of the happiest moments I have with my sister. However, we thought we snuck out unnoticed, but when we came back," Daisy paused, she seemed uncomfortable suddenly. "The duchess was awake. My sister got off with a warning. I was not so lucky."

Daisy moved aside her hair to expose her shoulders. Just barely peeking out from the neckline of her dress were small, white scars. She seemed self-conscious and quickly covered the lines back up with her hair. Her face contorted in the pain of memories. Abe dropped the trunk and grabbed Daisy's hands. He looked into her eyes and concentrated.

"What are you doing?" Daisy asked.

"Relax your mind for a moment," Abe responded. She slowly blinked and looked back. Tears were cresting her bottom eyelid. Abe allowed his mind to enter hers.

An image filtered through his head. A young girl stood in front of him. She seemed familiar to Abe, but he couldn't place it. Her hair was liquid gold and her eyes like two amethysts sparkling in the sun. She was young, but she had all the features to become something of pure beauty. She had delicate hands and facial features.

Abe felt happiness spark through him though it was not his own. Abe and the girl were playing in the snow, like Daisy described. He felt a cold spot on his back as a snowball hit him. A giggle escaped him though the sound was not his own.

The image flipped again and Abe stared at the back of a door. He felt wetness on his cheeks. He was kneeling on the floor. He could hear voices on the other side of the door but couldn't understand them. Then there were footsteps. They were coming closer and Abe could feel fear swelling in his chest. He scuttled away from the door and hid behind a chair, trying desperately to disappear. The door swung open and Abe tried to stay as quiet as possible, but it didn't matter. A hand clutched his arm and dragged him from out behind the chair. Abe struggled to try to get away, but failed. The grip only tightened.

The image changed again. This time he felt rope cutting into his hands then a crack and slice in his back. Stinging pain over and over again. Trickling liquid down his back, but not a single tear. He knew that he couldn't give them that satisfaction. He couldn't let them know it hurt him.

He pulled his hand away from Daisy's and was brought back to the here and now. Abe quickly averted his eyes, trying not to let Daisy see the tears creeping to his eyes. He was exhausted. Entering a mind could be taxing and Daisy's was no exception.

"What did you just do?" Daisy said accusingly. "Don't say nothing. I can feel you did something." Abe grabbed the trunk again and began walking again. Daisy followed reluctantly.

"Sometimes it is easier to watch than to talk," Abe explained. Daisy frowned at him, clearly not understanding. "I told you there are five forces. Do you remember them?"

"Earth, water, fire, air, and mind."

"Yes, mind. The ability to conduct animal and human minds. What do you think that means?"

"You can control minds."

"Partially. You can also read thoughts, control emotions, implant ideas, mend minds, and see memories. It depends how competent you are in the force."

"You watched my memory." For presenting as naive as she did, Daisy was quick to catch on and quite clever. But it wasn't her intelligence that surprised him. A sad understanding underlined her tone. "You didn't ask."

Abe paused. It never occurred to him. Mind was not one of his primary forces, so he didn't use it often. When he did, he used it mostly to his benefit that he never thought about asking for permission. The thought hit him like a brick wall. *How intrusive had he been? Why had he never considered asking?* Abe had been so accustomed to just going about his life. Never really caring about other people or their opinions. Daisy, however, was overwhelming his brain. She was quickly becoming all he cared about and her opinion was the most important thing to him.

"I hadn't considered it. Mind is not one of my primaries, so I don't use it often. It's often awkward and clunky for me to use," Abe explained.

"What do you mean by primaries?"

"I suppose you don't know much about the Conductors really. Most studies go through extensive trials and education before being tested by the forces, but for some reason the forces picked you before you were fully vetted. I don't fully understand it yet."

"That doesn't answer my question."

"Each Conductor has two primaries which correspond to their mismatched eyes. A Conductor can learn all the forces, in fact they have to, but there will always be two that are easier to learn and to understand. They are usually that Conductor's strongest forces."

"And what are your primaries?"

"My blue eye means water and my green eye means air."

"And what does mine mean?" Abe paused for a moment, uncertain of how to respond. Gold and silver had never been seen before, but studies' eyes often changed as they learned the forces. Usually by the end of the first month their primaries were set. However, a study's natural eye colour was usually the default for one primary, but silver had never been a natural colour.

"I am not sure," Abe finally decided to be honest with Daisy. He need not protect her from everything. Eventually, she would have to learn anyway. "Usually a study's eyes change in the first month as they experiment with the forces for the first time. I suppose we will have to wait and see."

Daisy smiled at him. Her pain was still palpable, but Abe could see she was getting excited. She was obviously looking forward to learning and Abe was looking forward to teaching her.

Chapter 17 - The Conductors

They entered the train station and stopped in front of a wall beside the ticket booth. Abe looked around before setting down Daisy's trunk.

"Wait here," Abe stated, "I will be back in a moment."

Abe quickly glanced around again before disappearing through the brick wall. Daisy was baffled. He just vanished into a wall. Clearly, there was more to conducting the elements than she suspected. It wasn't long before Abe reappeared from the wall.

"They are ready," Abe said. "Not happy, fair warning, but ready for you to enter."

He picked up the trunk and walked back through the wall. Daisy followed. It was a strange feeling passing through the wall. It felt like walking through a mist on a late fall morning but coming out the other side completely dry.

As she emerged on the other side, the first thing Daisy saw was the girl from the ball. She was closer this time and not hidden behind a mask. She had the telltale mismatched eyes of a Conductor: violet and crimson. Both deep in colour, and absolutely piercing. Her eyes were narrowed, her arms crossed, and her lips pursed in displeasure. Clearly she was not happy to see Daisy.

Three other people stood awkwardly behind the girl. There was another girl, who seemed very young and scared, and two men that seemed completely disinterested, more annoyed than anything, about Daisy's arrival.

"Daisy, these are my studies," Abe announced, indicating the small troop in front of him. "This is Brighid, Arlo, and Evander. I pointed them out to you at the ball. The lady on the right is Alina, who you've had the pleasure of briefly meeting. She is my assistant. Everyone, this is Daisy and I expect you to be nice."

There were eye rolls, smirks and scoffs at Abe's suggestions. Ignoring it all, Abe whisked away Daisy's trunk and disappeared down a hall, leaving her alone in the room of strangers. The studies disbanded and moved into other areas of the room, but Alina stood glaring at Daisy. Alina's gaze was nearly as heavy and critiquing as Dame Agatha's. It sent chills up Daisy's spine, but Daisy tried to act unbothered by Alina's apparent judgement. With her nose held high, Alina approached Daisy.

"So," Alina started. Her voice was stiff and not anything like the night of the ball. "What are you able to do?"

"What do you mean?" Daisy tried to keep her voice light, but could feel the defensive undertone building in each word.

"Can you do any conduction? Sorry, you probably call it *magic*." Alina began circling Daisy like a wolf stalking prey. She was obviously assessing Daisy.

"I cannot say I have tried anything yet. I just woke up from a five day magic induced coma about three hours ago."

"I see." Daisy's answer was obviously not satisfactory to Alina. "And why are you here?"

"Abe stated that I needed to learn how to control my magic for my safety and those around me."

"But why are you *here*?" Daisy could tell Alina was suggesting something, but wasn't quite sure what she could be indicating. Daisy made direct eye contact with Alina.

"I am here to learn how to conduct the elemental forces."

Alina was about to interrogate Daisy more when Abe re-entered the room humming a tune that was oddly familiar to Daisy. However, as Abe noticed Alina and Daisy, he cut his tune off and quickly came to Daisy's aid. He slid in beside Daisy and smiled at Alina, quickly shutting down anything else she had to ask. Alina turned on her heel and sulked over to where Brighid sat in the corner.

"This is the main room," Abe started to explain. He was clearly trying to distract Daisy which she didn't mind in the slightest. She enjoyed Abe's company. "It changes quite often depending on people's moods and particular skills they are practising. The hallway to the left leads to the dormitories. Each person has their own room. I quickly made your room, but as you learn you can adjust it to your style. It's the last door on the left. The right hallway leads to my study, the kitchen, and extra storage. Really only

Alina and I go down the right hallway. You will mostly spend your time here and in your dorm."

"Can I not go outside?"

"Until we can ensure you have proper control of your magic, it is best to avoid other people." Daisy pursed her lips in displeasure, but understood the situation. "I have some things to attend to, but I will be back to assist you in a bit. Brighid will likely be the most welcoming."

He winked at Daisy before walking away and disappearing down the hallway to the right. Alina quickly followed him which was a good thing in Daisy's opinion. Daisy wasn't interested in Alina continuing her inquisition. This also left Brighid alone.

Brighid sat in the corner by the fireplace. She had her hands outstretched and was making the fire within the firebox grow and shrink. She even changed the colour occasionally. She moved it from left to right and had it hovering above the wood. Slowly and with great difficulty, she pulled the fire out of the fireplace and had it floating just in front of the hearth. Daisy watched in amazement, inching closer and closer to the flame.

In a few short seconds, many things happened at once. In Daisy's amazement she did not see the cushion on the floor which she promptly tripped over and toppled to the floor. Daisy's fall caused Brighid to lose focus and drop her flame on the rug which promptly spread out of control. In turn, Evander snapped his fingers causing a cascade of water to fall from nowhere over the spreading flame and Daisy. Daisy sat, drenched on the floor, staring at the singed rug and people in front of her. There was an awkward silence before Brighid started laughing. Soon, everyone was laughing. Daisy was worried they might be mad, but this did not appear to be the case.

"That's your third rug this week," Evander chuckled. He snapped his fingers and the rug was replaced with a brand new, wool rug.

"Oh hush. You nearly burnt down the whole place when you started learning fire," Brighid teased. "Sorry about the water. Evander is always quick to put out fires since his mistake."

Brighid moved closer to Daisy. Her smile was wide and bright. She appeared younger than Daisy. Her hair was light brown like well-done toast. Her skin was unmarked and showed hardly any signs of age. Her eyes were a nordic blue and sable brown. Daisy wondered what her original eye colour was as both were beautiful on her.

"So," Brighid announced, "what can you do?"

"I'm not really sure," Daisy confessed. "I just woke from being in a coma for five days. My roommate said I hovered over my bed, made the room boiling hot, and flooded the room, but I don't remember doing any of that."

"You mean to say that you've already been tested?" Arlo asked, his voice was full of surprise. Daisy thought he was asleep as he lounged on a chair beside the fireplace seeming completely removed from the situation.

"I don't know what you mean."

"Most Conductors go through a series of mini aptitude tests to see if they can handle the elemental forces. Like seeing if you can hold water in your hands without it dripping," Evander explained. "The final test is full exposure to the elements. This is where the elements test your mental and physical capacity. It's not a controlled environment and the elements can throw anything at you. Most Conductors have some idea of what the elements are so they can navigate the final test easier. Some even have basic skills already learned, but they are generally quite weak. In most cases, you can't fully conduct the elements until you are tested. Typically, the tests are supervised by a graduate Conductor, like Alina or Abe."

"Oh, um, I didn't know anything. Abe told me stories about the Conductors, but I thought they were more stories than truth. Obviously, I was quite wrong." This earned a chuckle from the other studies which eased some of the tension in Daisy.

"Well, let's see what you can do then," Evander said, ejecting himself from his seat and moving towards Daisy.

"She won't know how to do anything,"Arlo retorted.

"Doesn't mean she *can't* do anything," Evander said snidely back. "Strong Conductors learn the ancient words for different things to conduct the elements. However, most of us just learn based on feeling. You have to graduate and get Grand Master approval to learn the ancient tongue. But when you are learning, it's about tapping into the natural energies of the world and exuding them in a concentrated force."

189

"But how?" Daisy asked.

"Close your eyes," Brighid explained which Daisy followed. "Slow your breath. Allow yourself to relax. Hear the sounds around you. The crackle of the fire, the dripping water, your breath. These are pieces of the elements. Focus on one. Allow the sound to overcome your senses. Allow it to fill you. Allow yourself to feel its energy. Then, when you're ready, tell it what you want to do."

Daisy focused on the dripping of water. She could hear the slow, repetitive splash on the floor. She could see the water forming in her mind. She could feel the power buzzing through it. She could feel the energy moving through her. She took a deep breath, and focused more on the sound, on the feeling, on the energy. She wanted the water to hover. She didn't want it to splash.

Her eyes opened and hovering just above the floor, were several drops of water. Nothing substantial, but certainly enough to be seen. Daisy stared at the drops of water in disbelief. She focused her energy and forced the drops into one ball of water. She quickly glanced at the others who also seemed quite surprised. Daisy didn't want to stop. She collected more water drops and grew the floating ball. Before long, there was a ball of water about the size of a melon hovering in the middle of the room. Daisy gently spun the orb and made it move in a slow circle. She was unsure of how she was doing this, but it felt oddly normal. It felt natural, like breathing or blinking. She didn't have to think about it really; it just seemed to happen.

"Impressive." The sudden interruption broke Daisy's focus and the orb of water splashed onto the floor. Daisy turned towards the voice and saw Abe standing at the hallway entrance staring at the scene before him. Behind him, stood a rather infuriated looking Alina. The other studies suddenly scattered and busied themselves with other things, attempting to look innocent, but failing.

"Studies are not supposed to do magic unattended for the first three months," Alina spat. Daisy was not sure if she was mad at the situation or at whatever Abe and her had been doing down the hall.

"Shut up, Alina," Abe interjected, which earned him an insulted look from her. "Daisy is simply experimenting just as they all did after their tests."

Abe indicated the other studies around the room who were ensuring they did not make eye contact with Abe or Alina.

"The difference is, Abe, they all had some basics under their belts before they did their exam."

"Clearly," Abe said, turning to face Alina. He towered over her with his nose just inches away from Alina's. "She can manage the basics."

Alina's face turned a deep shade of scarlet. Whether this was from embarrassment or anger, Daisy was unable to determine. Abe shrugged and moved into the middle of the room. He snapped his fingers, did a weird circling of his hands and everything in the room began to fly around. He then snapped his fingers again and furniture fell to the ground in neat rows. The plush comforts of before gave way to four hard desks with uncomfortable looking chairs.

Arlo, Brighid and Evander groaned from behind Daisy before taking a seat at a desk. Evander and Arlo sat at the back. Brighid took the third desk leaving a front desk for Daisy. Abe gestured to the seat, indicating that Daisy should sit in the chair. She followed the instructions.

"Let's learn!"

Chapter 18 - A Lesson in History

"As most of you know, the first month after a Conductor's initiation is crucial," Abe explained as the other studies groaned. "The elements don't always work with us, but often continue to test us. Learning to control and focus the forces is essential."

"We know this all, Ames," Brighid whined. "Why does this matter?"

"We have a new Conductor; therefore, we are returning to the basics for a short while," Abe responded. There were several sounds of complaint and displeasure. Daisy could feel guilt gnawing in her stomach as she was responsible for their dissatisfaction.

"Some of you have been sloppy with your techniques lately, so it will be good for all of you to return to the basics for a little while," Alina dictated from behind everyone. Brighid visibly rolled her eyes while Evander let out an exasperated sigh.

"For Conductors, control comes from understanding your thoughts," Abe started. "Forces are conducted through thought processes. Once you understand your thought processes, you can then control the forces to do nearly whatever you want."

"That's not true," Evander interrupted. Abe ran a hand over his face. Daisy smirked at Evander's remark. He appeared to be an expert and clearly tested Abe's patience.

"Evander, if you could please not interrupt me while I am teaching." Evander raised his hand as if to continue his comment, but Abe's stern glare silenced Evander into a pout. "Some magic is limited to graduated Conductors that undergo a second elemental test. Upon completion of the test, a graduate Conductor can learn the ancient tongue giving them access to more powers that are significantly stronger. Very few are allowed to take the test, even less pass the test, and a tiny minority can actually learn the ancient tongue."

"Do you know the ancient tongue?" Brighid inquired. Abe smirked at the comment.

"Yes, yes I do, but it's not something I use often. It's - unpredictable, hard to control and can corrupt your power if you are not careful." Abe shot a glance at Alina that Daisy caught but didn't understand.

"What happens when you corrupt your power?" Evander asked.

"For not wanting to return to the basics, you sure have a lot of questions," Arlo stated with an annoyed sigh.

"Corrupted conduction is broken conduction. Any forces you try to cast will come out wrong and unpredictable. You will ask water to boil but instead it will freeze. You will cast fire and instead you throw dirt. Your conduction doesn't work and, depending on the force, it can have catastrophic effects," Alina explained through clenched teeth.

"That is besides the point, we need to learn basic control before we can even consider advanced testing," Abe redirected. "Some forces require only thought. Other types require concentration of conduction through specific hand gestures and arm movements."

Abe handed out several pots and placed a small seed in each pot. He demonstrated what was apparently a simple growth conduction. He circled his stretched out hand around the pot in a slow motion and stated aloud, "Grow."

Daisy found it incredible as a small, brown seed, quickly grew into a beautiful gerbera daisy. Abe smiled at the flower and Daisy tried not to blush. With his flower fully grown, he directed his studies to imitate his actions. Evander was a flourish of unnecessary hands. Brighid struggled with her first attempt, but she was able to produce a small flower. With a lazy, yet successful, flick of his wrist, Arlo was also able to grow a flower. All eyes then turned to Daisy. She watched in adoration of everyone else, but she hadn't thought about attempting it herself.

Daisy swallowed hard and closed her eyes. She focused her mind on making the flower grow. She thought of a daisy like Abe's and slowly moved her hand around the rim of the pot. When Daisy opened her eyes, the seed sat untouched in the pot. Daisy scrunched her nose in frustration and tried again. This time, the room shook as Daisy focused on the seed and making it grow. The vibration increased until the seed suddenly sprouted.

The tiny sprout quickly grew into a single rose, but Daisy continued. The rose eventually grew into a full rose bush, but Daisy didn't stop there either. She focused on each individual rose and slowly turned them a different colour. She changed them from red to green, brown, orange, purple, and silver. Finally satisfied, Daisy lowered her hand back to the table and smiled. She looked up at Abe whose eyebrows were raised and mouth was slightly opened. He looked impressed as did most of the other studies. Daisy shied away from the attention, wanting to hide from the stares weighing on her. Even though it seemed like positive attention, she felt uncomfortable and uneasy.

"Well then," Abe announced, breaking the stunned silence. "Great job everyone. This was a successful lesson."

The first lesson was followed by a series of other exercises each focusing on basic control of water, fire, earth, and air. Abe explained that, if used incorrectly, the mind force could cause damage to the brain. As such, the mind force was not usually explored until a study had reasonable control of the other forces. However, with each exercise, Daisy excelled. She effectively conducted each force. With each exercise, Abe seemed more impressed.

"Your control is impressive," Abe stated during a break. He leaned up against Daisy's desk and stared down at her. "Usually, a Conductor doesn't show this amount of control so quickly. I suppose I have less to be concerned about with you. You at least haven't blown anything up like Arlo did his first time trying."

Daisy laughed at Abe's remark and felt herself relax. She had not realised how tense she was from trying to conduct the various forces. Her neck was tight and her head slightly ached from the strain of conducting. She rubbed her neck idly trying to ease the pain. Abe's face contorted in concern and Daisy dropped her hand. She didn't like receiving attention let alone someone showing genuine concern. It made her feel uncomfortable, and she wanted Abe to stop looking at her.

"Abe. Since my control is better than expected, I want to ask you about finishing school," Daisy stated.

"What about it? Want to go back?" Abe laughed lightly, but stopped when he noticed the seriousness on Daisy's face. "Do you want to go back?"

"Well, I can't just stop. My family is expecting me there, and I have responsibilities to my family. The expectation is for me to get married, and they already lost my sister. My family is important to me."

"Most Conductors don't have families or don't want to remain with their family. It's unusual and I keep forgetting with you. I am sure we can figure something out." Abe did not seem much interested in discussing this further. He moved back to the front of the room and called everyone's attention. Slowly, each study moved back to their desk.

"I thought we were done for the day," Arlo complained.

"There is one more thing that I want to cover," Abe stated. His voice became more authoritative than it had been previously. It sent pleasant shivers up Daisy's back. "I want to teach you all about the history of the Conductors."

"You mean that stupid story about the fountain? We all know it," Arlo stated disinterestedly from the back. He had his leg slung over the desk and was picking at his nails.

"No, I mean actual history about how the Conductors came to be." There was a loud thunk as Arlo's leg fell from the desk and hit the ground. Daisy looked at the other studies; they all seemed just as shocked. Daisy was unsure why. Shouldn't they already know this?

"You don't like talking about *that* history," Brighid said, her voice full of surprise.

"Quite right. However," Abe paused, glancing around the classroom before his eyes fell on Daisy. "I think it is important for you to know."

Abe stared at Daisy for a long moment, letting the words sink in. It seemed like Abe meant it was important for Daisy to know and not that it was important for the studies to know. The hairs on the back of her neck tingled with the weight of Abe's gaze. She swallowed and nodded her head slightly to indicate she understood, but the anxiety in her chest made her feel like she could never fully understand.

"Very well," Abe announced and cleared his throat. "I shall get started then. At the dawn of creation, there was an explosion that kick-started life. From that bang, there evolved celestial beings that would go on to create the world. Some that focused on life, others focused on land, but underlying all of them were the four elemental forces."

"Don't you mean five?" Evander remarked snidely from the back. The other studies snickered, but Abe's glare quickly shut them up.

"No, I mean four. Again, Evander, please do not interrupt me when I am teaching. There is plenty you don't know." Evander looked like a scolded puppy in the back corner but held his tongue. Abe continued.

"The four elemental forces, air, water, earth, and fire, played amongst the various celestials to help forge a cohesive plan that could support life. However, when these forces appeared to the celestial beings, they were always paired. Water with air and earth with fire. It was a perfect balance essentially. One pair could always balance, or correct, the other pair. They lived in unison as a perfect match and wanted to ensure the creation of life was successful.

"Eventually, not sure how long it took as time was not really a thing, the earth and its solar system were created. Other planets and systems were created, but the celestials flocked to Earth and so the forces followed. This place seemed the most hopeful for the creation of life. The forces first stepped on the planet and coalesced into two physical forms to better interact with the environment. To maintain their perfect harmony, one remained an embodiment of water and air while the other had the remaining two elements. They listened to the beings and helped form this planet in their image. The forces were excited to help and to forge. When the base was created, the beings vanished to different sections of the earth to create life in their image. No one image was correct or wrong, but each was different and important.

"But the forces felt abandoned and forgotten. They created the basis of life, but that earned them nothing. Hardly any of the beings created life that focused on the force's contributions. The forces were angry and hurt, but mostly unsure of what was left for them to do. As the beings created more and intelligent life emerged, the forces began to walk amongst the humans and learn their ways. In the early years, the forces existed in their natural form of pure energy. But as time went on, these forms began to scare the humans which was not what they wanted.

"The forces wanted to teach the humans, wanted the humans to learn about the forces' contributions and how the humans could learn the forces' ways. But the humans were reluctant to learn from monsters and beasts. So the two energies consisting of two forces formed themselves into human beings. Water and air transformed into a young man and from Earth and fire emerged a woman. They looked completely human but for the two coloured eyes. While necessary, the transformation had unintended consequences. The forces could no longer return to their natural form. They were trapped in the human form and had to live amongst humans as one of them.

"Together, the forces roamed the earth, showing humans the power of the forces. In the early years, the power of the forces amazed the humans. Some tribes were able to learn the basics and use them to help build empires and feed their people. They could move water where the land was dry. They could make soil fertile where plants couldn't grow. They could light areas that the sun never touched. People flourished under the ways of the forces and the celestials didn't mind for the forces didn't not change the human way of life, only supported it. The early forces called the humans that learned the forces the Conductors since they could feel the forces and use them. But humanity had a different idea.

"Eventually, as time wore, some factions of humanity grew fearful of the power of the forces. Those that could bear the forces were deemed witches and mages and put to death. War raged against those with magic and the population of the Conductors rapidly diminished. This was not what the forces wanted. The male force took to educating and listening to the people. He tried to understand what their fear was and how he could alleviate it.

"The female force saw no end to the horrors before her. Instead of trying reason, the female force took matters into her own hands. The living creatures were not created by the forces, but came from the basis of the forces. The female force found a way to tap into human energy. She began to control human and animal minds. She could feel their emotions, change their thoughts, control their movements. She created the fifth element and fought the slaying of her people by controlling those who feared the forces. The witch hunts subsided, but the fear did not. Instead of fearing magic in general, those that knew, feared the female. They hunted her instead. Anywhere she went she was hunted. Her face became the stories of children's nightmares. The male force faded into the background as he caused no harm, but he watched as his partner was villainized. He was unsure of how to help her and saw this as a rightful punishment for her desire for control.

"Many years passed, and she came to him to ask for help. She was scared and hurt, but the forces could not die. They existed in everything. She pleaded for his help and he felt like she had endured enough. Together, they developed a plan, a way to change her so that she would not be hunted. They learned of a way to transfer her essence into the soul of an unborn child and be reborn with the face of another.

"The male force ventured back into the world alone to seek out a human that they could use. The female force, however, stayed in hiding. In his journey, he interacted with humans and fell in love with their ways again. He had been separated for so long, he forgot the beauty of the human way. He even found a woman who he grew to love. She came with him throughout his adventures and eventually became pregnant with his child. Having been a perfect pair in perfect balance up to this point, the female force was envious of his relationship and decided their baby was the perfect transference. Without the male forces' knowledge, she implanted her soul over the baby's, but this change had unintended consequences.

"The mother grew sick and the male force tried everything in his power to save her. He was able to get the baby to term, but after giving birth, his love died. As he stared at his child, he noticed the dichromia of brown and purple, the first true emergence of the fifth element. At that moment, he knew that the female force had taken his baby. In his anger and pain, he dropped the baby off at an orphanage and disappeared into his pain. Years passed and he learned that the baby survived and was teaching humans the forces again. He remained hidden, not wanting to confront her or relive his pain. Even more so, he was terrified to emerge again and find another human that he could love just to have them taken away. Centuries evolved and humans changed, but the male force stayed hidden.

"It wasn't until the war of the Oppressors and Subjugates, did the male force appear. He saw their struggles and realised that he could change the war. So few Conductors existed and even fewer were strong enough to actually make a difference in the war. He came out of hiding and helped the Subjugates overthrow the Oppressors.

"The female force was excited to see him, but the male force held no positive feelings towards her. Finally willing to deal with his pain, they fought and fought. He did not agree with her methods of teaching or the process of transference. He thought her a murderer. Regardless of his words and absence, she loved him and wanted nothing more than to exist with him. They had always been a perfect balance and without him, she felt like a piece of her was missing. She used the fifth element against him. Because the fifth element was not a part of the original creation, the male force was exceptionally weak to its powers. Unlike humans, however, he was completely aware of her toying in his mind, but totally helpless against it. He eventually broke free of her grasp and another battle raged. In the end, the male force won over the female force.

"In the aftermath of their battle, he became a primary instructor to help guide and control the future of the Conductors, but his heart still ached from her betrayal. He longed for the woman he loved aeons ago, but she had long since turned to dust and returned to the Earth. He tried to overcome the pain, devote himself to his students, and focus on the future of the Conductors, but this proved difficult for him. He eventually disappeared again, but ensured to always keep tabs on the female force.

"Today, the Grand Master is said to be the female force and the male force has disappeared in his pain. He watches over the female force and only emerges when he feels she has done something wrong. Conductors started rumours that it is only the female force's love for the male force and the desire to appease him that keeps her in check. Some Conductors even believe that if the female force ever believes that the male force loves another, she will go on a murderous rampage again."Abe grew quiet. The other studies looked dumbfounded at the story. Clearly, this was not previously discussed and the content was shocking.

"It is also believed," Alina spoke from the back of the room. "That the male force's love is the reason for the emergence of a new force and not the female forces hate. Some Conductors believe that if he loves again, truly loves another, a new force will emerge. However, some do not think it is possible for him to love again after his heartbreak."

Abe's face paled, but none of the other studies noticed. All but Daisy had turned to look at Alina. Daisy couldn't take her eyes off of Abe. He braced his hands against the table. His arms shook. He appeared completely defeated and drained. As the other studies questioned Alina about the story, Daisy kept watching Abe. He rolled his shoulders back before standing upright and running his hands through his hair. The story seemed to age him. He noticed that Daisy was not distracted by Alina and his eyes locked onto her's. His face softened and some of the light seemed to come back to his eyes. He extended his hand to invite Daisy to follow him. She slid her hand into his. He led her away from the main room, down the corridor towards his office. She glanced back and saw Alina's eyes flare with fury as they walked away.

Chapter 19 - Windows to the Soul

Abe led Daisy towards his office. He had never really thought about how plain his office was until Daisy walked in. He had a simple desk in the middle of the room which was littered with papers, inkwells, and quills. On the corner of the desk there was a simple oil lamp that provided little light in the darkened room. Behind the desk sat a plain wood chair. It wasn't comfortable, but he rarely sat. Along one wall was a bed, neatly made and hardly slept in. He found he more often slept in the main room than anywhere else.

The only thing that resembled extravagance in his office were the books. Behind his desk, thousands of books lined the walls from the floor to the ceiling. The collection included everything from classics long since forgotten to the books that defined generations. Abe had taken to collecting books. Through his years of life, whenever something was important to a generation, he bought it. Whenever he met an author that he liked, he would buy all of the books written by them. He collected dictionaries to watch as language evolved. He kept atlases and encyclopaedias to see how the world changed. He made sure to collect whatever he could so that he could remember those generations later on. Books are the soul of a culture. They hold ideas that foster action. People loved and hated these books. There were controversies and ideologies that pushed society. The written word held power and it could change people, change societies, change the world if wielded properly.

Daisy immediately went towards the books. It was obviously intriguing to her which made Abe's heart jump. Everything he learned about her was always exciting. She ran her hand over the spines of the books, pausing to read a few titles here and there.

"They are beautiful," she said.

"Thank you. I have taken to collecting books over the years," Abe added, trying to keep his composure around Daisy's interest in the books.

"Some of these I've never even heard of."

"Some of these are older than the society you know." Daisy smiled. Although she often seemed confused by his unusual remarks, she never seemed overly deterred by his comments regarding time and age. He knew that people often didn't understand him because he was older than every human alive, but Daisy didn't seem to mind his unusual mannerisms and language.

"Which is your favourite?" In response to Daisy's inquiry, Abe reached over top of her head and grabbed a weathered and ancient looking book. The pages were worn from being turned thousands of times. The cover was faded and the words barely legible, but that didn't matter because Abe knew its story by heart.

As he brought the book down from the shelf, he realised how close Daisy was to him. He had not intended to be this close, but he could feel the heat radiating off her body in the chilled room. She smelled of sugar and vanilla with a hint of something slightly spicy. It was like she had been baking cinnamon buns all day. Her chin was tilted upwards to him so she could look him in the eyes. The gold and silver were a beautiful contrast. A piece of hair had fallen in her face which Daisy didn't seem to notice. With his free hand, he reached up and gently moved the hair behind her ear. Her cheeks blushed and Abe's heart raced. He quickly removed his hand to contain himself.

"What book is it?" Her voice was barely above a whisper. Abe was so focused on her that he nearly forgot he was holding the book at all.

"Oh, um, I don't know to be honest," Abe stumbled over the words. He was struggling to focus on what she was saying. He wanted to do more than just talk and she wasn't moving away. "I've read it so many times that the title has faded from its cover as well as my memory. I don't even think it is written in English. The story is ingrained in my memory, but not the title. It's the one book I always take with me."

"What is it about?" She blinked slowly and her long eyelashes fluttered. She was beautiful in a way he had not seen for a long time. She was all soft curves and simplicity. Even the ordinary rose held beauty and Daisy was extraordinary to him.

"A man learning about the importance of family and that it is not blood that makes a family. We get to choose our family by bond. Just because someone is blood does not make them family. We choose those we care about and that is what becomes our family."

"Why does that interest you?"

"I never had a family. I mean, I never had parents or siblings. I never had a natural family I suppose."

Her face saddened and Abe wanted nothing more than to put a smile back on her face. Yet, he couldn't help but answer her questions truthfully. She deserved more than lies and half truths and he would ensure that she got any answers she required.

"I am sorry to hear that." She took a step closer and placed her hand on his upper arm. She was trying to comfort him, but it only escalated the desire growing within him.

"It is not something I think about much anymore. When I first found the book, I connected, but now… it doesn't hurt as much anymore. I realised the moral of the story was true. Family is made by bond and not blood. As such, I decided to make a family. I found a family in my studies." Daisy smiled softly and Abe felt a spark of something unfamiliar in his soul.

She reached out and grabbed the book. The cover looked so fragile and the pages were slightly torn. Daisy idly flipped through the pages. Her hands were gentle as they grazed the faded words. She handled each with a care and concern Abe had never seen before. It was like she was holding a delicate bubble that would pop with the slightest wrong move. Eventually she closed the book and reached to try and put it away. She was shorter than he realised. He grabbed the book from Daisy's hand and put it away. They were barely inches apart and Abe longed to wrap his arms around her to close the remaining gap. Before he could, Daisy turned away from him.

"Why did you bring me here?" She hopped on top of the desk in a graceful yet unladylike manner and gently swung her legs. She cocked her head to the side curiously.

"I, uh, wanted your perspective on the story. I find your take interesting. Because you are a new Conductor that is."

"I don't really know anything to have much of a perspective. Everything is so new to me. Perhaps if I had a better concept of who the Grand Master is or understood the politics of the Conductors more, I would be able to provide you a more enlightened perspective."

"Well, what questions do you have?"

"Have you met the Grand Master?" Abe laughed at the question but cut himself short when he saw Daisy scowl.

"Sorry. Um, yes. I am an advisor of sorts to her."

"When was the last time you saw her?"

"Well, time works a little differently for Conductors." Daisy raised an eyebrow, inviting Abe to explain more. "When you start studying the forces, you begin to age differently. On the low end, five human years age a Conductor about one year. Brighid started studying with me when she was about twelve. She is roughly fifteen now, but has been studying with me for nearly twenty years. Things slow for us, so we don't interact with each other as regularly as humans do."

Daisy seemed amazed by the concept. Her eyebrows were raised and her lips pursed in awe. Suddenly, her eyebrows dropped as she looked at Abe with a curious expression. He imagined she was trying to figure out how old Abe was. He knew he looked young, maybe in his mid twenties, but he was much older than anyone expected.

"How old are you then?" Abe rubbed the back of his neck and smirked. He didn't like answering these kinds of questions, but Daisy asked.

"I'm unsure to be honest. I've been a Conductor for longer than I can remember anymore. Time blends when you are as old as I am."

"When did you start studying?"

"I was just a kid in all honesty. I hadn't really experienced anything to know anything different. I was young and this has been the entirety of my life. There is a reason I am the advisor to the Grand Master. I've been around for a long time."

Daisy seemed to ponder this statement for a moment. She slightly wiggled her nose and stared down at her shoes. Abe desperately waited for her to say something, but she seemed uncertain. She flicked something off her dress before looking back up at him. Silver and gold eyes framed by long, black eyelashes. Fine lips, the lightest shade of pink. Pale blonde hair that looked like white sand in the sunset. Her smile lit up her entire face even when it was barely more than a grin. He couldn't help but stare for she was absolutely stunning in his opinion.

"Abe?" Her voice was soft and sweet. He could listen to her talk all day. "Why am I here?"

"What do you mean?"

"I feel like there is more than wanting to hear my perspective on Conductor history. You could have asked me that in front of everyone, but you pulled me aside to somewhere private which is not proper form. So, why?"

Abe hesitated. He knew exactly why he pulled her aside. He knew exactly what he wanted, but this was not something that should ever be openly discussed. He wasn't even sure himself yet. He had grown to care about her deeply, but he wasn't sure if it was something more than that. The desire for her was growing and quickly, but whether it was more than a physical yearning was undecided. She had been in his mind for so long, and he knew so much about her, but she barely knew him at all. Even so, she trusted him, and Abe didn't want to ruin the trust he had built with her. He moved to sit beside her on the desk. He made sure to keep a respectable distance. He looked at the bookshelf to try and contain himself from blurting out everything he was thinking and feeling. She needed time and so did he.

"I want you to know that I am here if you need me," he said, feeling as though it was a partial lie. Of course, he would support her, but there was so much more to it. "When starting as a Conductor, it can be overwhelming and the other studies are not always the nicest. I don't want to show favouritism, but I am here to help."

He winked and nudged her playfully. She laughed a little before removing herself from the desk. She began to walk towards the door and Abe's heart fell. He was not ready for her leave. He was not ready to go back to the other studies. He wanted this moment to freeze. He wanted her to stay just a little bit longer. He knew, however, that they should be getting back.

As if knowing what he was thinking, Daisy said, "We should really get back to the others. I rather them not think me a favourite." She winked and opened the door. Abe reluctantly followed her out the door and down the hall.

When they arrived in the main hall, Alina was in front of the studies. Daisy's desk sat empty. The studies hardly noticed Abe and Daisy arriving, but Alina made it very clear she did not approve. Abe had gotten used to her sass and fury, but as of late, it had seemed to expand. Everything Abe did irritated Alina. She raised her eyebrows in her look of disapproval, but scrunched her lips in anger. Abe knew he would hear of this later, but his few moments alone with Daisy had been worth it.

Daisy quietly sat down at her desk. The others had been reading out of a book. Alina snapped her fingers and a book appeared for Daisy on an open page. Daisy took the cue and busied herself with the book. Periodically, one of the studies would try a different spell or motion to conduct a force. Daisy looked shocked and amazed each time. The other studies had become quite accustomed to random magic, but it was all new to Daisy and it showed. Abe loved watching her learn and experience magic. It had been so long since he had a new study that he forgot how amusing it was to watch the wonder on their faces.

After Brighid successfully completed a water transformation spell, a look came across Daisy's face. Abe was unsure of what she was thinking, but imagined it had something to do with the others completing magic. She looked at her hands, slowly flipping them over and over. She would spread them out then ball them into fists. He tried to make it seem like he wasn't watching her, but his curiosity won out. She eventually closed her eyes, which gave Abe the ability to watch her directly, then a look of intense focus came across her face.

Daisy's desk slightly vibrated and stones began to skitter across the floor. Eventually, several rocks appeared on Daisy's desk. She still didn't open her eyes. The rocks began to pile and eventually formed a rough cup. The cup slowly refined itself into a marble chalice. She still did not open her eyes. Water began to collect over top of the cup forming an orb. Slowly, the orb of water deepened in colour and eventually became a deep shade of merlot. She exhaled slowly, the liquid lowered itself into the cup.

Her eyes flew open. For a brief moment, her eyes flared brown and blue before fading back to her silver and gold. Abe was amazed and shocked. He snapped his head to Alina, who also seemed surprised. The other studies had quit doing their practice and openly gawked at Daisy. Daisy, who was inspecting her handiwork, didn't even notice that she was the centre of attention. She was admiring her work in complete bliss. She set the cup back on her desk and looked up with a pleased look on her face.

As she became aware of the heavy stares, Daisy's gleeful expression quickly dissolved into discomfort.

"I'm sorry, but why is everyone staring at me?" she asked innocently. Her attention turned to Alina and Abe. Panic was evident in her eyes, but her face tried to show her bravery. "Were we not supposed to be practising transformation? We were supposed to combine elements to make other things, right? I thought that was why we were reading the book."

The other studies snickered and Daisy's cheeks flared bright pink. Abe wanted to shield her, remove her from the situation, but he knew that would do her no good. Protecting her from the others would only isolate her more in the long run.

"Transformation was the lesson of today," Alina responded, but her voice was unkind with a hint of underlying hostility. Abe knew she was overcompensating for her brief moment of being impressed with Daisy. She disliked Daisy, and Abe knew that.

"Most new Conductors are lucky to move a rock. Your skills out match mine and I've been doing this for several years now," Brighid exclaimed. Her excitement and wonder were very apparent. Abe sometimes forgot how young she was, but it was moments like this where her youth shone through. Although Conductor's aged differently, they still seemed to mature in the same fashion and Brighid was only fifteen. Daisy looked towards Abe and he knew she was waiting for approval or critiques from him. At the end of the day, he was her teacher. He was their teacher and he needed to teach.

"Conductor skill is usually built upon the basics which are learned before a Conductor is tested by the forces," Abe explained. Everyone turned towards him like hungry wolves staring at a piece of meat. "In my years of teaching, I can't say I have directly taught a study that was tested by the forces before learning any magic. Perhaps, not knowing the basics changes how one learns to conduct."

The others considered this. Daisy looked embarrassed. Abe was uncertain about how to proceed. He didn't want to isolate Daisy or make the others feel inferior, but he really wanted to see what she could do. This was unseen power. She was stronger than any other he had seen before.

He watched Daisy as the other studies asked her questions. He couldn't focus on their words but noticed how Daisy shied away from answering. *Was it because she was uncertain? Afraid? Or was it because she wasn't used to being the centre of attention?* Abe knew from her memories that she had lived the entirety of her life in her sister's shadow. Her sister was the proverbial "golden child" whereas Daisy was more like the "black sheep". Abe wanted to ensure she never felt that way again.

He could tell that Daisy was getting overwhelmed. Instead of exploring her power more, he sent everyone to bed. His studies reluctantly obliged. Daisy seemed relieved as she made her way down the hall. When the doors clicked shut and the hall fell quiet, Abe found himself lounging in front of the unlit fireplace. He gazed absentmindedly at the charred stones where flames had licked the surface, eventually falling asleep in the chair.

Chapter 20 - Compromises

Daisy entered the room she had been assigned and sighed. It was, by far, the plainest room she had ever had. There was a small, wood bed in the middle of the room with a table to one side. A small, lit candle stick flickered on the table casting strange shadows about the room. Her trunk sat in one corner; it remained packed as there was not a wardrobe in the room. An empty shelf sat above the bed. A small cameo window with stained glass adorned the one wall. Outside of it, Daisy could see the twinkling lights of Grenich in the valley.

Daisy looked out the window and wondered what Rosie was doing. She had only been gone a day, but she had grown accustomed to Rosie constantly by her side. In her few months at the manor, her and Rosie had become close friends. She trusted Rosie with her life. Not having her here felt wrong in some way.

Daisy moved further into the room. Her shoes clicked loudly against the cold brick floor. The floor and walls blended together in a sea of grey stone. Some wood trusses in the roof broke up the dreary grey. She moved to the bed and sat down to kick off her shoes. The room depressed her.

She opened the book she brought from her lesson and flipped through it. The book was full of different hand gestures and thought patterns to conduct different forces. They had been working on transformation earlier, and Daisy was apparently exceptional at it. She read a few pages and decided to try some different types of conduction.

She closed her eyes and focused on the entity she wanted. A wool blanket dyed blue. She moved her hand in a figure eight and repeated the thought in her head. The room vibrated as it had earlier, but Daisy focused on what she wanted. She could feel energy surging around her, but she kept her eyes closed. When she opened her eyes, a deep blue blanket sat on her lap. It was soft and knitted. She stood up and draped the blanket over the bed. *What else could she do?*

She then thought of pillows and flowers. She thought of books she read at home. She thought of furniture like a wardrobe and a chair. Slowly, piece by piece, all she desired appeared in the room. Each time she used the magic, it was easier and faster. The room eventually stopped vibrating and she could conduct the magic without it being evident.

Finally the room met her expectations. It was cosy and warm with plenty of cushions, blankets, and pillows. There were heavily padded chairs and a wardrobe filled with clothes. She finally sat in a chair and looked around. She was thoroughly impressed with herself. As she surveyed the room, Daisy couldn't help but wonder what force she was conducting exactly. Wood, plants, and rocks made sense, but cloth and wool made little. She made a mental note to ask Abe in the morning what exactly she was using.

Daisy moved towards her newly created wardrobe and began to dress for bed. She looked at her clothes and thought of Brighid and Alina. While both dressed well, they did not dress particularly feminine. Brighid was even wearing pants which Daisy had never seen before. A woman in pants seemed odd. Alina, on the other hand, had worn her corset over her blouse and had a skirt that was short in the front and long in the back. She wore tall boots that disappeared just under the hem of her skirt. Daisy's clothes were all frilly dresses and constricting outfits. Her attire was hardly conducive to conducting. The frills and skirts were sure to catch on fire or get in the way. Her wardrobe needed a rehaul.

She thought of pants and blouses and tall boots. She thought of flowy clothes that gave her body room to move. Her dresses morphed into other clothes that were more suitable to her new powers. Satisfied with her outfits and her room, she laid in bed. Daisy closed her eyes, finally able to rest.

The next morning came early. Although she fell asleep quickly, Daisy found it difficult to stay asleep. The sun was just cresting the horizon as Daisy rolled out of bed and got ready for the day. Instead of her regular dress, Daisy donned a pair of pants, a blouse, and a corset over top of it. She slid on boots taller than she had ever worn, but she liked this alternative. Quietly, she crept out of the room and past the doors of her peers. She expected to be alone in the main hall to practice, but instead found Abe asleep in a chair.

His head was propped up by his arm with his hair cascading down. He looked peaceful, and Daisy really did not want to disturb him, but, as she approached, he suddenly sat up in panic. His eyes were wide and he frantically looked around before his eyes finally Daisy. His posture immediately relaxed and he let out a deep, slow breath.

"Sorry," Daisy said, "I didn't mean to wake you."

He rubbed his eyes like a small child being woken from a nap. He stretched his arms over his head before standing from the chair. His shirt was pulled out from his pants and several top buttons had come undone bearing his chest. Daisy tried not to stare at the exposed skin but could feel her gaze constantly shifting.

"What time is it?" he asked with a sleepy undertone.

"Early. The sun is just starting to rise," Daisy responded.

"Why are you awake?"

"I couldn't sleep anymore, and I wanted to practice without everyone watching me."

"Don't do well with being the centre of attention?"

"I am used to blending. Azalea always drew everyone's attention. My parents adored her, so I was never really a focus."

"Speaking of your family, I thought more about your request. Your control is exceptional, but you can't stop your studies. As such, I have thought of a compromise. Will you come with me?"

"Where are we going?"

"To show you my compromise." Abe extended his hand which Daisy gladly accepted.

They left the train station and headed for Grenich. The air was cold, and Daisy could see her breath. She didn't mind, however. The world was nearly silent as they walked which allowed Daisy to take in the views of Grenich. The sun casted deep shades of red, orange, and pink across the sky and reflected in the snow. The trees were heavy with snow, but the coniferous trees provided pops of deep green. The ocean was a deep blue nearing black in the distance. Everything was so quiet and peaceful. Daisy hadn't realised how chaotic that past few days had been until she was surrounded by calm. Abe seemed to notice that Daisy was enjoying the silence and didn't speak until they crossed completely through Grenich and entered the forest on the other side of town.

"I don't know how much you remember from the ball, but do you recall the stones I took you to?" Abe asked.

"Vaguely. I don't remember much of it though. I know there were five stones and I remember you catching me. Or I thought you did, but you said I hit my head. Did you catch me?" Abe let out a half laugh at Daisy's comment.

"I did catch you. When we are tested, we are usually scarred from it. We get different coloured eyes and a small scar. Mine is just above my lip. Yours is apparently on your head." Daisy touched the wound on her head. It hadn't fully healed yet. The scab was bumpy against her fingers.

"Scars and dichromia. Why do people choose to be Conductors?"

"Does the idea of *magic* not appeal to you?" Daisy could tell he was using the word magic for her understanding.

"It does, but I didn't choose this either."

Abe stopped walking and turned to face Daisy. Clearly, he hadn't thought about Daisy's choice or lack thereof. As she had learned, her experience and skills thus far were unheard of. She seemed different from most of the Conductors, but she still knew very little about it.

"I suppose you didn't get the opportunity to choose, before you were thrown into this all," Abe stated. "I am sorry about that. It wasn't intentional."

Daisy smiled and continued walking. They arrived at the stones and Abe stopped in the centre of them. They were stark, heavy, grey stones in a sea of white.

"So, my compromise," Abe started. "You can spend your days in finishing school with Rosie. I will meet you here every night to teach you the ways of the Conductors. You didn't get a choice about being a Conductor, but at least this way, you can maintain some semblance of your life for a bit longer. You will eventually have to choose though; this won't be sustainable long-term and no matter what you choose, you are marked as Conductor."

Daisy pondered his words for a moment. In all reality, she had no choice. She was a Conductor and eventually, she would have to dedicate herself to it. For now, Abe gave her the opportunity to balance things. She just needed some more time in order to get the closure she needed with her family. As awful as her family was, Daisy loved them dearly and didn't think it fair to just disappear especially after the loss of Azalea. She didn't want to stay, and moving to finishing school showed her that, but she also couldn't just leave permanently. She needed to do things properly and Abe just gave her that opportunity.

"Just give me until the spring when I can return home and say my goodbyes," Daisy explained. Abe beamed at her. He seemed truly ecstatic that Daisy was choosing to be a Conductor.

"Good. I am glad this will work for you." Abe shuffled side to side appearing unsure of what to do next.

"I suppose I should return to finishing school then. Will we start tonight?"

"Yes, I think we shall. Join me here after you are dismissed for the night. That path will take you back to the manor." Abe pointed to a path leading from the clearing.

Daisy started down the path heading back to the manor. She turned around briefly to wave goodbye to Abe who looked like a sad puppy watching her go. Daisy knew she couldn't linger much longer or Abe may try to persuade her to return to the train station. Besides, Rosie was waiting for her and Daisy had left so suddenly with very little explanation. It wasn't until she was headed back to the manor did Daisy realise the predicament she had put Rosie in.

Rosie knew why Daisy was at the manor and knew it was important to Daisy to stay at the manor. Knowing Rosie, she would cover for Daisy for as long as she could, but this meant lying. Rosie would have to keep covering up for Daisy and having reasons for her absence. It wasn't really fair to Rosie, but this compromise solved many of her current predicaments.

Daisy walked out of the forest and into the manor grounds. The gazebo Abe took her to the night of the ball sat in a simple, wonderless state as Daisy passed it. The sun was almost up but few lights were on in the manor. The snow crunched beneath Daisy breaking the silence. Daisy was paying attention to her feet and planning her next step in the snow when sudden smacking of feet on stone cut through the air. Running towards Daisy from the front of the manor was a frazzled looking Rosie.

Rosie kept falling through the snow as she stumbled towards Daisy. Daisy attempted to match her pace but it proved more challenging than expected. As their distance closed, Daisy could hear Rosie's light laughter. The situation was ridiculous and Daisy couldn't contain her glee either. They finally could grab hands and both collapsed in the snow, laughing like children.

"What are you doing here?" Rosie finally managed to ask when their laughter subsided and they pulled themselves to their feet.

"I am apparently a better Conductor than expected. I don't need as much supervision. Abe and I came to a compromise. I will be here during the days then I will learn with him in the evenings," Daisy explained.

"I am glad to see you. I was so worried about you!"

"I am also glad to see you, too. I've missed you."

"What are you wearing?" Rosie eyed Daisy's pant combo with apprehension and awe. Daisy had not expected to be returning to the manor today and certainly did not dress the part of a proper lady. She would have to change before their lessons.

"Conductors dress a bit differently. Skirts catch on fire apparently," Daisy jested not really knowing why Alina and Brighid chose pants over skirts.

Rosie laughed at Daisy's comment before linking arms and walking back to the manor. Rosie's clothes were drenched. Daisy knew they would both need to change now. They entered the manor, arm in arm, and walked directly into a displeased looking Dame Agatha.

Chapter 21 - Training

"What were you two doing outside in the snow and so early in the morning? Daisy is supposed to be in bed resting," the dame accused.

"I was feeling better and wanted to go for a walk in the fresh air, but the snow was deeper than expected," Daisy explained.

"And what are you wearing, Miss Bloomsbury?" Daisy had hoped to avoid this interaction. It would have been ideal to change before meeting the dame, but Daisy was not that lucky.

"It's a new trend apparently. All the fad in the new world. Daisy thought she would try it out," Rosie answered. Daisy smiled appreciatively at Rosie.

"Very well. Go change into something more acceptable of a lady in *our country* and get ready for breakfast. You will both be expected in lessons today." The dame turned on her heel and walked down the hall towards the dinner hall. Daisy and Rosie quickly scurried upstairs to their room.

As they entered their room, a realisation dawned on Daisy. All of her clothes were at the station; she had nothing to wear here. Rosie went to her wardrobe and started changing. Daisy opened her cupboard, hoping she forgot something, but it was bare. Rosie came up behind her in fresh clothes and stared at the empty armoire.

"You have no clothes," Rosie stated which earned her an eye roll from Daisy.

"I can see that." Daisy lowered her voice and looked around before saying, "Do you want to see something?"

Rosie nodded her head. Daisy focused on a dress she saw her sister wear a long time ago. She thought of the colour and the shape and the fabric. She thought of how it felt when she bumped into Azalea. When Daisy opened her eyes, the same dress hung on a wooden hanger in the wardrobe. Rosie inhaled sharply, clearly surprised by what Daisy could do.

"That just came out of nowhere!" Rosie exclaimed. Rosie ran her hand over the dress as if verifying it was real.

"I actually made it using the elemental forces. It is amazing what skilled Conductors can do. I barely even know what I am doing."

"It's impressive."

"Contractions, my dear," Daisy joked and nudged Rosie playfully. Rosie moved away to finish getting ready while Daisy changed.

After changing, Daisy and Rosie headed downstairs where the other girls were eating breakfast. Many of the girls expressed concern over Daisy's health, but happiness at seeing her well and out of bed. Daisy didn't like the attention and luckily Rosie took the brunt of it for her. After breakfast was finished, the girls were dispersed to their various classes.

The day dragged on with boring classes of etiquette, manners, ladyship, and reading various books about nothing of substance. Daisy tried to pay attention, but she was more focused on the evening's events. When the evening's dismissal finally arrived, Daisy was excited to go and see Abe. She had seen Rosie sneak out of the manor many times before and thought she would be able to do the same relatively easily.

That night, when the manor was quiet, Daisy grabbed a cloak out of the wardrobe, held her shoes in her hand, and crept down the hallway. She approached the top of the stairs and stopped dead in her tracks. At the bottom of the stairs, the dame stood talking with one of the instructors. Daisy was positive that if she moved, she would be seen. She stood as still as a statue listening to the dame's conversation.

"How did she do in classes?" she inquired.

"She always does well. The re-introduction of Miss Bloomsbury has focused her more than distract her," the instructor responded.

"I am still unsure about Miss Bloomsbury. She seems problematic at times and I do not want her to *distract* Miss Camden." Daisy had to contain a laugh at the situation she was in. They were complaining about Daisy being a problem while she stood at the top of the stairs trying to sneak out.

"I assure you, Dame, that Miss Bloomsbury is not her distraction. Perhaps you have been giving her too much leeway with leisure activities." Although Daisy could not see the dame's face, she could imagine the great insulted look upon it.

"It would do you well to remember who is your superior. It is my call what I do with my students."

Daisy could hear the dame's footsteps moving away from the stairs and down the hall. Eventually her door clicked shut. Whoever was with her also made a quick departure leaving the foyer empty. Daisy quickly made her way down the stairs and out the front door. She quickly put her boots on and headed down the path. As she entered the forest, everything darkened making it difficult to see. She wished she could cast a fireball with enough precision and finesse to provide light and warmth without setting the forest ablaze. The night was chilly; Daisy had to wrap her cloak tightly around her, but she knew it was worth it.

When she arrived in the clearing, Abe had several small fires burning around the stones. The fires added warmth and light, and Daisy appreciated both. Abe seemed ecstatic at Daisy's arrival. He came up to her as soon as she broke through the forest. His smile was bright which melted Daisy's heart.

"I thought we would learn a bit of fire magic tonight. Seems appropriate with the cold," Abe explained. Daisy nodded her head. She was eager to learn anything. "You seem to have excelled in transformation, but the problem with fire conduction is maintaining control. If you lose control of fire magic, it can quickly spiral and cause a great deal of damage."

Abe led Daisy to the centre of the clearing and moved away from her. He stood to the side to give her plenty of space.

"The objective is to make a ball of fire in your hand. If you do it properly, it shouldn't burn you. Now, follow me exactly." Abe stuck his arm straight out in front of him with his hand in a tight fist. His fingers faced the sky. He rubbed the knuckles of his other hand across his clenched fist which caused sparks. When he opened his fist, a small ball of fire hovered just above his palm.

Daisy followed his instructions. When she opened her hand, however, the ball of flame didn't hover. Instead, it sat on her hand. Daisy let out a scream of pain as the fire singed her skin. She quickly plunged her hand into the snow and listened to the sizzle as the flame was doused. Abe was at her side immediately looking at her hand with great concern. Surprisingly, there was no mark on her hand from the flames.

"You have to keep your focus. You need to tell the fire what you want it to do," Abe critiqued.

"You never told me what I had to think," Daisy snapped. Abe raised his hands in a defensive manner, but his grin suggested he found humour in the situation.

"There isn't really a specific thought -"

"Which is frustrating. I thought magic would use spells and words and wands. Instead, I just think. It's stupid."

"Firstly, this is not magic. It is conduction. Secondly, elemental conduction does use words and spells. But words hold a lot of power. You have to be able to control the basic elements before you can cast spells using words. I know it seems backwards, but when we were first teaching humans to conduct, we tried teaching them our language and ways, but many of them died. They would speak our words and then turn to dust and ash. It was as if the words drained humans of the elements that created them. The words were much too powerful, so we found a balance. We found a way to teach them and eventually those that were strong enough, and survived the exposure to the forces, could actually learn the language."

Daisy tried to focus on his words but questions began to cloud her mind. Abe retold these tales as if they were memories, not stories that had been passed down from generation to generation. Even with the slowed ageing process for Conductors, it would be impossible for him to look so young and be so old. *Was he actually there?* Daisy was confused at this possibility. She needed answers to make sense of this.

"You speak of these events like you were there at the very beginning, but…" she paused, "… that would make you thousands of years old." To Daisy's surprise, Abe looked stunned. *What surprised him?* After a few moments, he appeared to compose himself.

"I told you I am old, older than time, but maybe not that old," Abe explained. He clearly did not want to discuss it further and quickly moved on with the lesson. "Let's try again. This time, focus on hovering the fire ball above your hand."

By the end of the evening, Daisy was able to hover a fireball above her hand. She couldn't hold it for long and repeatedly burned her hand, but Abe was quick to heal her. As she left the clearing headed back for the manor, the sky was starting to lighten on the horizon. She knew she wouldn't get much sleep tonight, but this was what she agreed to. This was the only way she could balance both worlds, for now. She knew she wouldn't be able to do this for long based on how tired she was. Eventually something would have to give, and Daisy wasn't sure which would fall apart first.

Chapter 22 - Warnings

As spring came and the snow started to melt, Daisy was feeling excited. Both her training with Abe and at the manor had been going well. She was excelling with conduction and, as Abe regularly said, gaining remarkable control. There were still times where she made mistakes, but she was learning. She had learnt the basics of the four main elements, but Abe avoided the mind force as much as possible. At least once a week, Abe would take her to the train station for group lessons. Brighid always seemed excited to see her which helped Daisy settle in with the group. Evander seemed threatened, and Arlo appeared indifferent. But what really bothered Daisy was Alina.

Abe wanted Alina to teach some of the mind force lessons since it was her primary. However, Alina hardly attended the lessons, and when she did, she never taught Daisy what Abe asked her to. Furthermore, she was overly critical of Daisy. Because of this, Alina often reminded Daisy of her mother. Alina became cruel and judgemental; Daisy knew she would never be good enough. It never made sense to Daisy, but she tried to remain kind and friendly with Alina. This often infuriated Alina more. It almost seemed like Alina wanted Daisy to fight back, to argue, but Daisy refused. If she had learnt anything at the manor, it was how to remain a lady in all situations and a lady never shouted.

Because of Alina, Daisy often preferred her private lessons with Abe. He was more supportive and always focused on teaching Daisy what she needed to know. He always ensured that she fully understood a skill and could repeat it easily before moving onto the next topic. She would look forward to their lessons every night.

The days at the manor were slow and tedious, and the topics were often boring. However, Daisy quite enjoyed spending time with Rosie. They had become inseparable companions. Usually, students were moved into other rooms as they neared completion, but somehow, Rosie convinced the dame to not move Daisy. Daisy was immensely grateful for her friend's influence and relationship with Dame Agatha as Rosie often covered for Daisy. She helped Daisy sneak out at night, and she ensured that Daisy could get extra rest when she needed. Rosie had become Daisy's saviour in navigating both worlds.

Some nights, Rosie would join Daisy in the clearing for the lessons. She always seemed fascinated by magic, but had no interest in learning how to conduct. Daisy was just glad that Abe allowed Rosie to join them. Other nights, Rosie would sneak out of the manor with Daisy and head to town. Daisy didn't know where she went during those nights and never bothered to ask. As long as Rosie was there when Daisy got back from her lesson, Daisy didn't really care where she went.

In the few months following the ball, Daisy thought she could have everything. She was balancing everything, but sleep which often corresponded to sick days. The doctor came to inspect Daisy on more than one occasion which Daisy was always prepared for since she learned how to increase the temperature of specific targets. The dame was often frustrated, but let Daisy rest nonetheless. So far, everything was going well.

One night after Daisy had snuck out, Rosie laid in her bed trying to fall asleep. Suddenly, there was a knock on the door. Rosie thought it might have just been a dream, but a second knock indicated it was not. Rosie rolled out of bed and approached the door.

"Who is it?" Rosie called as she trudged towards the door.

"Mallory," answered the person on the other side of the door. "I have been sent to collect Miss Bloomsbury and Miss Camden for the dame immediately."

Rosie froze. She stared at the empty bed on the opposite side of the room. Daisy had gone for the evening and Rosie certainly didn't have time to run to the clearing and collect her without raising suspicion. However, Daisy's absence would also raise concerns. This was the first time Rosie had no way to cover for Daisy.

"Miss?" Mallory called again.

"Just a moment," Rosie quickly grabbed a basic gown to throw over her chemise. She knew it wouldn't be acceptable, but showing up in her night gown would be worse. Rosie opened the door to a small girl with brown hair and brown eyes that were the colour of coffee. She was one of the youngest girls in the manor and Rosie had not interacted with her much. Mallory cowered in the open doorway as Rosie looked down on her.

"And Miss Bloomsbury?"

"She is indisposed at the moment. Lead on." The girl squeaked and scurried away as Rosie trailed behind her, hoping, above all else, that Daisy was safe. Rosie walked into the dame's office. A large plush chair hid behind an ornate desk. Two small empire chairs sat in front of the desk. A gold globe on a pedestal stood beside the desk and sparkled in the moonlight streaming through the large bay windows. Several large paintings hung on the back wall. They were nothing of interest, but loud nonetheless.

Dame Agatha sat at her desk patiently waiting for Rosie's arrival. She gestured to one of the chairs and Rosie took a seat. She ensured to sit properly. Her bottom fully in the seat, but her back not touching the chair. Ankles crossed slightly and tucked under her skirt so as not to show her shoes. Her hands placed gently on her lap and her shoulders relaxed with her head held high. The dame took notice of Rosie's proper posture and gave Rosie a slight nod. In her years of being at the manor, she had learned this gesture meant the action was acceptable. The dame turned back to the door as if waiting for another arrival. Rosie understood that she was waiting for Daisy, but she knew not to speak until spoken to.

"How are your studies going, Miss Camden?" the dame asked. Clearly, she was filling time under the expectation that Daisy would arrive.

"Quite well, Dame Agatha," Rosie responded, ensuring to pronounce each word clearly. "However, they are becoming repetitive with my tenure here."

"Ah, yes. Well, most of my ladies do not stay here as long as you have." Her words were very factual and did not indicate anything besides the obvious. It was perplexing to Rosie.

"Dame Agatha, may I ask when you think I will be able to return home?" The dame looked intently at Rosie and tented her fingers in front of her face. Rosie could tell she was thinking, but of what, Rosie was unsure. It should not have been a difficult question to answer, but it always seemed a challenge.

"We can always reassess you, but as you know, your skills are adequate, your decorum is excellent, and your behaviour exemplary. It is not that you have not learned what you need to to be a good wife. It is your belief about marriage that keeps you here. As per your parents' request."

Rosie sighed. She knew she had passed all of the exams and could probably teach some of the classes herself. Her heart is what kept her stuck. She would never lie to herself or pretend to be someone she's not. Rosie averted her eyes. She was struggling to hold back tears.

"Do you think they will ever accept me?" Rosie's voice was barely above a whisper, and she could hear the pain in her own voice.

"My dear Rosie. There is nothing wrong with you, and I will keep trying to help you where I can. Unfortunately, I cannot release you until you are no longer considered a minor or your parents agree to release you."

It wasn't often that the dame was soft. She held a strong front before the other girls, but with Rosie's tenure, they had become quite familiar and comfortable with each other. For the first year, she was harsh with Rosie and tried to break her spirit. However, Dame Agatha's behaviour changed after she discovered why Rosie's parents sent her to the manor. Now, when they were alone, the dame acted more like a mother to her.

"Now," she said, clearing her throat and trying to change topics, "where is Miss Bloomsbury?"

"She is quite ill," Rosie lied, but it didn't seem adequate as the dame did not seem to believe her, so Rosie continued in a desperate attempt to make her story seem more legitimate. "Perhaps today was too much for her after her injury. She was vomiting in the lavatory when Mallory came to collect us. It was unpleasant and I thought it would be best for her to stay put and get some more rest."

Rosie knew she spoke too much. She was trying to sell something that didn't exist, but she knew she couldn't say that Daisy ran away with some strange man to learn how to do magic. Even saying it in her head sounded like complete madness. Had Rosie not been there herself, she never would have believed it either. Dame Agatha stood from her desk and walked around to stand directly in front of Rosie. Her towering presence made Rosie uncomfortable, but she tried not to show her fear. She directed her head up to maintain direct eye contact with the dame.

"This sounds like we should have the doctor in to examine Miss Bloomsbury. *Again*," the dame said as though waiting to be challenged. Rosie knew she needed to come up with something quickly.

"Perhaps we should write to her parents and ask for directions. Perhaps she needs more intensive care than what is being provided for her here." The dame eyed Rosie suspiciously, but Rosie held a flat face. She could not give anything away. She just needed to buy Daisy some more time. Dame Agatha moved back to her desk and sat down. She grabbed a piece of paper and began writing.

"You are excused," she said flatly as she scribbled on the piece of paper. Rosie stood and made her way to the door. "However, Miss Camden, it would do you well to not lie for others. I will write to her parents, but it will not be about her *illnesses*."

Rosie felt all the colour drain from her face and panic clawed at her throat. She'd been caught when she had tried to be so careful. Instead of buying Daisy time, Rosie served Daisy to the dame on a golden platter. Rosie stood frozen with her hand on the door knob, unsure of what to do or say.

"I commend your loyalty, but I suspect it is more than that," the dame spoke with the slightest hint of understanding and sadness. "Miss Camden, please make your next decision carefully."

Rosie twisted the door handle and exited the room. Once out of ear shot from the office, Rosie took off at a run. She sprinted to her bedroom, grabbed her travelling cloak, and headed for the front door.

She needed to find Daisy.

She needed to *warn* Daisy.

***

Abe met Daisy at the head of the path. He wore a white shirt with black suspenders and pants. Some of the top buttons were undone and his one shirt tail stuck out. It was as if he fell asleep in his clothes. Daisy knew it would not be proper to been seen with a man in such a state, but she hardly minded. Abe was always slightly unpolished. He smiled and waved to her as she approached. Usually, when they met at the path, it meant they were going to the station. Tonight was no exception.

They made their way back to the station in near silence. Abe seemed drained and was not very open to talking. Daisy didn't mind the silence. The manor was noisy and there were too many people. Daisy preferred the quiet environment of the station even when fire balls exploded and trees randomly sprouted. They crested the hill and Daisy could just see the station. Abe stopped unexpectedly and turned to Daisy.

"Dais. These last few months have been great and you've been doing amazingly, but we are getting to the point where you need to start focusing," Abe said softly.

"What do you mean by focus?" Daisy asked knowing full well what he meant, but wanting him to say it anyways.

"You have to choose. You didn't get the choice originally, but now you do. Are you wanting to stay at the manor or are you wanting to be a Conductor and stay with me?" The last few words sounded like a plea which made Daisy's heart flutter. *Did he want her to be a Conductor? Or did he want her to stay with him?*

"Not a lot in my life made sense before the manor. Everything felt disconnected, and I always felt out of place. Being at the manor helped guide me." Daisy watched as Abe's face fell. "But it wasn't the manor that allowed me to find my true calling; it was you. I believe I was always meant to be a Conductor and I have no plans on stopping my training with you."

"You will leave the manor then?" Abe asked with trepidation as if he wasn't sure of her answer. Daisy could tell he was trying to hide his emotions, but heard the spark of desire and longing in this voice.

"I will leave the manor."

"Will you stay with me?" Abe's voice was quiet, but full of hope. It was almost like he didn't want Daisy to hear the question but needed her to answer it.

"I will stay and learn from you." Abe smiled, but Daisy sensed a tension that she didn't quite understand. They continued walking without any further conversation and finally arrived at the station.

241

When they entered the main room, it was empty. There was a chair by the fireplace, but otherwise the room was completely bare. Abe let out an exasperated sigh and pinched the bridge of his nose. Usually when they entered, everyone else was waiting for them to start the class. The complete emptiness of the room was abnormal and clearly annoying to Abe.

"Alina must have dismissed them. They are likely all in bed," Abe stated. His frustration was very evident in his voice. "She knew I was going to ask you to stay tonight and this is how she decides to react. For as old as she is, she certainly acts like a child sometimes. I swear Brighid has more maturity and holds fewer grudges than Alina."

"Why does Alina dislike me so much?" Daisy asked.

"I am not sure honestly." Something seemed to unlock in Abe and everything he had held in started to pour out. "She didn't want to take on more studies. We are practically raising Brighid. Arlo and Evander need so much attention. She thought we were already overwhelmed. Then you showed up, and I took you on, and you excelled in everything. You are very talented, even more than we have ever seen before, so maybe she is threatened. She doesn't trust anyone. It took her months to trust Brighid and years to like Arlo. She still finds him lazy. She acts like a mother to everyone and has always been extremely protective of me since the last incident. She also thinks you distract me. I began focusing on you so much that she thought I was ignoring the rest of my studies. I suppose she has lots of reasons to be angry, but I think she is just upset with me and takes it out on you."

"Do I?"

"Do you what?"

"Do I distract you?" Abe paused as if assessing the situation to determine the best option. His face became a mask that hid whatever he was feeling or thinking. Daisy patiently waited for him to respond.

"Perhaps, tonight you should sleep here and we can share the news with the others in the morning. Your room is still set up."

"I am fine with that, but you didn't answer my question." Abe began walking away towards his office which was down the opposite wing to Daisy's room. As he reached the start of the hallway, he stopped and looked over his shoulder at Daisy.

"Very much so," Abe stated before disappearing down the hall.

Daisy stood, stunned, digesting what he just said and trying to understand it. Eventually, her feet carried her to her own room. She was grateful for the night of rest but found it hard to sleep. Her mind wandered trying to make sense of everything. She had just agreed to become a Conductor permanently which meant leaving the manor and, more importantly, leaving her family. Even more devastating was the idea of leaving Rosie behind. What stuck with her more than her decision was Abe saying she was distracting. Usually, that would be a bad thing and

Daisy could feel the guilt building in her. *Was she pulling Abe away from his duties? Was she preventing Abe from doing what he needed to do? Did she make the right decision?*

She closed her eyes and tried to sleep with her racing thoughts. Several hours passed and Daisy still hadn't fallen asleep. But then, the room shook. She opened her eyes unsure of what she felt. There was a loud bang. Daisy sat straight up. Another bang and Daisy was out of her bed headed for the door. She flung open her door to Alina standing in the door across from her. Alina looked terrified. *What was going on?*

Chapter 23 - Battle of the Main Room

The building shook. Daisy, Alina, and the other studies stumbled down the hall. Explosions rumbled the house, throwing them against the walls. Moving down the hallway was far more difficult than expected. Alina tried to use magic to stabilise things, but it seemed useless.

"What is going on?" Brighid shouted over the booms ahead. Lights flashed back and forth. Fire, air, water, and earth splattered the scene ahead.

"No idea," Alina yelled back. "But, we need to get there."

As they neared the opening to the main room, a sheet of ice stood in front of them. Behind the ice, they could see rapid movement and the elements flying in every direction. Arlo punched the ice. It was solid. He placed his hands on the ice. Daisy could see the heat radiating off of them as the ice began to drip and melt. Evander joined, quickly followed by Alina and Brighid.

"Why are we melting it? Can't we just use water magic to move it?" Daisy asked as she tried to find room to place her hands on the ice wall.

"You have to use the opposite force to negate a force," Alina explained through gritted teeth. "You can't use the same force on a force unless you casted the original spell."

Daisy looked at the ice wall in front of them. It was taking too long and the battle was getting more intense behind the wall. Daisy didn't understand why they couldn't just move the wall. It was water and they could use the water force. Just move the wall. Just move the wall. *Just move the stupid wall.*

Daisy closed her eyes, extended her hands and focused on the wall. She needed it to move. She thought of liquid water flowing away from the spot. Daisy heard a surprise squeak and opened her eyes. The wall was melting quickly and sliding to the side. The others stumbled back from the wall, but Daisy plunged forward.

The room behind the wall was in complete chaos. Rocks were being hurled about the room. A section of the roof was torn down, exposing the night sky. Some sections were wet while others smouldered. Roots and trees sprouted randomly amongst the rubble. Daisy casted a quick thought towards the embers, extinguishing them immediately. A loud pop caught Daisy's attention, and she ran towards the noise head-on.

Abe was backed into a corner on the floor. He held up a hand casting some type of shield. Above him stood a figure in a heavy black cloak with fire streaming from their hands. Abe looked exhausted. His shield was faltering as the stranger pushed further towards him. Abe's eyes darted in Daisy's direction when he noticed her standing behind the assailant. Abe tried to protest, but Daisy couldn't hear him over the roar of the flames. Daisy's presence seemed to send Abe into a panic. His shield split and flames licked his skin. Daisy could hear his scream of pain over the flames.

Something swelled inside of Daisy. This needed to stop. Everything needed to stop. In a blink of an eye, everything froze. The flames stopped moving, frozen in the air. Abe skittered back from the flames and pressed himself against the wall. The figure tried to cast a spell but nothing seemed to work. The stranger flipped around and caught Daisy in their eye line. Daisy couldn't catch a glimpse of what they looked like in the slightest as a large hood obscured their face. It didn't seem to matter however. As soon as the figure became aware of Daisy, something snapped. Fire hit the wall behind the hooded figure, meaning whatever force was holding them no longer existed. The attacker took the moment to flee and disappeared through the hole in the ceiling.

Daisy ran over and knelt beside Abe. His shirt was singed and the skin underneath bubbled from the burn. His face was contorted in pain as Daisy tried to peel away the shirt to assess the damage. Alina and the others appeared shortly thereafter; their arrival was marked with startled gasps.

"What the hell happened?" Alina exclaimed. Abe looked at Alina sadly, and Daisy's heart constricted. There was obviously a lot more going on than Daisy understood.

"It was - her." He winced with each breath. Every word and minor movement looked like it pained him. "She was - here and I don't - I don't know how she found - us."

Alina's expression changed from concern to pure fear. She started to pace back and forth. Abe's eyes lazily tracked her. Daisy looked at the others, and they all seemed to mirror Daisy's confusion. Clearly, they did not understand what Abe and Alina were talking about either. Daisy found some comfort in this.

"How can that be? We did everything right!" Alina seemed to be thinking aloud, forgetting that everyone else was there. "We went to a small remote community. We put in extra security measures. We did everything right. We have been here for years and there wasn't any inclination that she knew. How did she find us? Unless…"

Suddenly, Daisy was picked up off her feet and slammed against the wall. Alina was inches away from her face, pinning Daisy to the wall. Alina's face blazed with fury, and Daisy was confused as ever.

"Who do you work for?" Alina spat in Daisy's face. Alina pressed her arm across Daisy's throat, making it hard for her to breathe. "Why are you here? How did you find us?"

Daisy was starting to see black at the edge of her vision. She couldn't speak, but she tried to shake her head. She didn't have the slightest idea what Alina was referring to, but Daisy was unable to explain herself as Alina's arm was heavily fixed against Daisy's throat.

"Alina - no," Abe croaked. He tried to move towards Daisy and Alina, but he fell over and groaned in pain. Abe's suffering snapped Alina out of her rage, and she released Daisy who collapsed on the ground, clutching her throat and taking deep, gasping breaths. Alina went to Abe's aide and assisted him back into a seated position. As Alina touched Abe's arm, there was a flash of purple and Alina's face softened ever so slightly. Daisy looked at them as some hidden message passed between them that Daisy and the others were not privy to.

"I don't understand," Daisy whispered. "What happened?"

"Alina - believes that you - brought - her here," Abe muttered. His eyes were closed now and blood tainted his shirt. He was injured worse than she realised.

"We need to heal him," Daisy stated. Alina gave a slight nod and moved to get Abe to a standing position. Alina still seemed partially stunned from whatever passed between her and Abe. Alina grabbed one arm and Daisy grabbed his other. Together, they started moving Abe back to his office.

"Clean up the main hall while we tend to Abe," Alina yelled over her shoulder to the remaining students.

They dragged Abe back to his office. Alina cleared the desk of clutter and then assisted Daisy to carefully lay Abe on top of the desk. Alina tore Abe's shirt in half to expose the wounds. Daisy quickly took to applying pressure to his readily bleeding lacerations.

"You shouldn't have ripped the shirt off. It could have been helping the clots," Daisy exclaimed.

"I can't heal the wounds if I can't see them," Alina snapped back.

"Please - don't -" Abe tried to speak, but he lost consciousness before finishing his statement.

"Alina, what are we doing?" Daisy tried to sound calm but knew her voice shook with fear.

"Keep pressure on the cuts. I have to cool these burns with the opposite force. Elemental injuries can't be healed like normal ones. You have to try and reverse their damage with the opposite force. Water with Fire. Earth with Air." She placed her hands on top of the blackened flesh on Abe's torso. Water slowly started to collect around the gash.

"What about mind?"

"We haven't found anything that reverses the mind. There aren't usually wounds from the mind force, but we have found that, with time, the effects wear off."

"I apologise, but this opposite force thing seems like nonsense to me. I melted the ice wall with water magic." Alina paused and glared at Daisy for a moment before directing her attention back to Abe. Oddly enough, the skin seemed to be returning to a normal shade and smoothing out.

"What you are doing makes no sense at all. I don't know how you are doing anything you are doing. For being new, you seem to have incredible strength. As such, I do not trust you, but Abe does. That is the only reason you are here, and it is the only reason you will remain here…for now." Ignoring Alina's clear contempt, Daisy looked at another burn on his shoulder. Keeping one hand on the cut she was already addressing, Daisy moved her hand to the burn and followed Alina's lead. Alina seemed conflicted with Daisy's actions, but said nothing.

"I don't know who was here. I am not working for anyone. Abe met me on the train to finishing school. I

250

knew nothing of the Conductors before my arrival, but I learn by watching and doing. I just seem to pick things up quickly. I don't know what happened, but I know I care about Abe just as I believe you do." Alina's expression softened for a moment as she looked at Abe's unconscious face. The wound she was working on had nearly closed over and returned to normal. Some colour appeared to be coming back to Abe's face.

"I do care about him. We have been at this a long time. I was his assistant before he had any studies. He's been my partner for a long time and I can't imagine being without him."

"But you're not *together*, are you?" Alina flinched at the question, but Daisy pretended not to notice. Instead, she moved to address the next cut. Slowly, he was being patched back together.

"We were, a long time ago, but things don't always work out. I care about him deeply and continue to protect him, but it's not the same as loving him or being with him. There was a time when things made sense and Abe needed support. His last heartbreak was traumatic and he's never really been the same since. I helped him recover, and we grew close. I grew to love him, but I don't know if he knows what love is anymore." Her voice was sad, but factual. It was like she was talking about a death of a loved one that happened years prior; a death which she was still grieving. "He's a good man, but he's been through a lot. He's lived such a long time that things are very different for him. There will always be a part of me that wants to be with him I think, but the world of Conductors is small and we don't meet many people. Maybe he was right for me then, but now, as much as I wish it could, I don't think it will ever happen again."

Daisy wasn't sure what to say. Instead, she busied herself with fixing Abe's wounds. Eventually, the worst of them were healed, and Abe was breathing normally. He hadn't woken yet, but Daisy felt calmer. She felt like Abe would make it through. Some of the cuts were more difficult than others to heal as their elemental origin was not clear, so they had to use an approach based more on trial-and-error. Once the majority of the damage was healed, Daisy and Alina carried him to his bed to let him rest. Alina left the room to check on the others leaving Daisy alone with Abe.

Daisy gently wiped away some dry blood from Abe's face. He looked older somehow, like the years he lived weren't hidden when he was relaxed. This close, Daisy noticed he had a small scar beside his temple and another just above his lip; they had faded with time. Daisy looked down at his bare torso. She could see the scars this attack would leave. His torso looked like a treasure map of lines and x's. Even though his wounds were healed using magic, he would still be riddled with scars. She gently ran her hand over a scar that ran nearly his whole side. It had been the large wound that Alina had healed and somehow had knitted back together almost seamlessly.

"That tickles, you know," Abe croaked. Daisy startled and nearly punched Abe in the face. She wasn't aware that Abe had woken up. His eyes were barely open and he looked at her through long lashes. A small smirk grew from the corner of his mouth.

"I didn't know you were awake," Daisy stated, unsure of what else to say.

"Perhaps I didn't want you to know I was awake."

"Why?"

"People often expose their inner self when they don't think they are being watched."

"And what did you learn?"

"That is for me to know." He struggled to sit up and winced. Daisy tried to aid him, but he pushed her away. "Please, let me do it myself."

He propped himself up against the wall and opened his eyes more. He looked exhausted, but better than he did before. He clutched his side; Daisy imagined it was excruciating. His breath was shallow, but regular and Daisy felt relieved. He had at least survived.

"Abe," Daisy began, not entirely sure where she was going, "what happened? Who was that?"

"That would be an old rival." His words were less strained, but still seemed difficult for him. "A study, of sorts, that turned against me long ago when she didn't agree with my tactics anymore. We used to work side by side, but she diverted. She turned to other forces and wanted more power and control. She thought, thinks, herself superior to all others, but me. She hunts me in hopes

253

to convert me to her cause. Tonight, however, she was angrier than when we usually meet."

"That was a woman?"

"Quite right. However, I am not sure why she stopped when you entered the room. Previously, she just-" Abe stopped and his face whitened. Daisy thought he was in pain at first, but it wasn't physical pain. It was more like whatever he was thinking about was excruciating to remember.

"What is it?"

"The last time I came across her, she killed my studies. All of them. Dead. Gone in a mere instant." There was a deep horror and pain in his voice that Daisy could barely understand. She had lost her sister, but nothing quite like this to comprehend what Abe had gone through. "Alina and I barely made it out alive. Alina was just a study then. I had just taken her on so she got ignored as being a threat. We grew close after that and she helped me through that pain and loss. I took a long break before teaching again. I had to go into hiding for a while with her on my heels. I even moved countries to avoid her, and yet she found me."

"Who is it, Abe?" Daisy inquired. He averted his eyes and started playing with a bandage on his side. It was clearly not a subject he liked nor wanted to discuss. Daisy wasn't going to push the topic, but she gave him time to process and think. She was sure Abe would speak when he was ready.

"Like me, she has gone by many things. I am not sure her current name or even what she looks like exactly. Time can change a lot even when you age slowly."

Daisy had a multitude of questions to ask, but Alina came bursting into the room. She also seemed relieved to see Abe awake and alive. As Alina crossed the room to where they sat, Daisy couldn't help but wonder how much history there was between Alina and Abe. They had obviously known each other a long time and had experienced many things together. Abe laid back down on the bed and Daisy moved away. Alina looked over Abe , focusing on the few wounds that her and Daisy couldn't fix. She asked Abe questions about what caused the injury, tore off the bandages, and repaired the skin with the proper force. Daisy watched intently, mostly because she was curious about the magic, but partially because she was curious about Abe and Alina.

Alina's hands moved so gently and quickly over Abe's exposed torso. She examined each area with a familiarity that was clearly evident to Daisy. Daisy watched as skin slowly knitted itself back together and nearly all the injuries were healed. One persistent cut over his eyebrow did not seem to want to be fixed, so Alina bandaged it carefully.

"There are things we need to discuss," Alina stated. Daisy noticed Alina cast a quick sideways glance which made Daisy feel uncomfortable and unwelcomed. "Perhaps alone would be more appropriate."

Abe looked at Daisy. A sadness had settled in his eyes. It was like he didn't want Daisy to leave, but he knew she needed to. In order to save Abe the displeasure of telling Daisy to leave, Daisy excused herself and exited the room.

The door clicked shut behind her and she found herself leaning against it. The adrenaline that had kept her going was starting to fade and exhaustion was setting in. She closed her eyes and thought of heading to bed, but that didn't seem like the best option. Instead, she tried listening through the door, but no sound could be heard. Frustrated, she returned to the main hall. Evander, Arlo, and Brighid had already left for their bedrooms. Nearly everything was repaired, but the room lacked furniture. Perhaps they were unsure of what to add. Whether or not she wanted to, the only option for Daisy was to head to her room.

As she walked down the hallway towards her room, there was no indication anyone remained awake. No sound or light came from any of the doors. Daisy found herself disappointed; she had hoped to talk to someone else as she was not ready to be alone and needed to decompress. As she came to the end of the hallway, she opened her door and entered the darkened room. She quietly closed the door behind her, but as the door clicked closed, an odd feeling crept over her. She suddenly became aware that she was not alone in her room. Sitting on the bed, casually flipping through a book, was the hooded figure.

Chapter 24 - The Elements

"Ambrose," Alina started, but Abe held his hand up to stop her. He really didn't want to talk to her, but knew she wouldn't hold her tongue.

"Daisy is not responsible for this," Abe said without any sign of doubt. "She is not working for her. She barely knows anything about the Conductors."

"But -"

"I don't know why she is so talented with conducting the elements, but she was also tested by the elements before most other studies. A lot of things don't add up about her, but I can promise you, Daisy isn't working for her."

"How do y-"

"How do I know? I looked into her mind on many occasions. I practically controlled her for several hours during the ball. Not only was she not aware, but she had no memories that would suggest a connection. Furthermore, I've been working with her for months now and have gotten to know her fairly well. An opportunity you also had, but quite frankly neglected."

Alina looked irritated but satisfied. Abe could tell she had more questions, but those that were most pressing for Alina, Abe had answered. Abe leaned against the wall beside his bed. His head throbbed and his side felt like a knife was stuck in it. Although he had rested, he still felt completely drained, and Alina's questions were not helping him.

"If you were so concerned, why haven't you looked into her mind? You are more competent than me because it's one of your primaries. You don't even have to touch her to read her mind." Abe huffed. He already knew the answer, but he needed Alina to understand his frustration with her.

"You know exactly why," Alina responded quietly. Abe could feel the guilt coming from Alina. "Ever since… the accident… I don't use it anymore. I can't use it anymore. I don't want to hurt another person."

Alina stood up from the bed and began pacing back and forth. Obviously, more was weighing on Alina and she had to decide where to start. Abe tracked her with his eyes. Moving his head hurt. As she paced, Abe realised how much older she was starting to look. Not in the old matronly way, but more in the way of being mature. She carried herself with more confidence and wisdom. She held her head high regardless of what adversity faced her. She was stronger, emotionally and mentally, than Abe ever remembered her being. Being his assistant and working more actively with the studies had brought out something more in her. It was a good look on her.

She finally stopped pacing and faced Abe directly. Her hair was slightly messy, but she still looked as beautiful as ever. He knew why he cared about her so dearly once, but that feeling was clouded and muddled now. In this moment, he could see those emotions again in front of him, but trying to grasp those feelings was like trying to hold steam in your hands, nearly impossible and extremely painful. Abe tried to move on and away from the pain. Alina was family now and that was all Abe could see her as. She was important to him and he cared deeply about her. That was what mattered now.

"Why was she here, Ambrose?" Alina inquired. There was a hint of fear and distrust in her voice.

"Your guess is as good as mine. Usually, she is trying to take over my mind, so I can be her puppet of power and destruction. You know that," Abe retorted.

"But she was so angry tonight. Angier than I remember her being the last time we faced her."

"Agreed, but we didn't exactly talk. I didn't have time to ask about her motives before there was fire flying at me from every direction."

Alina sat back down on the bed beside Abe, looking defeated and tired. She fiddled with the hem of her shirt. Regardless of how Abe was feeling, she clearly was not done talking. There were several times where she seemed ready to talk, shook her head, and re-entered her thoughts. Eventually she spoke, but she completely avoided looking at Abe.

"Daisy did some absurd things tonight," Alina whispered. She looked concerned and unnerved.

"Which event are you referring to?" Abe half laughed, but that hurt his abdomen even more. He winced which earned him a stern glare from Alina. She helped him into a lying position.

"She moved the ice wall. She didn't melt it. She just moved it. Everyone else was melting it like we are taught, but she just moved it and it turned to water almost instantly. It was… amazing." Abe could tell that the last words pained Alina to admit. Alina had made her distaste for Daisy very apparent and admitting Daisy was good at something was certainly unpleasant.

"She stopped fire conduction in the middle of the air and stopped any further attacks. It is as if Daisy was able to disarm her. I don't understand it," Abe said while shaking his head in disbelief.

"She stopped someone else's conduction? How is that even possible?"

"I am not sure, honestly. I haven't the slightest idea. Things don't add up." The room became silent as they both contemplated Daisy's actions. Abe was mostly fascinated, but he could hear the concern in Alina's voice.

"Abe," there was a new pain in Alina's voice and Abe knew what was going to come next, "do you love Daisy?"

"If you are asking because you still believe that old prophecy, you need to stop asking. There is no evidence of it. I am fond of her, and I care deeply for her. She is fascinating to me, but I don't know if that is love exactly."

"But what if the story is true? What if your love creates a new force again? What if all this stuff she is doing is a new force? What if Daisy creating a new force is what brought that hag here? What if it attracts her somehow?"

"Alina." His voice came out harsher than he meant, but she hushed for a moment. She looked doe-eyed and scared. The thought of a new force was as terrifying as it was exciting. "It is all speculation based on an event that happened hundreds of years ago. It's nothing more than a story at this point. Something to learn from regarding the power and misuse of the forces."

"Then why tell them that part at all?"

"Because if I don't hold to the common narrative, it becomes more obvious who I am. I tell the story as most do, not as it actually happened. Maintaining my anonymity not only keeps me safe from her, but it keeps my studies safe and allows me to teach as I please."

"Are you ever going to tell them?" Alina asked just barely above a whisper.

"Tell them or tell her?" Alina bit her lip and looked away from Abe. Through the years, Abe had learned to read Alina like a book, and he knew she was uncomfortable.

"You know what I mean."

"And you know my answer. Think about how long it took me to tell you and how hard that was to do. When we survived her last attack, I had no other option but to tell you. If you weren't there, I don't know if I ever would have told you. I teach Conductors then they move on. I love them like family, but I live longer than most. They all eventually leave and that is just how things go, but I don't really tell anyone. You were the first exception in a long time and you know that."

"But you have to tell them, tell her. They need to know now. You are being actively pursued. We can't lose a whole group again. I can't go through that pain again and neither can you."

"But how? How do I tell people that I am older than the universe? How do I tell people that I was there when it began? How do I tell people that I am the embodiment of the elemental forces?"

Chapter 25 - Maria

The manor had grown quiet. Rosie waited until she was sure everyone, even the manor's servants, were asleep. She held her shoes in her hand and crept down the hallway, listening for anything that might indicate someone was awake. She hadn't really thought of a plan, nor was she even aware of where Daisy might be, but Rosie knew what she needed to do.

Rosie carefully descended the grand staircase. The old, wooden stairs creaked with each delicate step. To Rosie's relief, their noise did not seem to attract the attention of the slumbering residents. She reached the door and slowly opened it. As carefully as possible, Rosie closed the door and turned towards the yard. The moon was bright and casted long shadows across the snow spotted lawn. Warmer temperatures had melted some snow causing the ground to become soft and mushy. It was an odd comfort to be outside in the evening light again. This wasn't the first time she had snuck out at night, but this was the first time that it truly mattered.

Rosie ran out into the night barefooted. She headed to the path leading to the clearing. With the amount of mud at the head of the path, Rosie could tell no one had been down that way. There wasn't a single footprint in the mud or remaining snow. When she reached the front gate, Rosie slid her shoes on as she was sure no one from the manor would hear her now. She slipped out of the gate and headed towards town. Besides the clearing, Rosie was unsure of where else they would go, but she knew someone that might. She knew where the evening wateringhole of choice was and headed there directly. Abe had been around the town for a while. Rosie was certain that someone at the bar would know where Abe lived or maybe some clue she could follow.

As she rounded the corner towards the bar, Rosie could hear the loud ruckus of music, off-key singing, and laughter. Warm yellow light spewed onto the street which was a welcomed sight to Rosie. She entered the bar and glanced around. Several drunk men hugged each other and sang different songs at the same time. A lady and gentleman sat in the corner whispering to each other while the other corner was occupied by two men kissing quite passionately. None of the occupants she recognized. However, at the main counter, Rosie saw who she was looking for.

The barmaid that usually worked the evening shifts was making idle chit chat with a lone woman in a heavy cloak sitting at the counter. Rosie knew the barmaid as Maria while most regulars knew her as Madam Hooch. Maria's face completely beamed with happiness and excitement as Rosie approached the counter. A drink was immediately placed in front of Rosie. Maria gently squeezed Rosie's hand before moving away. Rosie knew she'd be back in a moment, but she had to make sure her other customers were comfortable first.

Just as Rosie finished her drink, Maria returned to Rosie. She nudged her head to the door that led to the cellar and Rosie smiled. Quickly and quietly, Rosie stood from her stool and made her way to the cellar shortly followed by Maria. As the door clicked shut, Rosie barely had a moment to process before Maria was on her. Maria kissed Rosie with a sweet desperation. She tasted of whiskey, but Rosie didn't mind. It had become normal to her. Rosie ran her hand over Maria's dress, feeling every curve of her body beneath the heavy layers and corset. It had become familiar to Rosie and she wanted to keep going, but the voice in her head kept nagging at her to stop.

"Maria," Rosie gasped between kisses, "Maria. Stop."

"Your body is saying otherwise," Maria tempted.

"I know. Trust me, I want to, but that's not why I am here tonight." Maria removed herself. She looked like Rosie had just slapped her across the face which Rosie felt. She understood the pain all too well.

"Why are you here then?"

"I am looking for a man -"

"Are you now? That'd be news to me, Hun. When you came bumbling in here three years ago, you weren't looking for a man's company then. "

"No, not like that." Rosie could feel Maria's pain, but Rosie was growing frustrated. "My friend ran away with a man, and she is in trouble. I need to find her."

"What friend? That girl you were at the ball with? You've never brought her for me to meet you know."

"I know I haven't. She's been occupied. And her name is Daisy by the way."

"Do you love her?" This time, Rosie felt she had been slapped. She was taken aback by the forwardness of the question, but that was just how Maria was. "She just seems awfully important to be just a friend."

"What? No. She has become a very good friend to me and I don't think she is interested in me that way. I care for her like family but not in the same way I feel about you. Besides, she's with a man that she is very interested in. Why does it matter?"

"Just checking if I still hold that cold heart of yours." Maria winked and Rosie felt a strong urge to push her against the wall and disappear into her kiss. Somehow, she restrained herself.

"My friend, Maria, please focus."

"Alright, so you mean business. What do you want to know?"

"The young gentleman with the messy black hair and blue-green eyes. He's been around longer than me, but he keeps mostly to himself. Apparently he is named Ambrose, but he goes by Ames or Abe, depending who you ask."

"I know the fellow. What did you want to know?"

"Do you know where he lives?"

"Sorry, Hun. He's never been drunk enough to need an escort home. I've been told he works at the train station though. Lots of people have seen him milling about up there apparently."

"That's something at least. Thank you, Maria."
Rosie quickly kissed Maria before running out of the cellar
and on to the street. For Rosie, leaving Maria was like
trying to convince herself to leave her warm, cosy bed on a
cold winter morning, but she somehow managed. Daisy
was important, and Rosie needed to make sure she was
safe. The train station wasn't much to go on, but maybe
someone there would know where Abe lived or could give
Rosie another lead.

Rosie hadn't been to the train station all that often,
but she knew how to get there. Guilt crawled in Rosie's
stomach at the thought of lying to Maria about Daisy.
Perhaps it wasn't lying. Rosie wasn't even sure if she loved
Daisy. Daisy was new and exciting. Maria was comfortable
and known. There was something enticing about Daisy, but
Rosie didn't see that as love. Maria was someone Rosie
could wake up to every morning. She had been sharing a
room with Daisy for months, but it wasn't as appealing as
the thought of waking up next to Maria every morning.
Rosie didn't fully understand her feelings about Daisy, but
she did know she loved Maria. However, one thing she did
know was that Daisy did not feel the same way.

She had seen the way Daisy looked at Abe. It was
the same way she looked at Daisy when Daisy was
unaware. It was a look of adoration, fascination, and maybe
even lust. Daisy did not look at Rosie like this. Daisy
looked at Rosie like she was just a friend and Rosie knew
it. Rosie knew that she did not hold Daisy's heart and that
was fine. Rosie had Maria, and Daisy could still be her
friend.

Being lost in her thoughts, Rosie had barely even noticed how far she had walked. As she neared the crest of the hill, she heard a loud bang. Looking up, she saw an explosion come through the roof of the train station. Without thinking, Rosie began to run towards the station. If Daisy was there, she needed help and Rosie would be there to do anything she could.

As she rounded the corner to the station, Rosie could see no clue as to what happened; the station appeared completely intact. She entered the station and went to the ticket desk only to find the clerk fast asleep despite the sound of the explosions. She rang the golden bell on the counter and the clerk sprung to life. His hat flew off his head and landed on the ground. He was a strange looking man. His freckled face was framed by tightly wound, fiery red ringlets. What made him look even more unique were his strikingly bright green eyes. Rosie hoped beyond hope that he would be able to tell her something.

"What was that explosion?" Rosie asked, cutting out the time wasting niceties.

"What explosion you talkin' a'but?" He had a heavy drawl that Rosie found amusing and had to contain a snicker. "I di'n't hear a nothin'."

"Well then, perhaps you shouldn't sleep on the job."

"Miss, you a ev'r work?"

"Not exactly sir."

"Ten shut er mouth." Rosie suddenly found his accent less humourous. He was not a nice gentleman, it appeared. Rosie barely refrained from rolling her eyes. This man was her ticket to information. Being nice would likely get her further.

"My apologies, Sir. The explosion just rattled me. I was on my way home when I heard a loud bang and thought I should investigate. I thought you might have heard something."

"I ain't heard nothin'." He leaned back in his chair and pouted.

"Perhaps you can help me with something else then?"

"Maybe. What sa init fer me?"

"I have some coin should you be able to help me."

"A'ight. I'm listenin'. Whatcha need?"

"I am looking for a man with black hair and blue-green eyes. He goes by Ambrose, Abe, or Ames. I was told by the barmaid that he spends a lot of time here. Maybe he works here?" He eyed her suspiciously as if determining if she was worth the information. He picked something from his teeth, examined it, flicked away and then glared at Rosie.

"I may, uh, know, uh somethin'."

"Anything you can provide would be appreciated."

"He spends a bit o' time here. Mostly comin' and goin', but sometimes, he examines the wall o'er tare quit a bit. Like he's lookin' for a door, but there ain't no door der.

269

He right in t' head?" Rosie imagined that there was a door in that wall, perhaps one the clerk couldn't see. In what she knew about him, Rosie wouldn't put it past Abe to somehow hide a door. Rosie grabbed some coins from her purse and slid them across the counter.

"Thank you for your help." He bit the coin before nodding his head. He leaned further back in his chair and stuck his hat over his eyes. Before Rosie even left the waiting area, he was already snoring.

She moved towards the wall and started inspecting it, looking for any sign that there was a door or something there. She ran her hand over the wall, knocked on different bricks but nothing worked. Quietly, trying not to disturb the clerk, Rosie began calling out Daisy's name. Maybe Daisy could hear through the wall. Rosie put her ear to the wall, listening for some type of response. Instead, she could hear shouts and bangs. There was something going on behind the wall and Rosie couldn't get there. She started pounding on the wall. Maybe they would hear her now, but there was no response.

The lack of response was disheartening. Instead of continuing to smack a brick wall repeatedly, Rosie decided to sit on a bench nearby and watch the wall. Eventually, someone would have to come out. They couldn't spend the entire day behind the wall. Slowly seconds became minutes and minutes became hours. There was no movement in the station, and it had fallen quiet with the exception of the snoring clerk. Rosie, however, was determined. She would not leave until she saw Daisy. She would wait all night and day if necessary.

Chapter 26 - Confrontation

Daisy stood frozen in place against the door. Her heart was racing. Daisy had just watched this person nearly kill Abe and now she sat on the bed, looking completely innocent, flipping through a novel. Daisy knew she hadn't entered the room quietly, but the figure barely even looked up at Daisy. Petrified, she was unsure of what to do. *Should she call for help? Run away? Fight her? What was the best option?*

Before Daisy could decide on anything, the figure snapped the book shut and directed her gaze at Daisy. The hood was still pulled up tight around her face so that Daisy hadn't the slightest idea of what she looked like because her heavy cape hid anything identifiable. Suddenly, and without a word, she stood from the bed and faced the window. Daisy still didn't move.

"Don't try to scream," she said, but not aloud. The voice sounded like it came from inside Daisy's head. The thought of this woman being inside Daisy's head was so intrusive and violating; it made her skin crawl. The voice was wispy and airy like a subtle breeze rushing by your ears, but more unnerving and uncomfortable. Daisy knew of the fifth element, mind, but she had not much experience with it yet. "I've made the air in the room heavier so that sound can't travel outside of it. Screaming would be futile."

Daisy stood and stared at the figure. She thought about the air around her and noticed it did feel heavier. Clearly she couldn't scream. She tried the door, but it wouldn't budge. The intruder impeded any chance Daisy had of getting help or escaping. Daisy could feel panic growing, but also anger. This made little sense to her. *What could this person possibly want with her?*

"You know I can read your mind, right?" she said rather sassily. There was slight pain building in Daisy's temple from the intrusion. "I know you are curious about why I am here and what I want with you so, please sit, and let me tell you."

Cautiously, Daisy moved towards a chair and sat down facing the trespasser's back. When Daisy finally sat, the figure turned around to face her. Her movements were familiar to Daisy; the way she swished her cloak as she readjusted, the subtle roll in her shoulders as she moved to face Daisy. But something was missing. Something was off. *Was one of the other studies toying with her?*

"I am not one of your little friends, my dearest," she announced in Daisy's mind. Her ability to read Daisy's thoughts and speak from within Daisy's mind became increasingly frustrating. Daisy wanted to block the invader, not let her in, gain back some of her privacy. "You appear to actually have some skill. How are you managing to block me?"

While trying to keep her focus, Daisy responded aloud, "I don't know. I've been told my powers are unusual."

The figure stood quiet for a moment and seemed to assess Daisy. Daisy could feel the stranger's gaze on her and tried not to shiver in discomfort. Everything about this situation made Daisy's stomach churn with nerves.

"You are quite talented. Tell me, what did you ask the forces to do when you stopped my fire ball?"

"I asked them to stop." Daisy saw no point in lying. The figure was likely going to kill her, but maybe something she could say would win over the intruder.

"To stop? You told them to stop?!?" Daisy could hear a low rumbling laughter under her words in her mind. It was like having two orchestras playing different songs at the same time. It was excruciating to Daisy. "How fascinating indeed. I imagine that - what is he going by now - Ambrose is also quite impressed with you."

"I haven't really had the opportunity to speak with him. I have been healing him from your doings."

"He will bounce back." She seemed disinterested and picked idly at her nails. "While I am quite set on taking him back, you are far more intriguing to me. I had to find out more about you before leaving."

"You're not going to kill me?" A soft laugh drifted into Daisy's mind. Although rather joyous, the sound unnerved Daisy more.

"No. I am not going to kill you. I care too much about you to do that."

"You don't even know me."

"Oh dearest, I know you better than you know yourself. Either way, you've answered my questions, and I must depart before Alina arrives."

She walked towards the window and snapped her fingers. The window sprung away from the wall, leaving a rosette shaped hole in the wall. It was just large enough for her to sneak through. She squished her body through the hole and looked back at Daisy through it.

"Lastly," she said through the hole to Daisy. "There appears to be a mortal waiting outside your hidey hole for you. I would pay close attention to her message. It might just be important." She let out a maniacal laugh that echoed in Daisy's mind as she disappeared into the forest.

Daisy sat in the chair, completely breathless, trying to comprehend what just occurred. Abe's adversary just had an idle chit chat with Daisy and Daisy did nothing to contain her or stop her. Daisy smacked her head wishing that she had done more. She felt like she failed Abe and let everyone down. Daisy picked up her feet, placed them on the edge of the chair, and hugged her knees. It was an oddly comforting position. She sat for a moment, replaying what had just happened, endeavouring to think of ways that she could have done better. The figure's words ate at her. She wondered if she should tell Abe, but that also meant admitting she let the person that just tried to kill him go freely.

It was messy and confusing, but then Daisy's mind landed on the last words spoken. There was someone waiting for her outside. There was only one person that could be. Daisy lunged from the chair and bolted down the hallway. As she reached the main room, she could see Alina carrying Abe down the hall towards her, but Daisy didn't stop.

She pushed through the wall. The cold and wet sensation overwhelmed her before emerging on the station platform, and there, sitting on the other side, appeared a tired and stressed looking Rosie. Before Daisy could say anything, Rosie was running towards her. Rosie ran straight into Daisy and wrapped her in a tight hug. Daisy squeezed her back and felt relief overwhelm her. She wasn't sure why the sight of Rosie was such a relief, but it was calming in light of all that had happened.

Daisy pushed back so she could look at Rosie's face. Daisy had never been this close to Rosie. She had freckles that were barely darker, and hardly noticeable, than her skin. Her eyes had flecks of gold and emerald. Even though they had only known each other for a few months, Rosie felt more like family to Daisy than any of her blood relatives.

"I am so happy to see you," Daisy beamed. She left barely twenty-four hours ago, but that one day had felt like aeons. "But, I have to ask, why are you here?"

"I tried to cover for you, but somehow Dame Agatha knew you were sneaking out, and she had already written to your parents. I don't know what she's said, but everything is falling apart" Daisy could hear the panic in Rosie's voice. Daisy smiled to try and ease her friend's mind.

"Perhaps I should go home for a while. Come up with some other story about where I am and what I am doing. Maybe I can sign up for a travelling school like my sister used to do. I can't leave the Conductors, Rosie." Daisy watched as Rosie's face fell. She could tell that Rosie wanted her to come back to the manor, but Daisy finally felt like she belonged somewhere, that she was someone. Everything she wanted was at her fingertips with the Conductors. So little was available to Daisy at the manor.

"I understand. You need to do what is best for you. Perhaps, I can ask the dame for a leave of absence and join you. I haven't really been anywhere."

"That sounds wonderful. How about you meet me back here for the one o'clock train to Stanford and Glenn?"

"Perfect. I will meet you here tomorrow." A weight seemed lifted off of Rosie's shoulders. Having a plan must have eased some of the worry Rosie had been carrying. Daisy hadn't really considered what she was asking of Rosie when she started training with Abe. It had been a few month's of Rosie lying and covering for Daisy. In all honesty, Daisy had not considered how much undue stress this may have put on Rosie.

Daisy hugged Rosie, grateful for everything she was doing. Rosie smiled and quickly departed to head back to the manor. Daisy watched her go until she was well out of sight before returning. Daisy's plan was starting to come together. Regardless of what the other Conductor's thought, Daisy had come up with a plan.

Chapter 27 - Decisions and Dreams

As Daisy entered the main hall, she was greeted by an extremely irritated Alina and very concerned Abe. Alina stood with her hands on her hips, her nostrils flared, and her foot tapped rhythmically. This was angrier than Daisy had seen Alina thus far. Abe sat in a chair behind her. He had his arms braced against his leg to support his head. He had worry lines and his expression showed his state of exhaustion. Daisy supposed it could be since he nearly died, but something about the way he looked at Daisy indicated it wasn't.

"What the hell were you doing?!?" Alina screamed at Daisy.

"Alina!" Abe corrected. "We heard everything. We know exactly what happened and what was going on. Don't be so harsh."

"How did you hear my conversation?" Daisy said feeling completely violated. Perhaps Abe had tapped into her mind again just like the hooded woman had.

"Security measures around the hall. Anything outside of the hall is amplified into the room to raise awareness of those entering and exiting. It was meant to prevent intruders, but it doesn't appear to have worked very well." Alina explained but there was still fury in her voice. Her words were filled with a venom that Daisy believed was undeserved.

"What element allows you to do that?" Daisy asked.

"We changed the shape of the train station to funnel sound then we charmed the air to amplify sound, but that isn't what is important. You can't leave right now, Dais. We have to plan and move as a group. Leaving by yourself would be incredibly dangerous," Abe stated.

"And staying here is safe? We were just attacked in your home with tons of security measures. I am the newest Conductor and the one that lady knows the least about. Going back to my parent's is probably safer than staying here."

Abe looked at Alina who shrugged. Knowing what she knew of Alina, it was unlikely for Alina to agree with Daisy, but somehow, Daisy's reasoning appeared to be winning. It felt like a victory to Daisy, but she tried not to show it. Maintaining a serious demeanour appeared necessary around Alina.

"We will decide in the morning," Alina announced. "In the meantime, we are safe for tonight. Everyone should go to bed and get some rest."

Taking her own advice, Alina immediately headed to the dorm hall. Daisy waited until she heard the click of a door to know Alina was well gone. Abe visibly relaxed with Alina's absence. He slouched back in his chair. His shoulders lowered and his eyes softened. He was looking a lot better than earlier. Clearly, the spells to heal him had worked after all.

"I don't know what is the best option here. I think we have a brief window of time before she will return for me, but I don't know if going to your family is the best option," Abe explained.

"They are my family, and I assume they will care that I am missing. Maybe. I don't know, but I feel like I owe them an explanation or something. They need some reason why I am gone and won't be coming back. I know my mother will only accept an engagement as a reasonable excuse, but I have to think of something. I can't cause undue stress on them for no reason."

Abe leaned forward and levelled his eyes on Daisy. She could tell he was contemplating her statement. Really, there was no reason for Abe to agree, but Daisy hoped beyond anything that he would consider it.

"Dais, you understand that my adversary not only knows your face, but she knows your power. While she may be after me, I think she'll come for you too."

Daisy kept quiet for a moment. She thought back to her conversation with the hooded figure; Daisy felt the hairs on the back of her neck stand up. Abe's words only reinforced that there was more to this person than Daisy understood. However, that wasn't going to change Daisy's mind. She was going with or without Abe.

"I am going," she finally announced. "I need to see my family so that I can properly focus on becoming a Conductor. You can come with me or you can stay, but either way I am going."

Daisy turned on her heel and headed for her room. Abe called after her but, either due to injury or exhaustion, he did not pursue her. Why Abe did not follow her, was the least of Daisy's concerns. She said her piece, and she had nothing left to argue.

The door to her room clicked behind her. This time, the room was empty. The window where the intruder had swiftly made her exit still hung open; Daisy quickly made her way to the window and slammed it shut. With a wave of her hand, an additional lock was placed on the window. Although she knew it would not protect her from other Conductors, Daisy felt safer having it there.

As Daisy slid into bed, her mind ran over the events of the day. The battle, healing Abe, conversing with the hooded woman, seeing Rosie, and deciding to go home. It was all so much in such a short amount of time. She kept replaying scenes and trying to identify things she could have done differently or ways she could have helped more. Eventually, however, extreme fatigue consumed her and she drifted off into a restless sleep.

Daisy stood on the edge of a cliff. The sky was grey and the ocean below her was choppy. Wind whipped past her face, spraying her with salt from the sea. The ground was a cold slate with jagged edges. Daisy looked around and saw nothing besides sea and slate. Although she was alone, Daisy felt like she was being watched. She felt like a rabbit being hunted by a wolf. Turning slowly, she looked for the source of discomfort. Before she could recognize any threat, she was ripped off her feet and started tumbling over the cliff towards the black churning water.

Stop. Daisy squinted her eyes and focused harder on stopping. Then the world went silent. The wind stopped whipping her face. She opened her eyes and noticed she had stopped mid air. Even more so, the sea below her stopped moving. A bird in the distance, barely a white speck against the grey clouds, stopped flying as if stuck in time. Everything froze but Daisy, who could somehow move freely.

She focused on the air and got it to move her back up the cliffside and back to safety. She simultaneously kept her focus on stopping everything else. Once her feet were back safely on the ground, she ran away from the cliff's edge. When she thought herself safe again, she allowed the world to move. The wind blew with such force it nearly uprooted her again and its howling was nearly deafening. Daisy was overwhelmed by the bombardment of sounds and sensations.

Then, she felt a tap on her shoulder. She turned to see Abe. His hair was tousled and danced in the wind. He wore a white shirt that was mostly unbuttoned. He wore black slacks that had his shirt partially tucked in. His feet were bare, and he wore black suspenders that hung around his waist instead of on his shoulders. His green and blue eyes were filled with tears. His skin was white making the scar on his face stand out like blood in the snow. Something was wrong.

"Why didn't you tell me?" he cried. His voice cracked and Daisy's heart broke. "You could have stopped all of this. This didn't have to happen."

Before Daisy could respond, a deep red stain blossomed on Abe's shirt. It spread across his chest and tainted his exposed skin.

Blood.

Daisy wanted to run to him, to heal him, but she couldn't move; she was stuck. She tried to talk and explain that she wanted to help him, but no sound would come out. Her voice froze in her throat. The blood continued spreading. The shirt quickly changed colour. He clutched his chest before collapsing on the ground. He gave one shrudding breath before ceasing all movement.

Suddenly, whatever force held Daisy relinquished its firm grip, and she was free. She ran to where Abe laid on the ground and held him in her arms. She sobbed over his limp, lifeless body. She needed to do something. He couldn't be dead. She held her hand over the wound as she desperately tried to figure out how to fix it. But, before she could do anything, she was ripped away from him. She watched as she flew away and Abe's crumpled body lay on the grey stone. She painfully screamed his name.

The scene changed. She was back in her childhood bedroom. Azalea sat in the chair reading a book. She looked up and gave Daisy a comforting smile. Azalea extended her arms towards Daisy offering a hug. Daisy accepted. She fell into her sister's arms and cried. There was so much pain.

"Men are never worth it, darling," Azalea cooed as she gently stroked Daisy's hair. "He didn't love you or he would have stopped this from happening. You are better off without him."

But the pain rang true. Daisy's heart felt like it was going to explode. Abe was dead, and she was back here because she had nowhere else to go. The school kicked her out, the Conductors all died, Rosie vanished. She had nothing left. Everything was gone but Azalea.

Azalea squeezed Daisy's hand before suddenly, Daisy was moving again. She sat in the same place but everything was different now. Her family home was diminished to rubble and ashes. Where a great castle once stood, now lay a pile of smouldering bricks. Daisy stood and walked amongst the rubble. She could see remnants of a life long since passed. Her mother's desk snapped in two. A library shelf tipped over with its contents burning. A large, four post bed tainted red with blood and black with ash. As she sifted through the rubble, she came across two bodies; Duchess Bloomsbury clutching her husband.

Daisy collapsed to the ground and held their dead bodies. Too much loss in such a short time. Her body shook with sobs and pain and anger. She was angry at whatever caused this. A familiar tune distracted Daisy from her anger. It was the song Azalea sang to her through the walls. The song was cut short as a tumble of rubble caused Daisy to look away. Standing on the top of the shattered staircase was the hooded figure cackling at Daisy's pain.

Daisy awoke breathing hard. Her body was wet with sweat and she shook with fear. Before she knew what she was doing, she was out of her bed and running down the hall.

Chapter 28 - Dismissal

As Rosie arrived back at the manor she noticed a light in the dame's office flickering through the window. Usually, this meant the dame was awake. It was no surprise to Dame Agatha that Rosie occasionally left during the night. During her four year-long tenure in the manor, Rosie had earned a great deal of trust and freedom. Unlike many of the other girls, her decorum was not the problem keeping Rosie at the manor. It was those Rosie chose to love.

As she entered the manor, she didn't bother sneaking or being quiet as she was going directly to the dame's office anyways. She hurried down the hallway towards the office and knocked on the door.

"Come in," Dame Agatha announced from the other side of the door. Rosie entered.

The dame sat behind her desk. She was deeply focused on the parchment in her hands. She looked concerned more than anything. The paper crinkled in her hands as her grip tightened on the pages. Her face reddened and Rosie knew the letter didn't not contain happy tidings. Whatever was on the page was highly offensive to her. She slammed the pages down on the table, temporarily breaking all rules of proper ladyship. Rosie tried to be placid and neutral.

"Were you at the tavern tonight? How is dear Maria?" she asked, trying to keep her voice light, but Rosie knew the tone running underneath it.

"She is doing well, but that was not the full extent of my journey this evening," Rosie responded. Dame Agatha's eyebrows raised with suspicion. "Not like *that*. I found Daisy tonight."

The dame's expression of surprise only heightened. Rosie felt uneasy. She wasn't sure what the dame was going to do or say, but Rosie knew what she had to say.

"And? Where was she?"

"She found a different instructor that has been teaching her content that intrigued her more than etiquette, manners, and ladyship. Daisy has found her calling," Rosie explained feeling nervous.

"With whom?" Dame Agatha narrowed her eyes at Rosie in a challenging manner. Rosie swallowed hard while trying to maintain a calm and strong presence.

"Alina and Ambrose. I am sure you have seen them around town? They were at the ball, and you met Abe after Daisy's injury."

"Yes. I remember him well and not in the most positive manner. I did not know that they taught."

"Nor did I, but Daisy seems quite content. However, there has been a recent development. It turns out you did not need to send for her family as her family has sent for her. Her mother has grown ill and her presence has been requested back home."

Rosie handed the dame a forged letter describing an ailment plaguing Daisy's mother and the request for immediate return of their daughter. Rosie had briefly stopped at the tavern to ask Maria's aid in writing the fake letter. She was sure that it would pass, but there was always the chance it would not. The dame idly read the note but stopped halfway through. She looked displeased and insulted at Rosie's attempt to con her. It appeared the letter did not work.

"What are you hiding?" she demanded. There was a force to the dame's voice that Rosie had not experienced before. "Why are you protecting her? What are you protecting her from?"

"What are you referring to, Dame? I have given you all that I know," Rosie replied meekly in a desperate attempt to keep up her ruse.

"I know Maria's writing as well as I know yours." Rosie's cheeks reddened with embarrassment. Rosie should have known that the dame would call her bluff, but the humiliation was far worse than she could have anticipated.

"I cannot tell you what Daisy is doing exactly, but she is learning from Alina and Ambrose. Furthermore, she is returning home tomorrow, and I intend to go with her."

The dame leaned back in her chair and looked at Rosie with squinted eyes as if searching for further deception. She pursed her lips and tapped her fingers on the desk in a syncopated rhythm. A long moment passed and Rosie was uncertain what was going to happen next. She felt uncomfortable in the unknown. She had never been this forceful with the dame, and it did not appear to be working in her favour. Although they had a different relationship than most students and teachers, Rosie felt uneasy with this level of demanding behaviour.

Finally, the dame sighed and grabbed a piece of blank paper. She began scribbling on the sheet. When she finished her message, she dabbed hot wax onto the page and pressed her seal in the wax. A bloomed lily on a background of stars was embossed on the page. She handed the sheet to Rosie with a soft smile. Rosie was surprised to see not a letter, but a certificate.

"I received a letter from your parents to request additional training. I was reading it before you entered, but I have taught you everything I know. I cannot train you out of who you are. I am completing your training, so you are free to do as you please. But Rosie," the dame's voice softened. She gently placed one hand on Rosie's arm and levelled her eyes to Rosie's. There was a motherly essence to this action that made Rosie's heart contract. "I hope you know what you are doing. When you are done, please know you always have a home, and a job, here at the manor."

Rosie hugged the dame and she returned the sentiment. As they embraced, Rosie felt two wet drops hit her shoulder. They pulled apart and Rosie noticed Dame Agatha was crying.

"Don't you dare tell anyone," she exclaimed, fiercely rubbing her eyes.

"A contraction! My oh my, how emotional this must be for you." Rosie smiled and the dame laughed. It was a strained, uncomfortable laugh and obviously not something she did often.

"Please be safe," Dame Agatha pleaded. Her eyes welled with tears and a supportive smile spread across her face. "Now, go before I change my mind."

Rosie needed nothing else. She exited the room quickly and made her way to her dorm. She began packing her trunk to allow for a quick getaway in the morning. As the dawn crested the horizon, Rosie crawled into her small bed, for a last bit of rest, before heading for the train station.

The morning came abruptly. Perhaps Rosie spent more time packing than she realised, but the morning bell was a rude awakening. She got ready and dressed. A servant arrived later to escort her to the train station and assist her with her luggage.

Rosie walked down the stairs to a small audience. Many of her instructors, the dame, and some of the girls she had mentored all awaited her to say their goodbyes. It oddly felt like leaving home. These people had become her family. She felt more sad leaving them than she had leaving her own family. She said her farewells, loaded her trunk, and was off. They made a quick stop by the tavern so she could explain to Maria before finally arriving at the train station. The servant carried her trunk out and placed it in the lobby of the station before departing. Rosie patiently awaited Daisy's arrival, hoping, above all else, she had not made a mistake in deciding to leave with Daisy.

Chapter 29 - Travel Plans

Daisy ran from her room intending to head for Abe's office. She needed to ensure he was safe, but as she entered the main room, Daisy came to a complete stop. Everyone was standing by the door with trunks looking ready to leave. Daisy felt a new swell of panic. It seemed as though they were going to leave without her. Alina eyed Daisy looking pleased with what Daisy assumed was the tousled and dishevelled look of having just woken up. She was sliding a glove on and looking as smug as ever. Daisy tried to not appear shaken, but her mind was running faster than she could understand.

"If we are to catch the one o'clock train, you best be getting ready," Alina announced. Brighid barely contained a giggle and Evander smirked. Arlo hardly even noticed Daisy had arrived. However, Daisy finally noticed that Abe was missing. She was not expecting an audience.

"I, uh, needed to talk to Abe," Daisy mumbled, trying to wiggle her way out of Alina's clutches.

"In your bed clothes? Weren't you at finishing school? That hardly seems lady-like. Besides, you really should be getting ready to leave. The train arrives in fifteen minutes." Daisy could feel the judgement in Alina's voice. Each word was like a slap trying to prove she was superior in some way to Daisy.

Daisy stopped for a moment to take in her words. They were getting on the train. The only train departing today was the train to Stratford and Glenn. They had agreed to leave, and they were leaving in fifteen minutes. Daisy nodded at Alina, turned back around and headed to her room to prepare. She quickly threw various things in her trunk and put on clothes. Her hair was a disaster, but she didn't have time to fix it. She was decent enough and time was limited. Not entirely sure what she threw in the trunk, she closed it and ran out of her room dragging the trunk along. This time, when she entered the main hall, Abe was accounted for.

"Alright," he said and smiled at Daisy, "now that everyone is here, we can leave. Make sure you have everything with you because we will be sealing this passageway. You won't be able to come back."

Everyone nodded, but Daisy. She hadn't really packed properly. She didn't even really know what was in the trunk or what was left in the room, but she didn't think anything that was left mattered. Everyone grabbed their trunks and exited the main hall into the train station.

Daisy saw Rosie patiently waiting with her trunk. Rosie immediately waved once she saw Daisy. As nice as it was to have Rosie along, Daisy also feared about bringing her. There was so little that Daisy knew about the Conductors and bringing someone that knew even less seemed like a horrible idea; however, Daisy knew she needed a friend. Alina was always so harsh towards Daisy, and the others were a very close group that Daisy could hardly interject herself. Perhaps with time it would change, but at least for now she had Rosie with her.

"What is this?" Alina demanded as Rosie approached the group.

"This is Rosie, and she is coming with us," Daisy dictated. Daisy raised her nose and crossed her arms across her chest daring Alina to challenge her more.

"You are bringing an outsider into our inner sanctum?" Alina sounded absolutely disgusted. Abe opened his mouth to interject, but Daisy held up her hand to stop him.

Daisy was tired of Alina's snide remarks and treating Daisy like an inferior. Alina was exhausting and Daisy did not have the time to deal with her today. She decided to take the lead and not allow Alina to continue to intimidate her.

"Firstly, Alina, we are going to my home, and I am bringing my friend to my home. It has nothing to do with the Conductors. Secondly, she already knows all about the Conductors and has watched several of my lessons with Abe. Thirdly, this is my plan and you could have chosen to not follow it, but you did. Now you are stuck with my decisions. Am I being quite clear?"

Alina placed her hands on her hips in protest and huffed at Daisy's remark, but Daisy held her ground. She wasn't going to back down now. The other Conductors watched the interaction in amazement, but no one dared to voice their opinion. The building tension between Daisy and Alina over the past few months meant that only Abe would say anything. This time, however, he was silent.

"If you have nothing else to say, we should board the train before we are late and running after it," Daisy stated. She walked past the group, linked arms with Rosie and headed directly to the train without even glancing back at Alina or the others.

They loaded up the trunks into the storage racks and sat in a cabin. Usually a cabin sat four comfortably, but they managed to squeeze all seven of them into one cabin. Alina seemed even more angry than usual with the introduction of another person. Brighid, on the other hand, seemed in awe of Rosie and quietly chatted with her on one side of the cabin. Abe flipped through a book with strange shapes on the cover that Daisy couldn't decipher. Arlo slept while Evander idly played with his jacket buttons. Alina tried to avoid looking at, talking with, or even just acknowledging Daisy or Rosie. Alina was clearly still upset about their earlier argument, but Daisy didn't mind her silence.

Everything felt unreal to Daisy. It was a merging of worlds that she never expected or intended to happen. She didn't think her parents would care that she was missing, but it was best to close all doors. She needed to give her parents a reason for her leaving the manor. Although Daisy was unsure who needed that closure more, her or her parents. The Conductors also needed somewhere to go and this seemed like a fine short term option. Then a thought hit Daisy hard. *How was she going to explain all of these people to her parents?*

"Abe," Daisy called quietly, trying not to draw too much attention from the others. He looked up from his book briefly to acknowledge he heard her, but did not say anything. "Abe, what are we going to tell my parents when we arrive?"

Alina scoffed at the question and rolled her eyes. Daisy glared at her and shook her head. It was an honest question and yet Alina seemed to think it was a ridiculous notion.

"It doesn't matter what we tell them. The fifth element makes this kind of stuff easy," Evander dictated without any sense of care or concern.

"These are my parents. Magic is the last option. I would rather explain something to them that is semi-believable than alter their minds. Is that too much to ask?" Daisy waited for a retort from Alina or Evander, but was cut off.

"We don't do magic, but that is perfectly reasonable, and I have already come up with a story. However, I must finish this section first as it may be relevant to my long-term plan," Abe stated and returned back to his book. Alina looked at him with great insult, but Abe flipped a page and continued ignoring Alina.

The remainder of the trip was endured in almost complete silence. The studies talked amongst themselves, and Daisy waited for Abe to elaborate further. However, Abe seemed completely lost in his book. Alina idly chatted with Brighid and ensured to ignore Rosie's presence. As they neared their final destination, Abe closed his book with a loud snap that caught everyone's attention.

"I expect everyone to be on their best behaviour, especially you Arlo, as we are guests in Daisy's home," Abe instructed. "You will follow mine and Daisy's lead.

There will be no interruptions, and you will speak only when spoken to to avoid any issues."

"So what is your story then?" Brighid asked, appearing mostly curious. Abe softly smiled at her.

"It's a slight twist on the truth. I am a professor at the University of Wimborne. I brought some of my students along with me on a research mission where I was introduced to Daisy and Rosie. I found Daisy quite intriguing and have come home with her to ask for her hand in marriage. It gives reason for our presence as well as her continued absence henceforth."

Daisy was flabbergasted by the notion of marrying Abe. She knew it was a story, but the narrative sang to a desire in her heart she hadn't fully realised until someone else suggested it. As she looked around the train car she noticed the expressions of the others. Evander and Arlo both seemed impressed while Brighid appeared indifferent. Alina had a clear expression of distaste and anger. Rosie, however, had a look of pure concern on her face. Daisy was confused by Rosie's expression but understanding of Alina's. Daisy raised an eyebrow at Rosie who shook her head and directed her attention at her shoes.

"Since no one has anything to say, I am assuming there is no better plan?" Abe paused for a moment to allow for any objections but none came. "Well then Daisy, might as well make it appear more legitimate."

Abe pulled out a small glass box with gold metal bars. Resting on a black cushion inside the box was a small, silver ring with a gold stone. It was unlike anything Daisy has seen before. She tried not to act emotional or amazed as this was all just a ruse which she had to keep reminding herself of.

"Don't you give her the ring after you've gotten permission from the family?" Evander piped up.

"Usually, yes, but I need to make my intentions clear quickly so that we don't need to linger longer than absolutely necessary, and we can get everyone to safety as soon as possible," Abe explained.

Abe grabbed Daisy's hand and gently glided the ring on to her ring finger. Daisy felt herself blush and quickly turned her face away from Alina's intense stare. Daisy could feel Alina's eyes glaring at the back of her head.

The train ground to a stop and Daisy was quick to move out of the cabin. Everyone quickly followed behind her and exited the train. There were two coaches available for hire outside the train station. Abe paid the drivers and Daisy provided the directions. Slowly, they loaded everything and were off towards Daisy's childhood home.

Abe, Daisy, and Rosie piled into one carriage which was a relief to Daisy. She could finally have a short reprieve of Alina's heavy stare. Clearly, this whole situation was displeasing to Alina, but it was not necessarily Daisy's doing. Abe had orchestrated the plan and Daisy simply followed it. However, Alina hardly seemed angry towards Abe. Perhaps it was Alina's love for Abe that blinded her impartiality. Daisy had never been in love to know what it could make one do, but she read stories of its symptoms and imagined that was what Alina was experiencing.

The coaches came to rest outside of the gates to her family estate. Usually there were attendants at the gate when guests were expected, but Daisy knew she was not expected. In place of servants, Daisy opened the gate for everyone. The Bloomsbury Estate sat on top of a large hill making it almost impossible to see from the gate. Daisy gave some brief details about her family as they climbed the hill, but it was hard to keep things positive. Her family had not been the most supportive of families.

As they crested the hill, all thoughts of her family suddenly disappeared. Instead of the castle as it usually stood, Daisy arrived into her nightmares.

Chapter 30 - Rubble and Ruins

Daisy dropped her trunk and stumbled up the remaining driveway. Where the large stone castle once stood, lay piles of smouldering rubble like Daisy had seen in her dream. She immediately started sifting through the rubble, afraid of what she would find, but knowing she had to. Daisy could hear everyone gasp and ask questions but the words didn't register to Daisy. She needed to know if the dream held true.

She kept throwing chunks of debris out of the way, looking for any signs. She tripped over all the furniture and found her mother's desk split in two. Daisy could feel her panic rising and clawing in the back of her throat. She tripped over something and fell to her knees. Instead of standing, Daisy found herself sobbing into the dust and debris.

Eventually, a pair of arms wrapped themselves around Daisy and pulled her against their chest. Whoever it was was warm and comforting. Daisy turned and cried into their shirt, not wanting to face the others that she could hear approaching.

"What are you looking for?" Rosie asked as she stroked Daisy's arms. Daisy shook her head against Rosie's stomach. Daisy wasn't quite ready to speak. "I know, hun, but we can't help you if we don't know what you are looking for."

"M-my p-p-par-ents," Daisy managed to sputter out between sobs. Daisy felt Rosie go stiff as though that thought had not bridged Rosie's mind until Daisy announced it.

Almost immediately, Daisy could hear more rubble moving. She briefly looked up from Rosie to see the Conductors shifting rubble by hand and conduction. Even Alina idly dug through debris. Daisy's heart warmed at their attempts to help her, but it also broke at the horror of what was to come. Some part of her knew they were dead, but she needed to see it. She needed her fear to be verified. Somehow, Daisy composed herself and began helping in the search. Hours passed and piles of rubble were organized, but no bodies had been found. The smallest bubble of hope emerged inside of Daisy's panic. Perhaps, somehow, they made it out. Perhaps Daisy's dream was wrong. Just as Daisy was sure there wasn't anywhere else to look, Arlo grabbed everyone's attention.

Daisy rushed over to where he stood. Lying on the ground covered in dust and dirt but otherwise looking asleep were Daisy's parents. Their hands were interlocked as if they didn't brace against the falling building. There were no marks or visible injuries, but Daisy knew they were long gone. This time, however, Daisy had no tears for her parents. They had already passed and this was just the confirmation she needed. She looked away from their greying bodies and noticed a hand sticking out from amongst the debris. She moved the remaining rocks and came across the body of Susan.

Unlike her parents, Susan's body looked mangled and crushed. Limbs extended at odd angles and there were visible gashes that had since dried. In her panic to find her parents, she had forgotten about the woman that truly raised her. Guilt and anger swelled inside her. She found herself on her knees sobbing again. Daisy felt immense pain and culpability. If she had been here, maybe she could have prevented this all from happening. If she had been there, maybe her parents and Susan would still be alive. In a quick moment, Daisy had lost nearly everything. They all searched for what was left of the day, taking inventory of the lives lost and what may be salvageable, but the sun was beginning to fall behind the horizon as night took over.

Daisy eventually stopped searching and sat on the bottom few steps of what remained of the grand staircase. Rosie and Abe sat on either side of Daisy while the others awkwardly stood looking at them. Daisy rested her head on Rosie's shoulder as Rosie wrapped one arm around her. Daisy felt completely empty and exhausted. Slowly, everything in her life was being dismantled. She lost her family, her house, the only other place she considered home. The Conductors were being threatened, and Daisy felt responsible. Everything was falling apart.

Alina turned to those sitting on the stairs as if ready to speak, but thought better of it. Evander looked at her and took her place instead.

"What are we going to do next?" Evander asked. Abe shot him a warning look, but Daisy didn't mind. She knew what she had to do next.

"There's a stable on the other side of the estate. If it is still intact, we can stay there tonight and you all can move on tomorrow," Daisy explained.

"What do you mean 'you all'?" Alina interrogated.

"I have personal matters to attend to now," Daisy retorted and gestured to the mess around them. "I have to deal with this estate and the bodies. I need to clean this all up. I have to determine who is the heir to the Estate. There are things I need to attend to."

"I will stay with you," Rosie offered and squeezed Daisy's shoulder. Daisy gave her an appreciative smile. She would need help, but she knew the Conductors were safe to stay here for a while.

"We don't know what caused this though. Are you sure you are safe here? Maybe you shouldn't stay and attend to anything," Abe said but there was a tone of pleading to his voice that made Daisy's heart hurt.

The feeling, however, quickly subsided. As if directly from her dream, Daisy heard the familiar tune followed by the cackle behind them. The hairs on the back of her neck stood on end as a shiver ran down Daisy's body. Quickly, Daisy dive rolled from her spot on the stairs and spun to face the familiar adversary. Rosie and Abe also scrambled away from the stairs. Daisy was the only one who seemed to immediately clue in, but, then again, Daisy had already seen this.

"Oh, yes, your parents and your poor little Susan are all dead. You poor little thing. All alone now, are you?" the hooded figure asked, but this time the voice did not sound in her head. It was out loud this time and there was a painful familiarity to it. It was the sound of a voice she longed to hear, but she knew that was impossible. Maybe,

Daisy thought, this Conductor could alter her senses. Daisy shook her head in order to refocus.

"I am hardly alone," Daisy responded. Everyone else stood around her prepared to fight. Daisy could see sparks of magic coming to light around her whereas Rosie, with innocent determination, wielded a frying plan.

"Is that so? Tell me, what do you really know about your beloved Conductors? Better yet, what do you really know about your family? Even about your *dead* sister?" Purposefully, the hooded figure began taking slow, intentional steps down the stairs. She moved any debris out of her way making a clear path down the deteriorated staircase.

"Why does that matter?" Alina barked. The figure stopped moving as if insulted by the outburst. Raising a hand, the attacker muttered some incomprehensible words and a flare of purple jetted from her hand. Alina fell to the ground clutching her throat.

"It would do you well to hold your tongue," the figure spat. She released Alina and continued walking down the stairs. Alina collapsed, gasping for breath. "Anyone else wish to speak?"

Daisy could feel their fear though their will to fight did not ebb. By the time the hooded woman was nearing the bottom of the stairs, Daisy had no idea what to do. She had expected Abe, or anyone really, to speak or fight, but they had not made a single move against her.

"What is it you want?" Daisy asked, trying to keep the terror out of her voice.

"Well, that is a multi-part answer, my dear. As usual, I've come for my love, but I see my love has turned his attention to another." Her head turned towards Abe to address him directly. "Something has changed in you, Abe. I can see your mind and you are not as you were all those years ago."

"I've also come for you, Daisy. After our last encounter, I had to have you by my side. You were never supposed to learn about the Conductors and yet, here you are amongst them. I tried so hard to keep you away as I knew you had an innate ability. I needed to keep away so you didn't get sucked into this all, but I knew there was one that would identify you. I knew there was one that you would find you. I tried everything to keep you away from him, from Abe." The figure stopped at the bottom of the stairs.

Daisy looked sideways at Abe. She could see that he was panicked, but waiting to fight. Daisy didn't understand what they were waiting for exactly, but it was obviously something. She turned her attention back to the hooded figure. More pieces started to slide into place. The voice was incredibly familiar now that it was outside of her head and this time, Daisy could see more. The figure was female, which Daisy knew from before, but the cloak was less bulky and showed off a more curvy shape. Her hands were exposed from her cuffs. They were delicate and very white almost like piano keys. Suddenly, Daisy could see the hands moving over piano keys playing that same familiar tune. But it was impossible. It couldn't be what Daisy thought no matter how much Daisy wanted it.

"What are you talking about?" Daisy finally managed to ask.

"My dear, Daisy. I know you better than you know yourself. I knew from a very young age that you possessed power and I tried to snuff it out. I tried to bury it. I tried to break your spirit, but somehow you prevailed."

"You said you didn't know me when we last met." Daisy saw a confused and terrified look cross Abe's face. She never did tell Abe about their meeting that night.

"I did and I didn't. I know you well, but I didn't know you in the moment. You've grown into something new." Daisy was starting to get frustrated with these riddles. She could feel her breaking point bubbling to the surface, and Daisy wasn't sure what she would do if she reached her maximum.

"Just answer the question."

"Or I could show you."

The figure pulled at the clasp that held her cloak on. She grasped the edges of the hood and pulled the cloak off in one smooth movement. Standing in the rubble of Daisy's home looking smug and menacing was a woman with blond hair, skin like ivory, high cheekbones, a full figure. She was essentially the definition of beauty, but her eyes. Her eyes were a deep purple and a fiery red. It was a discomforting look that took Daisy back for a moment. The different eyes made her look completely different. It was like staring at a broken mirror: the image is there and recognizable, but fractured and scattered making it hard to place.

"Do I need to say anything else?" The voice and the estate were the final clues to a puzzle that had been building over the years and Daisy hadn't the slightest idea it was even being built.

The hooded figure was very familiar. Standing before Daisy was Azalea.

Chapter 31 - The Truth

"Azalea? But…but you are dead," Daisy cried. She choked on each word. There was a different kind of pain heavy in her heart now. She felt betrayed and confused and so incredibly angry.

Overwhelmed with emotions, Daisy collapsed to her knees. Everyone else seemed concerned but wouldn't move their eyes from Azalea. Daisy couldn't believe that her sister was Abe's enemy. It seemed impossible that her sister was a Conductor, but Daisy watched her perform magic just a moment before. It was Azalea in front of her as clear as day. Alive and well.

"Daisy," Abe muttered through clenched teeth. "Daisy, you need to get up."

"Oh hush you," Azalea shunned Abe. "What do they even call you these days?"

"Ambrose, but I prefer Abe, which I know you know. You've already played in my mind."

Azalea was close, but she seemed to keep a specific distance. Her focus was on Abe now which gave Daisy a moment to process what was going on. She needed a moment. She needed to think. Daisy closed her eyes, she needed things to stop.

A sudden silence came. The wind stopped blowing and the birds stopped chirping. The world seemed to freeze. Daisy looked around. Alina was in mid step. Rosie's hair stuck out at an odd angle from her head. Arlo was mid-blink. Time had stopped and yet, Azalea and Abe seemed unaffected.

"Ah, you see Abe. You see!" Azalea shouted. "You're correct that I've been in your mind and I've seen how you feel, even though you try to hide it. The prophecy holds true even if you deny it."

"Daisy - Daisy, stop," Abe begged. Daisy could hear the fear in his voice. "Daisy, stand up and unfreeze time."

Daisy stood, but in terms of unfreezing time, she wasn't sure how to do that.

"I don't know how. I don't know what I am doing." Abe flicked his glance from Azalea for a moment to look at Daisy, but this was a dire mistake. A purple flash sparked from her hand and moved towards Abe, but somehow it stopped mid air. Daisy wanted it to stop, and it did. Abe stumbled back from the purple lightning in the air.

"No," Daisy said with a force she didn't expect. She could see the fury building in Azalea's eyes. Daisy had endured her sister's wrath many times before, but this was different. Daisy never knew this Azalea. Before Daisy could do anything else, the rush of sound hit them like a tsunami. All three of them winced. The silence of paused time was a rough adjustment.

"You still don't see it?" Azalea shouted at Abe. It seemed Daisy was no longer her focus.

"I don't know what to say. She can do things, yes, but that doesn't mean it's a new force," Abe responded.

Azalea clenched her fist tightly at her side. Daisy was sure that steam would have come out of her ears if it was possible. This was an anger Daisy had never seen before.

"Do you love her?" Daisy was shocked at the question. She didn't understand everyone's obsession with Abe's emotions. Abe, however, did not seem shocked. He seemed repulsed and irritated which slightly hurt Daisy. *Was the idea of loving Daisy so unpleasant? Wasn't it his idea to marry her?*

"That has nothing to do with anything." Abe clenched his fist and hunched his shoulders as if readying to fight.

"It has everything to do with everything. If you can't love me anymore then someone else must have your heart, and I know it's not Alina." Daisy expected to see a reaction from Alina, but her face held flat. Perhaps Alina was just better at keeping her emotions in line than Daisy.

"You have a superstition that you've embedded into our history to try and push your ways. My emotions mean nothing," Abe yelled, but it was like he was trying to convince himself more than anyone else.

Azalea stopped moving and looked around at the crowd before her. Everyone but Alina seemed confused. Daisy felt hurt mostly at their words, but the meaning was also confusing. Daisy hadn't the slightest idea what they were talking about. Azalea's eyebrows raised as some realisation suddenly dawned on her.

"You haven't told them who you are," Azalea announced in revelation. She let out a hearty laugh that put Daisy even more on edge.

"Told us what, Abe? What haven't you told us?" Brighid asked with distress clear in her voice. A look of immense pain crossed her face. A single tear fell down her cheek. Daisy did not understand her reaction entirely.

There were grunts of agreement from Evander and Arlo, but no one said anything else. Daisy watched Abe fight an internal battle. She could see the pain and fear playing across his face. He obviously did not want to tell everyone whatever he was hiding, but his options were limited.

"Tell them or I will," Azalea threatened. She turned to pick at her nails as if giving Abe permission to relax for a moment. Slowly, keeping his eyes on Azalea for as long as possible, Abe turned to face his studies and Daisy. Everyone appeared to relax slightly as Abe faced them.

"I recently told you about the history of the Conductors," Abe reminded them and everyone, but Rosie, nodded. Alina looked at her shoes as if wanting to avoid the topic. "Well, it's not a myth really. It's the truth and I know it's the truth because… well… I am the male embodiment of the forces."

Evander, Arlo, and Brighid all gasped. Rosie looked even more confused. Daisy, however, suddenly understood. Things made more sense with Abe being the forefather of the forces. While the others whispered between each other, Daisy noticed Abe was focused on her. His face was pained as if expecting rejection from Daisy. Based on the others' reactions, Daisy assumed most people did not take this news well. However, it had not changed Daisy's opinion of Abe in the slightest. If anything, it made things more clear. Daisy smiled encouragingly at Abe and saw some of the fear dissipate from his face.

"Also, she," Abe pointed towards Azalea, "is the Grand Master in a new body."

Unlike Abe's news, the announcement of Azalea being the Grand Master was earth shattering. Not only was her sister alive and a Conductor, but she was an incredibly powerful Conductor and maybe even evil. Daisy had so many questions, but so little time.

With the end of Abe's sentence, Azalea took the moment of surprise to send a quick purple blast at Abe. Daisy watched as he fell and crumpled in a heap on the ground. She ran towards him and felt for a pulse or any signs of life, but she hardly had the opportunity. Azalea stood over top of them and glared down at Daisy. For some reason, Daisy felt paralyzed with fear.

"You know, you were never supposed to happen," Azalea stated as if the words weren't supposed to hurt. "I don't mean you as a Conductor. I mean you as a person. Usually the fetuses I overwrite won't divide further into twins. You were the first. Perhaps what he loves about you is what you stole from me."

Before Daisy could do anything, she felt the familiar sting of a slap to the face. Azalea had raised her hand against Daisy. Sitting stunned, Daisy was unsure of what to do. She looked back at Azalea, keeping her face flat and trying not to show the pain.

"That is for stealing from me," Azalea spat.

"I didn't know anything. All I ever wanted was to be like you. All I wanted was for you to be my sister. You had everything I ever wanted. Our parents adored you and loathed me. I could never do anything right, but you were home, you were there to help me, save me. When you were gone, I was alone. You don't know what they did to me." Daisy subconsciously rubbed her back where the years of whip marks burned in her memories.

Daisy was speaking more than she intended. She wanted to keep silent, but at this realisation, she could feel the strange tingling in the back of her mind that meant someone was there. It was like her filter had been turned off and anything that came to her mind came out her mouth. The slap, the contact, was enough to break through anything Daisy was doing to prevent a mind connection.

Azalea looked at Daisy and almost seemed sad. Daisy was unsure of how to read her now. She didn't present like the Azalea she grew up with. Everything seemed wrong, but everything also made sense. Daisy's head pounded, and she wasn't sure if it was from trying to prevent Azalea's intrusions, Azalea breaking through, or all of the information she had received in a short amount of time.

"Why do you think I killed them?" Azalea stated as if she was handing Daisy a gift she should be grateful for. "I did this for you. Once I knew you were a Conductor, I knew they would prevent you from your full potential. I did this so we *could be together*."

"You did what?" Daisy was baffled by the confession.

"You were never supposed to exist, you certainly weren't supposed to fall in love with him, but I grew into this form with you and I developed a sort of soft spot for you. When I found you as a Conductor, I was excited, but I was also angry as I desperately tried to prevent you from becoming a Conductor. I suppressed your powers with various mind charms. I even tried crushing your soul by making your parents cruel. Often strong emotions cause power to erupt in younglings, so I had to remove any chances of you experiencing love or happiness. You hardly seemed predisposed to anger, so I wasn't worried about that. But, with you as a Conductor now, that meant I could take you with me. I didn't have to leave you behind. My attempts to diminish your powers failed, but this meant new opportunities. I just needed to remove the remaining obstacles. This included your captors, so I killed them."

Daisy sat horrorstuck. Never in her wildest dreams had she wished death upon someone. Her parents were horrible and abusive, but Daisy would never wish them harm. Too much information was coming at Daisy, and she didn't know what to do. She could feel something breaking, corrupting inside of her and it felt wrong. It felt so terribly wrong, but Daisy couldn't seem to stop it.

Daisy stood from the ground and fully faced Azalea who seemed interested, but unthreatened. Abe lay motionless at her feet and her parents lay dead a few feet

311

away. Azalea threatened her friends and played in her mind. Daisy couldn't sit idly by. She cast a quick glance back at her friends and realised they were seized in Azalea's trap. It was not that they didn't want to attack; it was that they couldn't attack. They had minor breaks in her hold, like Brighid's question, but Azalea was strong. Azalea was the creator of the mind force and had power beyond what Daisy could understand. However, Daisy for some reason, seemed unaffected.

"I would never have killed them," Daisy finally managed between clenched teeth. "I was coming here to say goodbye and to leave, but I wouldn't have killed them."

"I know that. You hardly have the backbone to squish a fly, so I did it for you. So you could be free. So you could come with me and learn the ways of the Conductors."

"Why would you want me? All you ever did was cast me aside. Furthermore, why would I go with *you*?"

"You are my sister. We were in the womb together which has never happened before. In all my transitions and implants, I've never had a sibling. I've always been an only as the process corrupts the reproductive system somehow. You were the first. You were actually family. You are a part of me just as I am a part of you. Besides, where do you have left to go?"

"Let them go Azalea." There was a fire to Daisy she had never felt before. Everything Azalea did was wrong. Everything she said was wrong and Daisy wouldn't let this continue. Azalea narrowed her eyes at Daisy. She seemed to weigh whether or not Daisy was worth it.

"Or what?"

"Or I will make you." Daisy didn't know if that was possible, but she would certainly try. Azalea clearly thought the notion humorous as she let out a laugh that made Daisy cringe.

"How quaint! You barely know anything. You haven't the slightest idea of what you can do. Your mark hasn't even been determined."

"Doesn't that make me more dangerous? Uncontrolled. Untested. I don't even know the extent of my power and you want to test it. So let's test it." Daisy quickly raised her hand and a large white light washed over everything.

Chapter 32 - Hostage

Abe felt the smash of the mind force as the Grand Master hit him with her full force. He remembered hitting the ground at Daisy's feet. He could hear talking and arguments. He could feel the Grand Master's grip getting tighter on his mind and controlling it. He had always been weak against the mind force since its emergence. When the world was created the four forces were in perfect balance. With the emergence of the fifth force, Abe was thrown off balance. He could never quite avoid its power regardless of who was conducting it. He had tried hard to learn to throw it, to not be overtaken, but the Grand Master was strong. Stronger than any other which made it almost impossible for Abe to prevent.

He felt her claws in his mind and he was helpless. He knew when he woke up, he would be her pawn and there was nothing he could do to stop it. He knew Daisy was close. Her touch broke through the mist of control, but it wasn't enough. He tried to focus on her touch, use it to ground him and pull him back, but it wouldn't work. He was lost.

Then, he felt a blast of warmth and saw a flash of silvery white light. The claws in his mind disappeared in a blink of an eye, and he was free. He opened his eyes and found himself sitting back on the stairs. Daisy sat beside him being comforted by Rosie. He saw the others awkwardly standing around them. He had been in this moment before. This was all familiar and known, but Abe didn't understand how this could have happened.

Daisy suddenly tensed, and he realised she recognized this moment as well. Quickly, she stood up and moved rapidly away from the stairs. Abe followed, knowing what was to come. Everyone else seemed confused. There appeared to be no understanding of what had or would happen. They mustn't have the memory Daisy and Abe did.

Abe couldn't fight the Grand Master and he knew that. Daisy was able to prevent her hold, but not forever. Abe had to get them out of here before the Grand Master showed. He turned to Daisy who seemed to be waiting for him to say or do something. Abe knew he needed to protect everyone. He needed to ensure his studies and Daisy were safe, and there was only one way he could think to do that. He locked eyes with Daisy and could see the fear on her face. Time was limited. He needed to act.

"You need to take everyone and you need to leave," Abe stated with determination. Daisy frowned and shook her head in protest. "Dais, we can't fight her. You don't know how to use your conduction, and I can't beat her. She is here for me. Take the others and go while you can."

"Abe, she will take you," Daisy said and a tear fell down her cheek. Abe reached out and brushed away the tear resting his hand against her cheek. He was going to have to leave her and it nearly broke him. Her hand reached up and held his. He could feel the cold metal of her engagement ring against that back of his hand. As much as he tried to avoid it, loving her didn't seem out of the question. He was going to ask for her hand in marriage as a ploy, but maybe it wasn't as much a ruse as a true desire.

He had only known her a few months and yet cared for her like no other.

"Dais, we really don't have time. Take the others. Let Alina train you. I will find you. I will figure this out and then I will find you. I promise." Although Abe was trying to convince Daisy, he was also trying to convince himself. He knew he was weak with the Grand Master, but Daisy was worth everything in the world to him.

Daisy nodded her head. She turned to go, but stopped. She ran back to Abe and threw her arms around his neck in a tight, crushing hug that hurt, but in a good way. His hands tangled in her hair and a waft of sugar and cinnamon filled his senses. If this was his last moment, he would savour it. She pulled back to look him in the eye. Abe could see a battle waging inside her, but he knew he had to let her decide. It was the same battle warring inside him. The battle between social edicate and true desire. He knew he couldn't make the decision for her.

Between one blink and the next, Daisy's lips were pressed against his. There was a brief moment of shock before Abe abandoned himself into the kiss. Her lips were warm and soft. His arms wrapped around her deepening the kiss. He quietly moaned so desperately wanting more of her, but knowing he couldn't. He recognized this as the last moment he had with her, perhaps for a while, but more likely for good. He savoured the sweet taste of the kiss and etched the feeling into his mind. He would keep Daisy there, in his mind, locked in time so he would never forget her. It would give him something to fight for. She was worth fighting for.

Finally she pulled away, leaving Abe feeling hollow. She grabbed Rosie's hand and started running away from the rubble and down the otherside of the hill. Alina looked confusedly at Abe before turning and following after Daisy. Evander stood staring back at Abe with an expression of pure anger. Abe grabbed the book he had been reading on the train out of his pocket and stared at the glyphs on the front. Evander seemed to be waiting, and Abe knew he needed to give Evander something else.

"Here," Abe said and threw the book to Evander, "help them."

"What is this?" Evander asked, looking confusedly at the book in his hands.

"My journal from the beginning of time. It will need to be translated, but I trust that you can do it. I trust that you can help them." Evander smiled and Abe could sense Evander's feeling of pride and joy. Abe knew how much this trust and faith meant to Evander. Realising the others were all gone, Evander took off clutching the book to his chest.

Eventually, they all left, leaving Abe alone on the top of the hill. Each step they took away from Abe craved away at his soul. When they disappeared through the gate and out of sight, Abe felt like he might fall apart completely, but he didn't have time to dissolve. Abe watched until he could see them no more then turned to the stairs and waited for the Grand Master to arrive. He would protect them with all he could even if it was the last thing he did.

He didn't have to wait long. For some reason though, it all seemed to take longer the second time. Perhaps because he was alone, or perhaps the Grand Master was confused by time travel. Either way, Abe waited, hoping beyond all hope that the others got away safely.

There was the familiar tune of transportation. Abe and the Grand Master were able to travel differently than other Conductors, but there was always an odd sound, like a song, that rang through the air before they arrived. Hers was different from his, but somehow he knew it. As the song neared the end and the shimmer of the Grand Master arriving appeared at the top of the stairs, it hit him. The tune was the same song Daisy hummed. Of course, Daisy didn't know that is what it was, but in the silence of being alone, the tune would hold a different meaning.

The Grand Master solidified from the shimmer at the top of the stairs. She immediately threw her cloak down. There was no reason for theatrics now. Abe assumed that, like he and Daisy, she also knew time had been reset somehow. She marched down the stairs and directly up to Abe. Her golden hair flew behind her as she marched with a surprising speed. Even from afar, Abe could see her bright purple and red eyes flaring with anger. Her fists were clenched and her jaw was tight. As angry as she was, Abe didn't fear what was coming next.

"What the hell happened? Where did they go? What did you do?" Azalea demanded. Her hand glowed purple by her side which Abe knew to mean she was planning on getting the information regardless of what he said or did. There was no point in lying to her.

"Daisy happened. I don't know how as we haven't really had the opportunity to explore her abilities yet. I sent them away before you could get here. You won't be able to hurt them. I don't know where they went," Abe responded with longing and pain. He wished he could have stayed with them, with her. The Grand Master narrowed her eyes in assessment of Abe.

"You love her, don't you?" Abe weighed telling her the truth and lying, but he felt her mind force wrapping his brain making lying seem impossible.

"I think I may."

"Why can't you love me?" Abe stared blankly at her. She seemed genuinely hurt. It had been a long battle of her wanting him and Abe not returning the feelings.

"Do you really need to ask why? Look around you! You do things like this. You hurt people. You used the mind force to corrupt minds rather than help them. You killed Daisy's family because you thought of them as a barrier to whatever you are planning. I don't harm people, but you do. You corrupted the good and killed the evil. I cannot sympathise with you and therefore I cannot love you. "

"But we are so much more than people. We created everything. If you joined me, we could rule everything again. We don't need to kill to rule. Instead, you sacrifice yourself for such measly humans."

"I care about them more than I care about myself. At the end of day, we both know you won't kill me. You don't want them. You want me."

"Not true. I want Daisy. What I said was true. She is my family."

"But her parents weren't? They are the same flesh and blood as her, as you."

"You know how the transference works. They are merely hosts for my being."

"I do, but Daisy won't. You killed her parents and admitted it. She isn't going to come back to be with you."

"You're right. She won't come back for me, but she will come back for you. Your sacrifice was just giving me the perfect bait to lure her back."

There was a flash of purple and Abe could feel the sting of the fifth force. He tried to cast it off, to focus on staying in control, but he could feel it growing. He could feel her digging deeper and pulling at recent memories. She was learning all he knew about Daisy while setting her grasp over his mind. He tried to fight it. He focused on a beacon to keep his mind tethered, a strong memory of who he was. It proved futile. He felt her final push and her eventual victory over his mind.

It was a weird feeling, having someone completely take over your mind. It was like an out of body experience. He could see himself doing things, saying things, but there was nothing he could do to prevent it. Abe sat in the back of his mind and waited for time to wear down her hold so he could rejoin his body.

"Much better," she announced. "Now, stop calling me the Grand Master. I go by Azalea, just as you go by Ambrose, apparently. No, you prefer Abe. I don't know why you rarely use the mind force. Things are easier when people can't filter their thoughts. Lies are complicated whereas the mind is simple. Come now, we have plans to make."

Abe's body started following behind Azalea as she made her way down the hill to the back side of the property. Azalea snapped her fingers and her tune began to play. Sher grabbed Abe's hand and they dissolved into a mist. At the very least, Abe was relieved she was going the opposite direction of Daisy. For now, Daisy would be safe without him.

Chapter 33 - Time

Daisy didn't look back as they rounded the gate. She clutched Rosie's hand and just kept running. She could hear the others behind her, so she kept moving. She was leading them back to the train station. They would take the next train out of Straford-and-Glenn, transfer to another train and another and another until it would be too hard to track. This would give them time to find somewhere they could hide; a safe haven to plan their next steps. The others shouted at Daisy, wanting answers, but Daisy just kept moving. She shook her head every time they asked questions. Occasionally she threw out responses about it not being the right time or it wasn't safe. It wasn't until the third train that Daisy could feel herself starting to relax.

They sat at the very back of a train headed for Smithsonite. From there, they would get on a train to Baytown then to Haysville then to somewhere else. Ideally, they would leave the country. Maybe even head over the mountains or across the sea. Daisy wasn't sure what exactly she was doing, but everyone just kept following her and she kept leading them. She had to get far away and make it almost impossible to be tracked. The more modes of transportation and the further away they could get the safer everyone would be. She was certain of it.

Everyone sat in the train car looking absolutely haggard and exhausted. They had left everything on the hillside. They dropped their trunks so they could run, but this meant they had nothing with them. Luckily, Evander had become quite good at using the mind force and could mask their lack of tickets to any train master. He was even able to get them food at one point, but Alina did not approve of this behaviour. She ensured they were aware of her disapproval, but Daisy enjoyed the food nonetheless. Even if they couldn't pay for things, they still had to eat and survive. Regardless of Alina's disapproval, Evander was helping all of them.

It was the middle of the night on their second full day of travelling. Everyone was tired and annoyed. Daisy felt it in her bones, but she needed to keep everyone safe. Arlo slumped against the wall. Rosie sat beside Daisy occasionally dozing off with her head bobbing until she woke up and apologised to Daisy for falling asleep. Brighid was curled up against Alina trying to rest. She looked young in the moment, and Daisy's heart hurt with guilt.

When Daisy met Abe all those months ago, she never thought this would be her future. He was witty, handsome, and kind, but Daisy didn't know the power he held. She wanted a husband so she could leave her family, but she never intended to meet someone with power other than political prowess. Another duke or prince, maybe, certainly not a Conductor. Now, since they met, everything in her life and the Conductors' lives had spiralled out of control. She felt responsible and needed to fix it, but she hadn't the slightest idea of what to do.

As they sat in the final train car and Daisy assessed the situation; she knew they were alone and she had decisions to make. It was quiet and the train was empty. Now seemed like a good time to discuss what had happened and what was going to happen next.

"The Grand Master is my sister, Azalea," Daisy explained. She could feel Alina wanting to blame Daisy for everything, which was partially accurate, but Daisy held up her hand to silence Alina. "I did not know she was a Conductor let alone such a powerful one. I had never heard of the Conductors until I arrived in Grenich and met Abe. She was originally not looking for me, she just wanted Abe, but now she wants me as well."

"So you have put us all in her line of wrath by running away then. You threaten all our lives and couldn't even tell us what you were doing until now," Alina accused. Daisy swallowed and tried to hold her ground.

"Abe told me to take you and run, so that's exactly what I did. I trust that Abe knows what he is doing," Daisy replied.

"What were you and Abe talking about before we left?" Rosie asked. Everyone else seemed equally curious. Alina still seemed hostile however.

"We knew the Grand Master was going to come. Based on the past and the Grand Master's mood, everyone would have died if we stayed. We had to get you all out of there as soon as we could," Daisy explained

"How could you know that?" Brighid inquired.

"We had already lived through it," Daisy replied.

"What do you mean you already lived through it?" Arlo asked and sat up right to look at Daisy.

"Well, um, I appear to be able to do things no one else can, but I have to learn how to control it. Abe thought you could teach me Alina." Daisy looked pleadingly at Alina who stared back with a cold, distant glare. Brighid elbowed her in the side. Alina seemed insulted at the gesture but looked back at Daisy.

"What exactly can you do? What exactly am I teaching you?" Alina questioned.

"Control of any force firstly, and then how to use my specific abilities."

"And...what *abilities* are those?" Alina said as if acting like there wasn't anything possible that Daisy could do that was special.

"I've made a sixth force. I can control time."

Manufactured by Amazon.ca
Bolton, ON

26846125R00179